"As an author who has a clear predilection for strong female protagonists I found myself very much taken with David Debord's Shanis and her story. He has eminently succeeded in achieving that all-too-rare accomplishment: a believable heroine---and a believable fantasy heroine, at that---by a male author. Shanis can be, and probably will be, placed on the same plane as such classic heroines of heroic fantasy as Robert Howard's Belit and Red Sonja, C.L. Moore's Jirel of Joiry or Leigh Brackett's Ciaran. The Silver Serpent is a superb story told believably and unpretentiously by a superb new fantasy author."
Hugo Award-Winning Author Ron Miller

"I was quite impressed with the book. The characters were well-crafted, the pacing excellent, the prose was straightforward but accomplished, and the story was an enjoyable blend of adventure, intrigue, and humor. In fact, as far as traditional fantasy goes, I think fans of Terry Brooks and David Eddings could easily enjoy The Silver Serpent..."
Fantasy Book Critic

"The Silver Serpent is a gripping epic fantasy in the tradition of Robert Jordan, Raymond Feist and David Eddings. If you are looking for a fresh, new voice in the traditional form, I highly recommend this first installment of what promises to be a memorable series."
The Asgard Oracle

"As a voracious fantasy reader, it's hard these days to find a new series to get excited about. So, as you can imagine, I'm giddy to share a new discovery. I found The Silver Serpent a truly enjoyable and entertaining read... His presentation of the world initially is fuzzy and nebulous, but as the characters move out of a small village and step into this world's legends (ala Eddings or Jordan), you've found solid footing within his world. The fight scenes are well done with impressive clarity and brevity. The prose is straightforward, but engaging. Though the characters are flawed, your affection grows fast. Its ending seemed disjointed, vaguely described, and abrupt, but it leaves you wanting more. As book one of "The Absent Gods" series, I thought it provided a great foundation. I'm just happy to have found a new series that's right out of the gate. Now I have something to look forward to again within fantasy."
Elizabeth Mock's Slush Pile

The Absent Gods by David Debord

The Silver Serpent
Keeper of the Mists
The Gates of Iron (forthcoming)

KEEPER OF THE
MISTS

DAVID DEBORD

Gryphonwood Press
545 Rosewood Trail, Grayson, GA 30017-1261

Published by Gryphonwood Press
www.gryphonwoodpress.com

ISBN 13:   978-0-9825087-9-4
ISBN 10:   0-9825087-9-4

Printed in the United States of America
First printing: October, 2010

The author would like to thank Susan Boswell, Cindy Seguin, and Cindy
Wood for their invaluable contributions to this book.

To my mother Barbara
For all the stories you read to me.

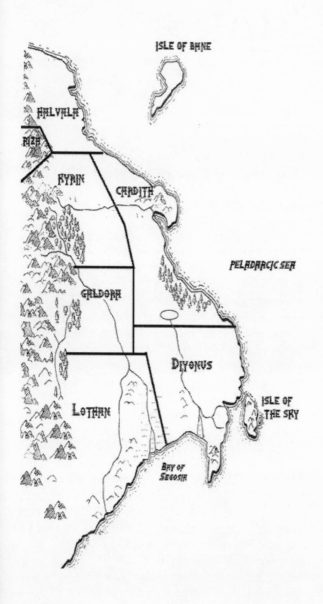

CHAPTER 1

"You can not find me now, Harvin." Jayla giggled and pressed her body deeper into the farthest recess of the tiny cave hidden behind a stand of brush. The cool stone surface leached the warmth from her hands and her belly as she lay in the dark, listening for the sound of her brother's approach.

At six summers, she was still small enough to wriggle in and out of tight places where Harvin, nearly nine, and big for his age, could not fit. When chores were done each day they would spend hours exploring the warren of rock ledges, chimneys and tunnels they called "the castle." Neither of them had ever seen an actual castle, but they agreed that a real one could be no more majestic, and certainly no more fun than this, their special place. Hidden by thick stands of blue-gray panon trees and dense tangles of briar, the network of caves, crevasses, and passages wended its way down the steep side of Marlat Mountain. One could climb down if he or she was very careful, though incaution could lead to broken bones, or worse. It was a much faster way down, however, than the meandering switchbacks of the old mountain road the grownups traversed.

One of these days Jayla was going to surprise Mama and Papa when they took the cart to Galsbur. She would clamber down through the castle and be waiting for them when they finally reached the bottom. She would lean against a tree, looking bored, and when they finally arrived, she would say, "Hello Mama and Papa. What took you so long?" Mama and Papa would want to know how she reached the bottom first, but she would tell them it was magic, and they would laugh again.

Harvin was taking his time about finding her. He was bigger, stronger, and faster than her, but he was a daydreamer. He had been known to let the smallest thing distract him—a colorful bird or an oddly shaped rock—and forget all about their game. Where *was* he? She did not want to wait all day for him to remember to look for her.

Careful to remain quiet, she slid toward the front of the cave and, squinting against the afternoon sunlight, she saw nothing but forest. The snows take him! She had not spoken aloud, but she immediately clapped a hand over her mouth. Mama would punish her for even thinking such a foul oath, but it *would* be just like her brother to leave her hiding in a cave all afternoon. He had done it before.

When she was certain she had given him sufficient time to discover her hiding place, she crawled out of the cave and began her climb back up to the top of the castle, where the dakel bushes lined the road and hid their secret place from passers-by. The going was more difficult on the way up, but she had made this climb countless times, and she raced up the rocky face like a squirrel dashing up a tree.

She had almost reached the top when she heard hoof beats and men's voices. Lots of them. She slowed down, wary of what might wait at the top. Few people lived in their tiny village nestled in a valley in the foothills of western Galdora. She was taken by the conviction that these were strangers, and therefore to be looked upon with suspicion.

"Nothin' but a farming town. And not even a town at that. More like a village. Told us we would have all the loot we could carry home. All the women, too. But what do we get?" The speaker cleared his throat and spat. "Farmers. No gold, no silver. Not even a copper among them. Bah!" Several other voices muttered in general agreement.

"But there was women, wasn't there, Garge?" The second voice was soft, and oily, putting Jayla in mind of the squishy brown newts that lived under rocks in mountain streams. "Healthy farm women and a few young girls, too. Can't complain about that now, can you?" Someone barked a sharp, mirthless laugh.

Jayla did not know what the men were talking about, but it frightened her. She stayed very still, her feet and legs braced in the sides of the cleft in the rock face. She was getting tired and her arms burned, but she was not about to move. She closed her eyes, and whispered a prayer to the forest fairies, asking them to lead the bad men away. Harvin did not believe in the little people of the forest, but Jayla did.

"Not hardly enough to go around." Garge was closer now. "Though we made a fair job of sharing them around like good little boys, didna' we? I tell you, Tarn, there'd better be sweeter pickings when we come down outta' these hills, or some of the boys just might up and leave this outfit."

Other voices chimed in, most echoing Garge's sentiments, others disagreeing.

"You can't do that. You made a blood pledge. Do you think they'll let you out of it just like that? You know what they do to deserters. Besides, every farming village we raid brings us that much closer to the cities. And in cities there will be gold."

The voices began to fade.

"I declare, there had better be gold, or blood pledge or not, I'll walk right..."

When she could hear them no more, she counted all her fingers and toes twice before climbing the rest of the way to the top. Trembling from fright and fatigue, she crawled beneath the shelter of a dakel bush, careful to avoid the thorns, and sat clutching her knees to her chest, and rocking to and fro. Silent tears ran down her chin, dripping onto her plain woolen dress. Where were Mama and Papa and Harvin? She wanted to know what had happened, but she was too afraid. She hurt all over and she wanted to go home.

Something scraped on the dirt road. Someone was walking toward her hiding place. Her heartbeat pounded out an angry rhythm in her ears, and she felt as if the whole world could hear her.

"Jayla? Are you here?"

"Harvin?" she called back, her voice thick with emotion. "Is it really you?"

"Where are you?" The panic in his voice was plain, and it frightened her all the more. "I can't see you. Are you all right?"

"I'm in the bush, over here." She was still afraid to come out, so she waited as he crawled to her. It was a relief when his broad, freckled face finally peeked out through the wall of greenery. She wrapped her arms around his neck and tried to squeeze some courage into her heart.

It did not work.

"Jayla, you must listen to me." He gently untangled himself from her embrace and held her at arm's length so he could look her in the eye. "Something very bad has happened. You cannot go back to the village. Mama and Papa say that you must climb down the castle as fast as you can."

"Wait! How do they know about the castle? Did you tell them?" The surprise had momentarily driven all thoughts of the bad men from her mind.

"That does not matter now. You must climb to the bottom and then go east. Do not walk. Run. Do you know which way is east?"

She nodded. In the morning, east was toward the rising sun. In the late afternoon, the shadows pointed east. At mid-day, or if there was no sun, you just put your back to the mossy side of the tree and turned left.

"Good. Go east as fast as you can until you come to a village. Keep to the forest and hide if you hear anyone coming. Do you understand?"

"I want to go home." She hated the way her voice sounded right now—like a little baby, but she did not care. Hot tears streamed down her cheeks and she tasted the salt in the corners of her mouth. "I want Mama and Papa."

"We will come for you." Harvin's voice was soft, but insistent. "We will come east, too, and we'll find you. But you have to get away as fast as you can. Promise me you will."

"But what will you..."

"Promise me!" He gripped her shouldlers and gave her a shake.

She nodded, and Harvin seemed to accept that as her oath. "Time to be going then. Come on." He crawled out the way he had come. She bit her lip as he vanished into the foliage.

"You there. Stop!" The man's voice froze her heart. Who was out there? More bad men? She heard a rapid scuffling and she knew Harvin was running away. Booted feet pounded the dirt, chasing after him. She had to help him!

She crawled out of the bush, thorns raking across her back as she went. At the edge of the bush, she thrust her head out and looked up and down the road. To her right, she saw a tall, lean man with silvery hair and a gray cape dashing down the road.

"You leave him alone!" She screamed as loud as her little lungs would permit. She regretted it almost immediately.

The man stopped in his tracks and whirled about with cat-like grace. His eyes narrowed as his gaze met hers, and then his whole body seemed to... ripple.

Jayla gasped as he changed before her eyes. In a span of two heartbeats the man had transformed into a creature from her worst nightmares. He stood as tall as a man, but his muscled body was covered in sleek gray fur. His hands were tipped with wicked black claws, and his head was that of a cat, something like the puma that Papa had killed last winter, but she was sure that no puma's eyes had ever shone with the cunning malevolence with which this beast gazed at her. It threw back its head and screamed a primordial cry, dropped down to all fours, and took off up the road toward her.

Survival instinct took over, forcing her paralyzed limbs to move. She scrambled back through the bush, ignoring the scrapes she received. Reaching the ledge, she dropped feet-first down into the crevasse. There was precious little slope, and she had to use her feet and hands as brakes to keep her from plummeting to the bottom. The stone was mostly smooth, but her hands found every imperfection as she slid down, and soon they were slick with blood.

She hit the first ledge hard, the pain shooting up through her legs and into her back. She was too afraid to permit so much as a whimper to escape her lips. She ducked down into the little tunnel on her right and crawled to the next chimney. She heard a scrabbling sound like claws on rock somewhere far above.

The monster was still chasing her.

She slid down the next chimney in the same manner she had done the first. Her hands were now numb to the pain, or perhaps her whole self was numb. She did not care. She no longer thought of Mama, Papa, or Harvin. She only wanted to get away.

At the bottom of the next chimney, she wriggled beneath a low-hanging rock, coming out at a ledge above a precipitous drop off. She hoped the monster would be too large to force itself through the tight space through which she had just come, but she would not wait around to find out.

She took a deep breath and looked out at the gap that lay before her. She could not climb around it—the sheer rock face to her right offered no handholds. The only way across was a thick vine that spanned a gap thirty paces wide. To cross it, one had to stand on the vine and scoot across sideways, keeping his hands against the wall for balance. Lean too far, though…

She shook the frightening thought out of her head. Harvin had done it once, but she had never tried. If Mama knew of Harvin's reckless indifference to his own safety, she would have taken a stick to him. Now Jayla would have to cross it. She took a deep breath. This was going to be the scariest thing she had ever done.

Gingerly she stepped out onto the vine, and was pleased to discover that it supported her weight with ease. She placed one hand against the rock wall and found her center of balance, just the way she had seen Harvin do it. Holding her breath, she slid her right foot onto the vine. It continued to hold her. As quickly as she dared, she scooted across the vine, letting out a small moan each time it swayed beneath her feet.

She heard the monster sliding down the chimney, and she started to cry, but she kept moving.

Don't look down. Don't look down.

She remembered Harvin saying that same thing over and over as he made the crossing, so she took his advice and kept her eyes on the rock. So surprised was she when her foot touched solid ground that she almost lost her balance, but caught herself just in time.

She could still hear snarling and scraping as the monster climbed down. He was not moving as fast as she, but he was coming fast enough. If only there was something she could do.

She spotted a broken stone with a sharp edge, snatched it up, and began hacking at the vine where it met the ledge on her side. She was strong for her age, thanks to hard work and lots of climbing, but the vine was tough. She struck it again and again, feeling each blow all the way up to her shoulder.

She had cut almost one-third of the way through when she heard the creature's ragged breathing. It was close. Reluctantly forsaking her task, she scooted away on her backside, squeezing into a narrow fissure. Surely the thing would be much too big to get to her back here.

The beast appeared on the other side of the gap. It stood on its hindquarters and peered down over the ledge.

And then it looked up.

Its eyes fell upon her. It dropped down again on all fours, and tensed to jump, but seemed to think the better of it. It took a long look at the intervening gap, its silver-flecked eyes taking in every detail. Making its decision, it bared its glistening fangs in a sinister mockery of a grin, and once again stood on two legs.

As Jayla sat mesmerized in horror, its form blurred again, and once more a man stood before her.

"I did not mean to frighten you. I was afraid you would fall over the edge, and my cat form is much faster than my normal shape." He smiled. Perhaps his intention was to reassure her, but the shadow of the beast was on his face and in his eyes, and he looked every bit as deadly as he had moments before. "Just stay there and I will come and help you back across. You have nothing to fear."

As the man-beast crossed the vine, Jayla tried to press deeper into her hiding place, her hand gripping the sharp stone, seeking comfort in it, but it was no good. She could not get away.

Her pursuer was much heaver than either her or Harvin, and the further he moved out onto the vine, the farther it sagged. Soon his bottom half had sunk out of her field of vision.

There was a loud crack, and the vine gave a little. He gritted his teeth and snarled like the cat he had been, his fingers splaying out against the rocks. Jayla imagined she could see claws sprouting from their tips. But the vine held, and the man-cat thing crept toward her, slower this time.

The vine gave again, dipping the beast lower. She realized it had not noticed the cut she had made in the vine. As this thought occurred to her, the vine gave way again.

Please fall. Please fall.

But the vine continued to hold. He was now ten paces from the edge. As he looked up at her, his mouth twisted into a depraved grin and he made a noise in his throat that sounded nauseatingly like purring. He took another step across the space that measured the moments of the rest of her life.

She tore her eyes away from his and looked at the place where she had cut the vine. With the added weight, the vine had almost broken in two! Not pausing to think about it, Jayla squirmed out of the narrow cleft and dashed to the cliff's edge. Startled by her sudden movement, the beast froze for a moment.

That was all Jayla needed.

She raised her sharp stone above her head.

"No!" The man beast realized what she was doing a moment too late.

She brought the stone down with all of her might.

Crack!

The vine snapped clean in two. The man-cat monster, whatever he was, seemed to freeze in mid-air for a moment, the malice in his eyes having given way to disbelief.

Then he fell.

He clawed at the cliff face as he plummeted to the ground far below. Down, down he fell, screaming with insane rage, until he finally struck with a wet sound.

And then it was quiet.

Jayla sat there for a long time, wondering what she should do next. She wanted to climb back up and find Mama, Papa, and Harvin. She knew other paths up, so the broken vine was not an impediment. But what if she reached the top only to learn that her family had already left? In any case, she did not know if she had enough strength left to make the climb.

She did not want to climb down. The monster thing was down there. But he was dead, wasn't he? She peered down over the cliff, and her eyes fell upon the tangled remains of his body lying broken on the ground. He was definitely dead. Still, she would keep her distance. She never wanted to be near one of those things again.

Her mind was made up. Mama and Papa wanted her to go

east, and they had promised they would come for her, so that was what she would do. She would make her way east as fast as she could, and one day, she would find her family again.

CHAPTER 2

The world was tilting, spinning. Shanis's memory shattered into miniscule fragments; images she could not understand dancing through her consciousness like fireflies, always evading her grasp. She bolted upright, her heart racing, and gasped for breath. She felt a strong hand grip her own.

"Relax. You are safe." The calm soothing voice was strangely familiar, and in her state of delirium it seemed to hold a mystical power of command. Her breathing eased, and her confused eyes took in her surroundings.

She was in a hut. Its walls were supported by rough posts, the gray, peeling bark still clinging to them in places. The walls were of woven branches, with gray-green moss stuffed into the largest holes to help keep the weather out. Something dark and solid, probably deer hide, formed the outer layer.

She lay atop a thick, soft bear skin, and her legs were tangled in a rough blanket. A smoky peat fire in a stone ring at the center of the hut provided a faint light. The room began to seem familiar, as if she had been here before, but the haze of smoke made her feel as if she was still dreaming.

Her thoughts returned to the dream in which she had just been immersed.

She walked at the head of a solemn procession, followed by attendants dressed in fine clothes, but of a style she had never seen. A young man, tall and muscular, but with a stern face, looked at her through tear-filled eyes. She forced herself to look away from him, and instead focused ahead, where a man in a dark robe stood behind an altar, upon which lay a stone sword...

"You are finally awake, then?" Larris knelt beside her. His eyes were bleary and his hair disheveled as if he had not slept in days. "I am glad. You gave us quite a fright in more ways than I care to count." He smoothed her hair with an air of familiarity that seemed inappropriate, but strangely, she did not mind. Perhaps it was the fatigue.

It was coming back to her now. She and her friends had fled their village, met up with Larris and Allyn on their journey, and gone with them in search of the Silver Serpent. They had journeyed into the mountains and…

"Where…" Her own voice sounded strange in her ear. How did I get…" The questions died on her lips. There were too many things she wanted to ask, so much she did not understand, and the whirlwind of confused thoughts was more than her weary mind could bear. She fell back onto the bearskin and closed her eyes. "I don't remember…"

"Shanis, I need you to think." Larris sounded uncomfortable. "Tell me, exactly how much do you remember?"

She tried to recall the events of the previous days. Of course, she had no idea how long she had been in this hut. How long ago had her most recent memory been?

"I remember the golorak." She shuddered at the mental image of the grotesque creature that had nearly killed them in the caverns beneath the mountains. She felt his hand on her forearm, and she did not pull away. "We found the chamber. Then the snake came alive and I lost my sword. I was so scared and confused; I tried to grab the stone sword from the statue. Everything is fuzzy after that. Mostly I remember strange dreams of flying through the air and fighting a giant serpent. All my dreams have been… odd."

"It was not a dream." Larris spoke softly, but his grip on her tightened. "You did fight the snake. The stone sword became a real sword, and you used it against the snake. You hurt it and it tried to flee, so you followed it out through a tunnel and…" His voice grew hoarse, and he seemed to choke on the next words. "…and into the sky. Somehow you took us up with you. When the fight was over, we were lying on a hill in Lothan. Horgris found us the next day. This is the encampment of the Hawk Hill clan—his clan."

She grew increasingly numb with each word. It was impossible, but in the depths of her soul she knew it to be true. Her old obstinate nature welled up within her, and she sat up, her ire rising.

"That is the most ridiculous heap of goat dung I have ever heard." She looked him in the eye, and he met her gaze with a level stare. As desperately as she wanted to cling to her disbelief, she could not deny it. Her anger fled as quickly as it had come and, to her horror, she began to cry, the firelight sparkling like diamonds through her tears. "How can it be?"

"That stone sword is the reason." Larris looked up at the ceiling, then back at her. "It is the Silver Serpent."

"No," she gasped. "It was for you, not me. You have to take it." She realized she was babbling and clammed up. Her thoughts now spun so fast she was surprised Larris could not hear the buzzing they seemed to create in her mind.

"I cannot take it. I tried. When you came down from… the sky, you dropped it on the ground. I tried to pick it up and it felt like my entire body was afire and frozen at the same time. I was certain it had burned my hand off, but there was nothing. Hierm tried as well, but the same thing happened to him. Allyn refused to even attempt it. Finally, we used our swords to push it onto my cloak. Once it was covered, we were able to bundle it up and carry it away, but no one can actually touch it. A few of Horgris's men have also tried and failed. They finally gave up."

He inclined his head toward the far wall. The sword leaned there, the firelight dancing on the image of the serpent etched in the blade, seeming to bring it life. The jeweled eye sparkled back at her in sinister silence. Larris clasped her hand in both of his. "For good or ill, I fear you are now the bearer of the Silver Serpent."

She did not know what to say. It was all too much to take. She shook her head. "There must be some way to give it up. It can't be me."

"It has marked you. Look here." Gently he grasped the low neckline of her loose-fitting tunic and slid it down to uncover her chest just above her left breast. It was a measure of her stupefied state that she permitted him to do so.

A silver serpent, the twin of the one she had seen carved in the rock above the lost city of Murantha, shone on her chest. Instinctively, she tried to wipe it away, and then claw it away, but to no avail. It felt like stone affixed to her skin. Larris pulled her hands away. Her first instinct was to fight him, but then her whole body sagged. She let her head fall against his chest, and she cried tears of confused despair.

Her entire world had changed. Who was she? What was she? Had this somehow altered her very nature? Was she still the farm girl whose father had taught her to use the sword? Was she even human anymore? Suddenly, she wanted nothing more than to be back at home with her father and her friends.

Her friends.

She pushed away from Larris. "Where are the others?"

"Hierm is nearby, sleeping in one of the huts. He offered to take a turn sitting with you, but I didn't mind." He shrugged and looked away.

"Allyn is out hunting. He has not been himself for some time, but he's been especially out of sorts ever since…" He neither finished the sentence, nor mentioned their other companions.

"What about Oskar and Khalyndryn? Where are…" Another memory formed in her mind. She did not want to believe it, but the look on his face confirmed it. "They fell, didn't they? They fell and I could not reach them." The tears came anew. Larris pulled her close. "We have to go back for them," she said with little conviction.

"You know we cannot," he said. "Once we made our way back, how would we find them again? Who knows where that chasm ended, or where they might have gone by the time we got there? That is, if they…"

"Don't say it." He was probably right, but to speak of it made her feel as if she was giving up what little hope remained. "They have to be alive." She sat for a long time in the silence, grieving for lost friends and the loss of her life as she knew it. "What do we do next?"

"Go back to Galdora I suppose. Prophecy holds that the

Silver Serpent is crucial to the crown in some way. Until we know what that means, I would keep you close by my side."

"Only until then?" She jerked away from him, not sure why his words angered her. Perhaps it was because suddenly her life seemed to no longer be her own. "Have you forgotten the other prophecy? Didn't Martrin say that whoever bears the Silver Serpent will reunite the clans? Won't they try to keep me here when they find out?"

"Shanis, I…"

"I am right, aren't I?" She did not wait for his reply. "Well I have something to say to you and everyone else. I might have been branded like an animal, but I am not your cow to be herded along wherever you please. I will do exactly what I want, when I want to do it, and no one will stop me." She clambered to her feet, slower than she had intended, but determined not to let Larris see any weakness in her. "Where are my clothes?"

He pointed to a neatly folded pile next to the sword.

"Thank you. Now get out."

Larris stalked to the doorway, turned and folded his arms across his chest. He looked as if he were about to argue, but he changed his mind. He gave her a curt nod and pushed his way through the thick skins that hung from the door frame.

Getting dressed was no easy task. She was still weak, and she felt like she might faint when she leaned over to lace her boots. She had been provided a basin of tepid water. She scrubbed her face, determined to erase all signs of the tears she had shed. She hated crying, and she hoped she never did it again. Her hair was a tangled mess, but she combed it out the best she could and tied it back.

Finally, she took a long look at the sword. Her sword. The thing that now apparently marked her new identity and her new purpose in the world. At least until she could figure out a way to get rid of the thing.

Forcing herself to ignore her fears, she picked it up. She touched it gingerly at first, but when she was certain that it was not going to burn her arm or carry her up into the clouds, she took a firm grip and held out in the dim light so she could examine it more closely.

It was beautiful. The craftsmanship was exquisite, and the etched serpent seemed to writhe as the light played along its scales. The hilt, shaped like the open mouth of a fanged serpent, was deadly looking. She noted how light the sword felt. That could not be right. This sword was a hand longer than the one her father had gifted her, yet she could easily wield it with one hand. She chuckled. If the thing could make her fly and fight giant snakes in the sky, she supposed making itself almost weightless was a relatively small matter.

She was pleased to see that someone had provided her with a simple scabbard and a shoulder harness. She slid the blade home and slung the strap over her shoulder. Taking a deep breath, she steeled herself before striding forth from her dim, smoky hut and into the damp morning air. It was time to face the world.

The cool autumn mist clung to her face, teasing her senses into wakefulness. She inhaled the cool mountain air and felt life returning to her sleep-fogged mind and weary body. Her eyes took in the haunting, lonely beauty of the fog-shrouded hills. They looked like she felt: desolate and somehow private, as if the fog hid their true nature from prying eyes.

She wended her way through the waking encampment. Smoke from cook fires hung low in the moist air, snaking through the gaggle of huts like ethereal serpents. A chill ran down her spine. She did not want to think about serpents of any kind.

A few of the Monaghan acknowledged her with a nod or curt greeting, but most just stared. She heard their whispers as she walked past. "That be her. She be the one."

"Shanis. Over here!" Hierm's voice was blessedly familiar. He hurried over to her, his damp, white-blond hair plastered to his face. He clutched her in a bear hug, and she returned the embrace with gratitude. "I'm so happy you're all right." He looked her over, as if trying to convince himself that she truly was well. A frown suddenly marred his face. "Did Larris tell you what happened?"

"Yes. I don't know what I'm going to do now. Larris wants

me to stay close to him because he thinks I'll be important to Galdora's future. But I just don't know. I thought I was trapped back home, but now I wonder if my life will ever be my own." She pulled away from him, keeping her head up and her gaze level. She was disconsolate, but felt herself already growing impatient with her feeling of helplessness. She would not be ordered around.

"There you do be, girl." Horgris lumbered up to her, his eyes shining and his face more open and friendly than she had ever seen it. The remains of his breakfast clung to his beard, and he held a half-full tankard of ale in one hand. He smiled and clapped her on the back. "Good to see you awake, it do be. Wondered if we ever would, that we did. Come with me and we will talk." Having nowhere else to go, Shanis followed, taking Hierm along with her.

When they reached his hut, Horgris went on in without any formality. Shanis assumed she was invited, so she followed him inside. They settled down on bearskin rugs laid out around the fire ring. Horgris stoked the fire, added a chunk of peat and blew on the coals until it caught. She watched the heavy, pungent smoke spiral up to the smoke hole in the ceiling and out into the foggy morning sky.

"I don't need to be telling you how surprised we all be. What with you being the one. We kept council about it over the whole night, arguing and such." He took a swig of ale and wiped the foam away with a hairy forearm. "They don't all be liking it, but here be the way it is. If you be willing to lead us, we be willing to follow." He placed his mug of ale on the ground and stared at her, waiting for a reply.

"I don't know what to say. Lead you?" She had been prepared for him to make demands, even threats if she did not take up the Silver Serpent and follow them, or perhaps find a way to give it over to them. But to lead? Lead them where? She shifted uncomfortably and looked at Hierm, who only shrugged and moved his head side-to-side in a non-committal way. She looked again at Horgris and wondered how he felt about giving his allegiance to a young outlander girl. What must it cost him to even make this offer to her?"

"I never expected to find the Silver Serpent, much less bear it, so I was not at all prepared for what I woke to find. One thing I can tell you, though, is that I am no leader. I never have been."

Horgris laughed.

"You don't need to be worryin' about that now. You are destined to lead, and the power of the serpent will guide us. And whatever you don't be knowing, I can help." He raised his hand to silence the protest that was forming on her lips. "Hear me out before you be arguing with me.

"When I was a boy the fightin' be not going on for so very long. I remember me Pap tellin' me about how it was before. You know we used to have games? Every year the clans would gather for games and feasting. We did no fight with the Malgog, either. They no be our favorites, but we were at peace. It was a place our children could be growing old." He paused and stared into the fire, as if his memories were visible within its light. "My daughter be expecting my first grandchild. I would see that child grow up in a different world than that which I do know. You can change that."

"I cannot change anything." How could he believe her capable of such things? She was a farm girl. "I have never done anything right in my life." Hierm laid a hand on her arm, but she shrugged it off. She did not know why she was unburdening herself to Horgris, but now she had started and would not stop until she had her say. "I am the most selfish person you will ever know. I spent my life believing I should have whatever I wanted. The only thing I am good at is using a sword, and you have plenty of those. I am no good to you or anyone else."

"Stop it, girl." Horgris winced. "You be making my head hurt something fearful. Let me say this. It takes character to be admittin' your faults, but I'll wager you be no as bad as you be thinkin' you are. You did no have to take part in the quest, but you did, and you fought for your friends. I also hear tell of that other thing you did. I don't know what it be meaning, but it took courage. In any happenstance, the prophecy say you be the one to bring us back together, and if I believed nothing else, I believe that. We need someone to reunite us, girl, and you be the one. Help us. Please."

Shanis sat dumbstruck. He wanted an answer. Needed one. But what could she say? No matter what she decided, it would be wrong. Larris was convinced that she was critical to the safety of their homeland, and did she not owe something to the place from which she came? But what of these people? Horgris's words had touched her heart in a way she would not have thought possible from the brutish chieftain. Lothan had suffered for so long. What would her answer be?

She was saved the trouble of giving a reply when a familiar young girl burst through the draped hide doorway.

"Be it true? Do he really be here?" The girl's eyes fell upon Hierm and she let out a cry that was at once both joyous and despondent. Hierm had scarcely reached his feet when she hurled herself into his arms and began sobbing.

"Rinala!" Horgris bellowed. "What be the meaning of this?" He lurched heavily to his feet and stared at the two with a look of utter confusion and helplessness that was entirely out of place on this forceful man. "What you be doing, girl?"

Shanis looked at the young woman, then back to Horgris, and she understood.

Rinala finally loosened her grip on Hierm, who was staring at her in astonishment. Tears flowed freely down her lightly tanned cheeks, and her smile brightened the dim, smoky room. She took his hand and laid it on her rounded belly. "I am only a few moons, but I will give you a son. The bone woman told me so."

"A son?" Hierm's face went ashen. "What..."

"You be the only man I am ever laying with. No one before you. No one after. I will give you a strong son, I promise. And I will be a good wife to you."

Hierm's lips were moving but he made no sound. Horgris bellowed so loudly that Shanis reached for her sword, but there was no need.

"My boy!" Horgris thumped him on the back so hard that he took a step forward. "A pleasure to welcome you to the family it will be. This girl been no telling me who it was, but now I be seeing why. Fearful for your life, she was." He pumped his fists and laughed. Wait until the other chiefs be hearing that me daughter be marrying one of the Six! Good blood, I tell ye, and a good omen." His celebration finished, he wrapped his arms around his daughter and the still-dumbstruck Hierm. "I am proud of ye, Rinala. You done good."

Suddenly remembering Shanis, he smiled at her. "Do think about what I have said. We'll be talking more later, girl. I do have a wedding to arrange."

Chapter 3

The wedding took place three days later. In accordance with Monaghan tradition it was held on a hilltop and in the moonlight. Hierm, though stunned by Rinala's revelation, was determined to do what he believed was the right thing. Horgris's enthusiasm at having a member of "The Six," as he called it, had rubbed off on his clansmen. Hierm was suddenly a well-loved member of the community, never without a companion or a mug of ale. He wandered the camp dazed by shock and strong drink in equal measure.

Shanis worried about what would happen to her friend. He was now an expectant father and about to become a husband, married to a young woman from another country and culture. On the other hand, honesty compelled her to admit that she rather enjoyed the thought of Mistress Faun being introduced to her new daughter by marriage. The mere thought of Hierm bringing the young clanswoman into the Van Derin home made her laugh. If Faun had felt Shanis did not know her place as a woman, she had a hard row to hoe with Rinala, who was strong-willed even for a Monaghan woman.

She was also grateful that the wedding had somwhat distracted Horgris from pressing her for a decision. He had not entirely left her alone, occasionally making mention of their previous conversation, but he had, for the most part, left her to make her mind up. She assumed that, once the wedding was over, she would have to make her decision.

Larris sidled up to her as they joined the crowd of Monaghan circled around the crest of the hill. He had surprised her by also not insisting on a decision. She knew he wanted her to go back to Galdora. That possibility had upset her more and more over the past few days, because she had gradually come to the disconcerting realization that if it was *her* Larris wanted, and not just the Silver Serpent, she probably would go with him. When had her feelings for him changed? In any case, she was much too proud to say anything to him.

"Does the moon look brighter to you?" He stared up at the silver orb.

"Is this a joke, or a poor attempt at being romantic?" Strange. She craved his company, but still took great pleasure in needling him.

"I'm serious. At first I thought it was my imagination, but I've noticed it for several days now. It's brighter and seems closer. I thought perhaps the air here is clearer than other places I've traveled, but we've passed through this territory before. I don't know, what do you think?" He scratched his head and continued to gaze at the sky in a manner, in Shanis's estimation, unbecoming of a royal.

"I don't know. Truthfully, I haven't thought of much besides myself and that ice forsaken sword. When that hasn't been on my mind, I've been busy trying to talk Hierm out of this wedding." She turned her eyes toward the sky. "I suppose it does seem brighter, now that you mention it." He was right. The moon did look different. Larger, brighter, more real. Strange.

"You are not the only one who does not want this marriage to take place. Rinala has no shortage of admirers, and several young men sound almost mutinous over the clan chief's daughter marrying an outlander." He fell silent for a moment.

"Does it bother you so much?" Larris's voice was light, but his expression grave. "Hierm's marriage, I mean." He turned to stare at her in that way he had of seeming to delve into her thoughts. She was finding it less annoying than she once had. Her verbal jousts with Larris were a fresh return to normalcy, an opportunity to forget about the sudden, drastic change in her life. "Or is it the entire concept of marriage to which you are opposed? The mighty warrior girl needs no man, and such."

"Oaf!" She shoved him away. "What bothers me is that my friend is about to marry a girl he has known for three days. How can that possibly be a good thing?"

"Three days, plus one evening," Larris added, grinning wickedly. He took a step back as if to avoid another push. "I am only joking. I can understand your concern. Among the nobility, our marriages are arranged for us and, more often than not, both parties are at least... content with the arrangement."

"Are they truly, or is that merely the face they put on for others to see?"

"I don't know," he confessed, "but I admire that Hierm is willing to stand behind his convictions. There's precious little honor among the nobility, I fear. All the court intrigue, the manipulation, the games that are played in the name of power. I find a bit of old-fashioned morality refreshing, if you want to know the truth."

"Give me a sword any day. There's no deceit in that. Just two people and two blades." It was perhaps the most pompous thing she had ever said. It sounded like something Master Yurg would say, or perhaps a storyteller. She hoped Larris would let it pass, but he did not.

"No deceit in swords? Hmmm." He rubbed his chin and frowned in an exaggerated look of thoughtfulness. "Though you are probably correct in the main, I think I still might be inclined to disagree."

"So would Hierm." She thought of Pedric Karst and the tournament they had not finished. She wondered what had become of Karst. The last time she had seen him, he was with Lerryn's party, and she had been convinced they were after her. But there had been no repeat encounter, thank the gods. Most likely Karst was now studying at the Prince's Academy, preparing to be an officer in the Galdoran army. A shame. She would have loved to cross swords with him. Such an eventuality was now highly unlikely.

"Truly? You will have to tell me about it sometime." The high-pitched trilling of pipes and the gentle thrumming of a hide drum interrupted their conversation.

The clan elders strode single-file up the hill, the light of the torches they bore casting eerie shadows on their weighty expressions. The onlookers parted to let them pass. They took up places in a semi-circle near the apex of the hill. Arborator Bomar, clan priest to the god Dagdar, came next. He was clad in the traditional clan garb, but wore a thick silver chain around his neck to denote his office. Hanging from the chain was a cylindrical pendant, which Shanis had been told contained soil from Amangdar, the sacred burial ground of the Monaghan. His snowy hair showed only traces of the red it had once been. Unlike the other clansmen, he was cleanshaven, revealing a round, kindly face that appeared misplaced on his short, powerful body.

Hierm strode to the top of the hill to stand beside the arborator. Granlor, the young man for whom Rinala once had eyes, stood at Hierm's right as his second. Hierm had wanted Shanis to stand with him, but like so many other traditions, she was excluded because she was female. A pity Oskar was not with them. He could have stood with Hierm. Her throat knotted at the thought of her lost friends, and she feared she would cry. Seeing the look on her face, Larris slipped his arm around her shoulders and smiled. *He thinks I'm emotional because it's a marriage ritual!*

"I wish Oskar could be here," she whispered, her voice thick. Larris's gaze dropped a little and his features sagged. He nodded and drew her closer to his side. She took a deep breath and forced her thoughts back to the moment at hand.

Rinala looked positively radiant as she came up the hill. Shanis had only seen her dressed in ordinary clothing and usually dirty from whatever daily tasks she had performed. In general, Monaghan women tended to be sturdy and handsome, but tonight Rinala was beautiful. She was garbed in an ornate silk dress, obviously old, but well-cared for. Perhaps it was an heirloom from a more peaceful time. Her hair was woven in a complex web of tiny braids, and mossflower adorned her head like a fine dusting of snow in early winter.

Horgris escorted her, wearing his clan garb, which looked to have actually been washed for the occasion, as no food or drink stains were evident, along with his tall, hawk-feathered hat. She noted with detached amusement that a few additional feathers had been strategically placed to cover the hole Allyn's arrow had made in it months ago. The clan chieftain smiled and walked with a jovial bounce to his step, clearly enjoying the attention the moment brought. Considering he had intended to kill her the first time they met, she rather liked the man. He was a ferocious warrior to be sure, but a good and decent leader as well as a doting father. Miliana, his wife, followed behind, dressed in a simple gown. It was obvious where Rinala had gotten her lithe build and good looks. The only things she appeared to have inherited from Horgris were his coppery hair and, if the whisperings were true, his prodigious temper.

The wedding party reached the top, and all turned to face the arborator. Shanis noticed that Rinala and Horgris were bound together at the wrist with a strip of fabric. A hush grew over those assembled as the ceremony began.

"In the sight of Dagdar, who brings life to the earth, and upon whose benevolent hands we stand, may these two who stand before us be blessed upon their path. May their household be blessed with a solid foundation, strong walls, and a warm fire. May the fruits they bear be abundant, and may they remain united in marriage, in service to their clan and to their god.

"Hierm Van Derin, of the clan Van Derin of Galsbur. You stand before this assemblage to make your pledge to Rinala ni Miliana, of the Hawk Hill clan of Monaghan. Do you pledge upon your honor and your life to be a husband to her, to provide for her with the toil of your labor, to protect her with the might of your sword, and to love her with the strength of your heart?"

Hierm knelt and scooped up a handful of dirt. Rising, he held his clenched fist before him. "In the sight of Dagdar who brings life to the earth, I so pledge." He opened his hand and let the soil fall to the ground.

Granlor handed him something. It was the ancient wreath he had been given by the Thandrylls. A soft murmur ran through the onlookers as he placed it on Rinala's head. Shanis had paid no attention to it when he received it in the Thandryll's trading ritual, but now she took a closer look. It was masterfully woven, the twisted coils of ancient vine were shaped into the semblance of flowers: daisies, mossflowers and moonblooms. Had human hands truly woven such a creation? The gray-brown vines were smooth and shiny with age, and glistened in the combined light of the torches and the full moon. Rinala's eyes shone as she saw the gift her new husband had bestowed upon her. Horgris nodded in approval.

"Rinala ni Miliana of the Hawk Hill clan of Monaghan. You stand before this assemblage to make your pledge to Hierm Van Derin of the clan Van Derin of Galsbur. Do you pledge upon your honor and your life to be a wife to him, to bless him with the fruit of your loins, to serve him with the work of your hands..." Many people chuckled at that, including Horgris. "...and love him with the strength of your heart?"

Rinala repeated the ritual just as Hierm had, scooping up soil, making her pledge, and sprinkling the soil onto the ground. For her part, she placed around Hierm's neck a braided leather hawk claw necklace. The process was awkward with her left arm still bound to her father, but she managed. She stepped back, beaming up at Hierm, who smiled in return.

He does seem happy. Perhaps he really does care for her. Shanis marveled at the realization. She had assumed that he was only doing this out of a sense of duty and obligation, but Hierm appeared happy. He had been such a brooding young man under his father's constant disapproving gaze and his mother's suffocating control, that she had forgotten what it was like to see him relaxed and at peace. The thought warmed her heart. Without realizing what she was doing, she slipped her arm around Larris's waist and pulled him close.

"Do you, Horgris ni Lamana, Chieftain of the Hawk Hill clan of Monaghan," Bomar continued, "grant your blessing upon this marriage and accept Hierm Van Derin of the clan Van Derin of Galsbur into your hearth and home?"

"That I do," Horgris said, his voice strangely soft. He kissed his daughter gently on the forehead, and stood smiling as Bomar untied the cloth that bound him to his child. He stepped back and took Miliana's hand. The two watched, Miliana tearfully, as Bomar now bound Rinala to Hierm.

"In the sight of Dagdar," the arborater boomed, "I declare you are husband and wife. May the road before you be smooth, the rain be gentle, and may the earth always be soft beneath your feet."

At that proclamation, the pipes sang out and the drums struck up a joyous beat. The onlookers roared as they moved apart, creating a path down which the new husband and wife descended the hill. They pelted Hierm and Rinala with chunks of the gray-green moss that grew in the lower branches of nearby trees. Well wishes from the women and bawdy suggestions from the men chased the couple down the hill where a blazing bonfire, food and drink awaited them.

CHAPTER 4

The new couple was the center of a loud and ebullient celebration, with everyone wanting to give blessings, advice, or both. Shanis was finally able to draw Hierm aside. He had abstained from drinking, but was in a fine mood. His face had a relaxed quality that made him look like the Hierm she remembered from their early childhood. No longer did he appear weary from the strain of their adventure. The fatigue and worry had made him look too much like his father for Shanis's comfort. Now he seemed renewed.

"Are you all right?" Shanis asked. It seemed impossible that marriage to an almost-complete stranger could have such an effect on him. "You seem happy, but I just wonder..."

"Yes. I am happy." He said the words as if they came as a surprise to him. "I was shocked and frightened at first, but the thought of being a father and a husband appeals to me. I want to be the sort of father I did not have. And Rinala is a kind, beautiful girl. She also has a temper, but that just makes her more interesting. In many ways she reminds me..." His voice trailed off and he looked away for a moment. "I'm sorry. I only meant..."

"I am flattered." Shanis squeezed his hand. "Truly I am. We were always close, but it never seemed exactly... right between the two of us, did it?"

"No, it didn't." He shook his head and looked back at the cluster of well-wishers that encircled Rinala. "But with Rinala, it's almost as if this is my destiny. Ever since we left home I've felt that something was directing our lives— some force beyond our control. This marriage feels like a part of it."

He shrugged. This was not the sort of conversation in which Hierm normally took part. This was more Oskar's domain. Each thought of her missing friends was another dagger to her heart. Hierm's sudden downcast look matched her feeling. "I had better get back. It would not do to make Rinala jealous on her wedding night."

"Good luck." She turned to find Larris standing behind her. "Spying on me?" She smiled to make certain he knew she was joking. "How are you enjoying the festivities?"

"This is my first Monaghan wedding. It is quite interesting. Not so liturgical as that to which I'm accustomed, but it has its own beauty." He held out his hand to her. "Would you care to dance?"

Shanis protested that she could not dance, but he would not hear of it, reminding her of their last visit to Horgris's village. He seemed to have forgotten that the evening of which he spoke had not ended so happily. But, despite her reservations, he was soon leading her through an ancient promenade. He danced like he fought— with confidence and practiced grace.

She found herself drawn more and more to this young man, and she stared into his brown eyes, as if trying to read his intentions. He had definitely seemed interested in her when they first met, but she worried that her almost-constant rejections had dampened his spirits. Foolishness! He still paid plenty of attention to her. It was up to her to decide what she wanted.

The drummers now struck a faster beat, and they flew into a raucous, foot-stomping Monaghan traditional dance. Neither of them was familiar with it, but they made a good approximation of the steps, which mostly involved stomping, clapping and turning while working your way around the bonfire. Partners switched several times during the dance, but she found herself back with Larris at the end.

Horgris interrupted the dancing to make a speech, in which he praised his daughter, mostly due to her fine bloodline and upbringing. This part of his speech drew loud laughter and derisive comments at the appropriate times. He went on to praise his new son by marriage and proclaim his blessing upon the union. He then grew very serious.

"It be Monaghan tradition that the father must be givin' his daughter a marriage gift. Were times bein' as they once were, I would be proud to grant you a piece of land to call yer own. It is my vow," he continued, turning to look across the crowd directly at Shanis, "that things be changin' in my lifetime. I pledge to you that, in my lifetime, I be makin' good on yer gift."

The clansmen and women cheered, but only Shanis and Horgris knew what had passed between them, though she supposed a few of the elders also knew what he was suggesting. How dare he? It was her decision to make, and she would not be guilted into making it one way or the other. She turned and stalked away.

"Where are you going? It's almost over." Larris hurried up and fell in step with her. "Rinala's brothers kidnap her and Hierm has to fight them to get her back. It's not as serious as it sounds, but it should be fun. What's wrong?"

"I can't take it any longer. You are all pulling me in too many directions." She stopped walking and turned to face him. "You want me to go to back Galdora. Horgris wants me to stay here and unite Lothan. As usual, no one seems to care what I want."

"All right. What *do* you you want, Shanis?" Larris moved closer, their faces almost touching, and lowered his voice to little more than a whisper. "Tell me you don't want to go to Galdora with me, and I will accept that. Reluctantly, to be sure, but I will accept it."

How could such a simple question confuse her so? Was he asking her to go to Galdora for the good of the realm, or was it because he wanted them to be together? There was a world of difference between the two, but her pride had kept her from asking. Now was the time.

Shouts arose from the far side of the camp. Hoofbeats thudded in the soft earth. Not many riders. She suddenly remembered her sword back in the hut. "I'll be back." She left Larris standing alone in the dark as she sprinted away.

"I'll find you later," Larris called out, his voice a blend of annoyance and amusement.

Her feet slipped on the damp loam, and she stumbled on protruding rocks. The cries had died down, and there were no sounds of fighting. She slowed and looked back, but she could see little in the foggy air, save the glow of the bonfire and dark shadows moving around it. She hurriedly retrieved her sword and made her way back.

Most of the villagers were clustered near the fire, and she had to force her way through the crowd in order to find out what was happening. Breaking through the throng, she came upon a group of elders tending to a dozen or more newcomers. All were injured, some more serious than others. One was dead. Blood, looking slick and black in the firelight, soaked his tunic and obscured his tartan so she could not tell if these people were of Horgris's clan.

"...set upon us without warning. We been trying to skirt around them, but their outriders spotted us and chased us down," one of the men was explaining to Horgris while Amia, the bone woman of the Hawk Hill clan, tended to his wounded shoulder. "We be havin' no chance except to flee. Dagrim put arrows in a couple and I took a few down me'self. They finally leave us be when it be plain we no be coming back their way." His voice broke a bit as he spoke. "Little Lissie, she been hurt something fierce."

"Ye no be worryin about her," Horgris said in his gruff voice. "We be takin' care of her." Shanis could see the lie in his eyes. "You say the Three Oaks be doing this? We no be havin' trouble with them for a long time." His voice heated. "Why they be this way to you? Do you be knowin?"

"They thought we be spies or the like," the man said, grimacing as Amia bound his wound. "They no be lettin' anybody close to their camp. They do have Badla."

The murmur that had filled the crowd erupted in cries of surprise, anger and, in some cases, joy.

"Badla! We be takin' her from them for sure!" Granlor raised his fist in the air. "Honor to the Hawk Hill! Honor to Monaghan!" Other young men joined their voices to his. Chants of "Badla! Badla!" rang through the hills.

Shanis turned away, disgusted by the hunger for pride in the face of so much hurt. Vengeance she could understand, but to be so easily distracted by the opportunity to steal a corpse?

Her thoughts were distracted as her eyes fell on a little girl who lay gasping for breath in her mother's arms. Blood soaked the blankets in which she was wrapped and smeared her face. Her mother looked up at Shanis with eyes as dead as her daughter was soon likely to be. This must be Lissie.

"She did take an arrow." Her mother spoke in a vacant tone that matched the look in her eyes. "We did remove it out, but her body be so… small. She be only six summerss old. Why my little girl?"

Rinala, who was attempting to comfort the woman, looked up at Shanis with tearful eyes aglow with unrecognizeable thoughts.

"You be the one," Rinala said. "You able to be helpin' her." While Shanis stood dumbstruck, trying to find the words to protest, Rinala lifted the little girl from her mother's arms and thrusted her upon Shanis. "Use the Silver Serpent. You can do it." Others heard Rinala's words, and gathered around.

"Yes!" someone cried. "You be havin' the power. You save Lissie then you be punishin' the Three Oaks!" A few shouted curses at the Three Oaks, while the rest pressed in on Shanis, speaking to her in urgent tones, begging her to believe in the power she supposedly possessed.

What could she say? She looked down at the little girl, who gazed up at her with big, green eyes. The courage she saw there broke her heart. She wished she could help, but she didn't know how. She wanted to shout at them, to tell them that she neither knew what the power was, nor how it worked. She could not even remember using it the first time. But when she looked around at their desperate, pleading faces, she knew she could not disappoint them.

How did magic work? How did sorcery work? Kneeling down beside the little girl and taking her hand, she closed her eyes and fixed her mind on the sword strapped to her back. She imagined power flowing out from the blade, through her body and into the little girl. She opened her eyes and looked down at the child.

Nothing.

Her vision misted, her throat pinched, and she sagged under the twin burdens of expectation and despair. She could not do it. She didn't know how. She was helpless.

I give up.

The serpent on her chest suddenly burned with an intensity that made her gasp. Her back stiffened straight as a post as something she could only call power surged like an avalanche through her body. It raged down her arms and into Lissie. The little girl uttered a small cry, and her eyes widened in surprise, but not pain.

Shanis could not see what was happening, but she felt it. She felt the little girl's body mending, the wound closing up. Her heartbeat strengthened and steadied, as did her breathing. With a contented sigh, Lissie curled up against Shanis and closed her eyes.

"Lissie!" Her mother wailed and she snatched the girl away, but her despair turned to joy as she realized that her daughter had not died, but was sleeping peacefully. The woman stripped away Lissie's bloody clothes to expose the girl's fully healed body. She held her daughter in her arms, stood, and turned for all the others to see. They were too amazed to cheer, or even smile. Lissie awoke and vehemently protested her state of undress and the effect of the chill night air. Still laughing, her mother held her tight as someone led them to a nearby hut.

And now Shanis remembered. She could recall the moment of absolute surrender in which she pushed her own limitations aside and let the power of the Silver Serpent take her over. She remembered the battle with the serpent, and the words it had spoken to her. Most of all, she remembered the torrent of power that surged through her then just as it did now.

"Girl! Help me now!" someone shouted.

"No! Me next!" cried another.

She could not.

Right now she was struggling to control the storm that raged within her. Her body felt as if it would explode as the force grew within her. She imagined herself swelling from the sheer volume of power. She focused her mind on the serpent on her chest.

Stop! No more! The flow cut off, but the power still stormed within her. Crying out in agony, she fell to her hands and knees, clawing at the turf. She was aware of Larris at her side, asking if he could help. Hierm was there as well, and Rinala. Allyn was nearby, but he cringed and drew away at the sight of her struggles.

She had to do something with all of this power. She could no longer contain it. Her thoughts turned to the sword. It seemed to beckon to her, and she willed the power into the weapon. The sword drank it up. She could feel it draining from her body as it filled the ancient blade. Finally, the weapon could take no more. Energy still surged within her, but now she could contain it.

"Help me stand," she whispered to Larris. He took her by the arm and aided her as she rose. She chose the person who appeared to be the most badly hurt and laid her hands on his temples.

"I have only done this once before, so I make no promises." She closed her eyes and allowed the power to flow forth through her fingertips and into the man. This time, she was ready for the shock as it poured forth, and she barely flinched. She felt the healing energy flow into him, finding and mending his wounds. It was as if some unseen force controlled the energy. She was simply the vessel that carried the power. When she finished, the man smiled and thanked her profusely. Too tired to do more than nod, she moved on to the next person.

Larris and Hierm remained by her side as she tended to more of the injured. By the time she had healed the fourth person, she was completely spent. The energy that had surged within her was gone. The serpent on her breast pulsed and tingled, wanting to unleash another torrent, but she was too weak to manage it. If another such flow of power entered her body, she would be unable to control it, and she was certain it would destroy her. She forced herself to stand up straight, but Larris read the look in her eyes.

"She has done all that she can," he told Horgris, his arm now wrapped protectively around her. "She needs rest."

"Aye," Horgris replied. "You done well, girl. But if you going to be a leader, you no let them see you be weak. Can you be walking on your own?" She wanted to tell him that she was not going to lead anyone, but she lacked the energy to argue, so she merely nodded her head. Larris let go of her arm, but he did not move away.

"My kinsmen," Horgris shouted. "Today be a blessed day. Not only do my daughter be gettin' married, but today we be seein' the miraculous power of the Silver Serpent, and she who do bear it. Glory to the Hawk Hill! Glory to Monaghan! Glory to Lothan!"

Cheers exploded and shouts of *Hawk Hill!, Monaghan!,* and even a few of *Shanis!* rang out. The crowd parted for her and, with the last of her energy, she made her way back to her hut.

She did not bother to undress, but fell heavily onto the thick bearskin sleeping mat. Larris covered her and extinguished the light. She did not know if he planned to stay with her or not, but she hoped he did.

Sleep devoured her, filling her head with dreams she did not comprehend. When she woke the next morning, she had come to a decision.

CHAPTER 5

Oskar had sometimes tried to imagine what death was like. This was definitely not it. It was cold, wet and utterly devoid of light. And he hurt all over. The next life was supposed to be a pleasant reward for a life well-lived, but this…

Wait a moment! Cold, dark, painful… He was in the underworld! He had never truly believed all his mother's warnings that his sharp tongue and irreverent attitude were offensive to the gods. Perhaps she had been right. All the misdeeds he had ever done came rushing back. What was he going to do? If this was how he was to spend eternity…

He realized his arms were bound. He struggled to move, but he could not get loose. Something was crawling on him. He felt its cold tongue on his face. He thrashed and twisted, trying to break free. What was it going to do to him? He tried to scream, but no sound would come.

"Oskar… Oskar…" It whispered his name, and he imagined a dark wraith ready to take him in its chill embrace. He tried to turn his head, to shake loose from its cold kiss. "Oskar… Wake up. You're safe…"

He would not believe its lies. He flailed about, and a groan escaped his lips.

"Open your eyes. You are all right. I'm here with you." A red-orange glow filled his field of vision. The beast stopped licking his face, and the air around him grew warmer. So the beast was trying a new tactic—trying to entice him with warmth and light.

"Please come back to me. Just wake up. Open your eyes." The voice was feminine, enticing... He felt a light pressure on his chest. It was touching him, but the feeling was not so disconcerting this time. Perhaps he would open his eyes just long enough to see what torture eternity held in store for him. He had to find out sooner or later.

Opening his eyes was no mean feat. It was like loading heavy sacks onto a wagon. Finally, with significant effort, he parted the lids enough to see smoky light shining on a rough stone ceiling. Someone was leaning over him. Someone familiar...

"Thank the gods you're awake. I don't know how long you've been unconscious, but it seems like days. I tried to keep you warm, but everything got so wet when we fell. I..."

The person kept talking, but Oskar was not listening. He was trying to remember.

Falling... falling... falling.

He remembered falling, but not from where, or how it had happened.

He searched his mind and recalled the golorak coming after them. The chamber with the seastone coffins. The battle with the serpent. He had raised his staff and tried to do... whatever it was he had done back in Thandryll.

And then nothing...

He forced his eyes to open wider and tried to sit up, but a wave of nausea swept over him and he fell back. He groaned again and wished that he could have been dead after all. Being alive was not worth this misery.

"Once I was certain you were not going, I did a bit of exploring. Really, I just felt my way around. I didn't want to use what few firesticks we had. I found bits of wood and such, and I finally was able to make a fire. Can you believe it? Me! I made a fire the way Shanis does it. It isn't much, but it gives a little light and warmth. I had to use some of your parchment, Oskar, but I made certain it had no writing on it. I hope that is all right. I needed something dry to burn."

He finally realized who was speaking. No one else could talk for so long without need of someone else taking part in the conversation.

"Khalyndryn?" he croaked. "Where are we? Where are the others?" His mind no longer moved like cold molasses, and thoughts coursed through his mind. Where were Shanis, Hierm, Larris and Allyn? Had they survived the battle with the serpent? They had heard the bellows of more than one golorak. Were more lurking somewhere nearby?

"I don't know," she said, though she did not indicate which question she was answering. "Do you remember the fight?"

He nodded.

"Shanis took the stone sword off of the statue in the center of the room, and something happened. It looked like the statue turned into a real sword, and she started fighting the serpent with it. But when she took the sword, the statue sank out of sight, and the floor started sloping down toward the hole where the statue had been. You fainted, or something, and I tried to hold on to you. But we fell."

Khalyndryn had tried to save him? He remembered a little bit more now. He was holding out his staff, trying to call down the lightning again, but when Shanis touched the sword, a blinding flash of agony burst in his mind. Somehow, the sword had done it to him.

"I have no idea what happened to the others." Her voice was rife with sadness. "I hope they are alive, but I do not know. We fell into deep water and we were carried a long way. I don't know how I found you, but we drifted together, and I was able to keep your head above water. You float on your back quite well, by the way."

"Thanks," he grumbled, trying again to sit up and managing to prop up on an elbow. "So, where are we now?"

"When the water was shallow enough, I managed to drag you onto this ledge. Our packs held up very well, being oilcloth and all. Our spare cloaks were dry, as were our food and fire-sticks. I only wish we had more. What we have will not last very long, I fear. We left so many of our belongings up on the mountain above Murantha that there just is not much left. I found one other pack. I think it is Allyn's. That gave us a little more food and a spare cloak.

At the mention of food Oskar's stomach rumbled. He suddenly felt as if he had not eaten in weeks. "Can you spare a little for me?"

"I think so," Khalyndryn said. "I haven't had an appetite. I did manage to warm some water. No tea, unfortunately, but warm water takes the chill off."

Oskar ate a small piece of cheese and a hard crust of stale bread, washing it down with a cup of hot water. He still felt worse than he'd ever felt in his life, but he was alive and, hopefully, so were his friends.

"What should we do now?" He was surprised to hear himself asking Khalyndryn such a question, but he was not in any condition to make a decision on his own. "We can't stay in the dark forever."

"This ledge follows the stream. I suppose we should go in that direction." She sighed and looked away into the darkness. "The gods willing, we'll find a way out." She did not remark on what would happen if they did not find an escape before their food ran out.

For a fleeting moment, Oskar imagined wandering alone in this abysmal darkness, buried beneath earth and stone, far from sun and sky. He shuddered.

"I hope you aren't taking a chill." Khalyndryn misunderstood the reason for his trembling and scooted up against him to try and add her warmth to his. The feel of her touch was like a shock, but in a good way. How many times in his life had he admired her from afar, knowing she had eyes only for the most handsome young men?

"I know it's cold and damp down here, but I did the best I could for you..."

He placed his finger on her lips, surprised at himself that he would touch her in such a familiar way.

"Thank you, Khalyndryn, for taking care of me. I would not have survived if you had not been here for me."

Her smile warmed his spirit as her body warmed his. She had never been strong or independent, but she had certainly been self-reliant while looking out for him.

Much too soon, she pulled away from him and stood up, hastily brushing non-existent dirt off of her clothing. "I suppose we should gather our things and start walking."

They wandered for what seemed like days, feeling their way along the cold, smooth passage. They saved their meager supply of wood for the occasional fire, so they might have a little extra warmth when they stopped to sleep. They lay on spare cloaks when they slept, but the stone floor leached the heat from their bodies.

The ledge on which they walked narrowed in places, or even disappeared entirely, and they found themselves slogging knee deep through the dark, icy water. It sapped the feeling from Oskar's legs and feet, and drained him of what little warmth and energy he had. They were forced to stop all too frequently, always at his behest. He still did not feel right. Every time they paused, he found himself wanting to lie down and never get back up again. But every time he faltered, Khalyndryn would get him moving again.

"Come on Oskar!" Her voice cracked like a whip. "Get up and move. You are not going to curl up and die on me down here after I've worked so hard to keep you going."

And they would go on. Step by mind-numbing step, neither of them giving voice to what they both wondered—would they ever again ever see a glimmer of light, a reason for hope?

The longer they remained in this black prison, the further his spirits fell. One time, half-conscious, he staggered into the water and felt something long and slimy slither past his leg. He shouted and scrambled away, sputtering and shaking. After that he clung to the wall, fearful that something might reach out and grab him.

He tried not to voice his fears, but from time to time he would let slip a comment about the hopelessness of their situation.

"We will get there, don't you worry." Her voice never wavered, and she gave no indication that she might entertain even the slightest possibility that she might be wrong. To drive her point home, she seized him by the front of his damp cloak and yanked him forward. Either she had grown stronger or he was still very weak, because she guided him around like a cow led to milking, and she kept him going that way until they reached the end of the passage.

The tunnel finally ended in a blank wall where the stream formed a deep pool. They felt around for any opening at all. They searched about for the faintest light, or breath of fresh, dry air, but they found nothing.

They lit a fire and repeated their search by its faint light. Finally they took flaming brands and worked their way back up the tunnel in case they had missed a side passage or egress, but they soon gave up. They returned to their campfire too disheartened to speak.

They would die here.

Oskar had neither the energy nor the desire to retrace their steps, and their food would not hold out much longer. They shared a silent meal and fell asleep by the dying embers of their tiny fire. As his eyes closed, he wondered if he should bother to wake again.

"I see light! Oskar, I see light!"

Khalyndryn's voice roused him from his slumber, and he returned to consciousness like a swimmer coming up for air. Slowly, slowly, slowly... then gasping for breath. The meaning of her words finally broke through the haze of sleep, and he bolted up, afraid to believe what he had heard. Surely it had been a dream.

Khalyndryn took him by the arm and led him to the water's edge.

"Look down there under the water. You can just see it. It must have been after dark when we reached this spot. I suppose it's morning now. That has to be light from outside!"

He lay down on his stomach and peered down into the dark pool.

He saw it—a shaft of light far beneath the surface. It was the first cause for hope since he had awakened in this dark, dank place, but he could not permit himself to feel optimistic. It might be an opening to the outside, but what if it was too small to get through? What would they do then? Might it not be better to die in the dark than to die so close to freedom?

"We'll just have to swim down to it and see where it takes us." Khalyndryn's voice trembled with excitement. "We did it! We found the way out!"

He did not have the heart to voice his concerns to her. Instead, he began stuffing his things into his pack in preparation for a swim.

CHAPTER 6

"What do you mean you are staying here? Are you out of your mind?" Larris threw his hands up and looked up at the sky as if searching for a source of help there. They had taken a walk away from camp in order to speak privately. "You are a Galdoran. The prophecies say that the Silver Serpent..."

"I know what you've told me the prophecies say. The prophecies also say the bearer can unite the clans in Lothan." She already knew how this argument would likely play out, but her mind was made up.

"Those are different prophecies." He frowned. "I have read them, and I am uncertain about their reliability."

"Well, I haven't read any of them. It occurs to me that I have been doing a remarkable amount of listening to other people, and it's time for me to make my own decision." She put her hand over his mouth before he could interrupt her again. His eyes flared. This was probably the first time someone had done that to the prince. "Please, just listen to me. I held that little girl in my arms, looked into her eyes, and I realized that if there is any chance at all that I can stop the clan wars, I have to try. What is happening here is too terrible to just turn away from them when there is a chance I can help."

"Your heart is in the right place, but what can you truly do? You aren't a clan leader. You aren't a Lothan at all. Why would they listen to you?" He had regained control of his temper and was now speaking calmly.

"Because I have this." She pointed to the serpent on her chest. "But most of all because the prophecy says I'm going to." She folded her arms across her chest and waited for him to argue, but he just stood there. Might there be a chance he would listen to her?

"I could use some help. I don't know how to lead people. I need you." That was as close as she was going to come to opening her heart to him, until he did some opening of his own. "Will you help me?"

Larris stared at her, his expression blank. For a moment, she feared that he was not going to say anything at all, but finally he broke the silence.

"You should begin with this clan. They have witnessed your power firsthand, and right now there is no one here more beloved than you. Besides that, Horgris has already pledged his support. Capitalize on that. Get them behind you today. Right now."

"All right." She had asked for his help, but she was a bit taken aback by his quick turnaround. "How do I begin?"

"The people need not only a person to follow, but a vision in which to believe. What is your vision?"

"Well, I..."

"No! That will never do. You must know your vision and believe in it. You must be ready to speak from your heart any time someone asks. Tell me, from your heart, what will you do to change the lives of this clan?"

"I would heal their broken country. Give their children the chance to grow up. Their grandchildren could know peace and prosperity. I would bind Lothan's wounds and make her strong." She didn't know where that had come from, but it was what she felt.

"That's a good start." He suddenly reminded her of Master Yurg criticizing her sword technique. "But tell them what you *will* do. Not what you hope to do, or want to do. They must know that you will do what you say." His brown eyes burned with intensity.

"I can do that."

"Very well. Now, tell me how you are going to do it."

"What? I don't know. I suppose..."

"You cannot suppose anything. Tell me, without pausing, stammering, or showing the least bit of doubt, what specifically you plan to do. Even if you're not completely certain. Go ahead." He sat down on a nearby stump and stared up at her with an expectant look.

"We will start with the Monaghan." Larris had annoyed her, so her words were firm, even harsh. "We will march up to the holds of each clan one at a time. I will heal their wounded, show them the sword and the serpent, and then I will tell them that the time of clan war is at an end. I will call them to unite, and then I will move on to the Malgog."

Larris just stared at her, the morning sunlight framing his face in golden light. Finally, he smiled. "It's a start," he said. "Your plan will likely change as you go, but it is enough to get the people behind you. Listen to those you trust behind closed doors, but always be strong in front of the clan. Do not let people know that I am advising you. The last thing you want is for them to believe that you are somehow under the control of the Galdoran crown." His eyes softened. "In fact, I should probably leave for that very reason."

He let his gaze fall to the ground, and her heart fell along with it. He was going to leave her? Oskar was gone, Hierm was married and now Larris was going to leave. She didn't want him to go, not only because she was lonely and in need of his counsel, but she was finally able to admit to herself that she wanted him there. But the frost would take her before she spoke first.

"But I don't want to go." He sat there, staring at the ground. "I should be back in Galdora. It was childish of me to leave without telling my father, and I am probably needed, but I don't want to leave."

"Then why don't you stay?" She tried to keep her voice casual.

"Because a royal cannot wed a commoner," he said quietly, his voice strained as if the words pained him. "And I would never treat you the way Lerryn treats women."

She could not believe what he was saying. Her eyes burned, but she was determined not to cry. Her throat choked off the words she wanted to say.

Larris rose, came to her, and caught her in a crushing embrace. She wrapped her arms around his neck. Before she knew what was happening, his lips were on hers, their bodies pressed together. Too soon he broke the kiss and pressed his cheek against hers.

"I am sorry. I know I should not have done that." His breath was warm in her ear. "You must know I would never shame you."

"Stay with me." Her voice was almost a sob. "All the rest we can figure out, but please stay with me. I need you here. I want you here."

The space between her declaration and his reply seemed interminable. They stood there, locked in their embrace, and she hoped it would not end. She felt a warmth she had not felt since she left home, a feeling of belinging, of being home. What if he said no?

"All right. I will stay for as long as I can. If you are certain you want me?" He drew back to look her in the eye. Their noses were almost touching. She was suprised to see a touch of fear in his eyes.

"You be out here, girl?" Horgris's voice boomed from somewhere nearby. She pushed away from Larris and wiped her face. A moment later, the big man appeared through the trees. "Apologies," he said when he noticed Larris's annoyed expression. "I know we already been talking about this, but the elders be wanting to speak to ye. After last night, they be hoping to convince ye..."

"There is no need to convince me," she said, grateful for the distraction from Larris. She had wanted him to admit that he cared for her, but now she was even more confused. What sort of future could they have? "I have made up my mind. I would like to speak to the entire clan if I may."

Horgris smiled. "That be the spirit! You be doin' the right thing girl. You'll never regret the decision you make, and you always have Horgris to support ye." He beckoned for them to follow him back to the camp. He led them through the shady patch of forest, and as she stepped out into the daylight, it seemed to her as if she were stepping into a new world.

She stood atop the hill where Heirm and Rinala had wed only the night before. The clanspeople were gathered round. She felt sick; her heart pounded, her stomach was icy and sour, and her hands were clammy. What was she doing? She was a farm girl from a village in Galdora. Who was she to presume she could unite a nation? The very thought was absurd.

And then her eyes fell upon Lissie, the little girl she had somehow healed. She smiled up at Shanis with total adoration. This was why Shanis had to to what she was going to do. By no choice of her own, she was destined to heal, and she would begin by healing this land and its people. She had agonized much of the night over what she would say, and the talk with Larris had fueled her desire and focused her thoughts. The words seemed to come unbidden.

"I am Shanis Malan," she began. "I bear the Silver Serpent." Cheers erupted all around her. "And I have been so marked." She pulled her tunic down far enough to reveal the silver marking on her chest. "As you know, I have been granted the power to heal." A few cheers again, but most people were listening closely to what she said.

"In the short time I have spent among you, I have grown to admire and appreciate your courage, your strength and your kindness. My heart weeps at the suffering of such a proud people and a noble land. Monaghan deserves better." Loud shouts of agreement answered this statement. "Lothan deserves better." More cheers, though less enthusiastic. "I would heal your people, and I would heal your land. Lothan must again be united and stand as a proud, powerful nation. I would do this so that ones such as these..." She picked up Lissie and held her up for all to see. "...may grow old. That your grandchildren and their grand-children might prosper."

They were quiet now. Some were frowning at her, suspicious of her message.

"I do not promise you peace. At least not yet." Sadly, that drew nods of approval. "Nor do I demand that you come to me on bended knee. I offer to you my sword and my service. The power of the Silver Serpent can both heal and destroy. It is my most fervent hope that this power be used only to heal, but if it must be used to break those who oppose peace, so be it. In any case, I promise you this: the days of interminable clan war are at an end."

Utter silence met her proclamation. Some looked at her in confusion, while a few smiling women wept silent tears of hopefulness and thanks. A few young men stared down at the ground or shook their head. But many were nodding.

"I call upon those who will join me to come forth and make yourselves known."

This was the moment. Horgris stood in the back. He could not be the first to come forward. As clan leader he could not seem to be in her thrall, nor could he give the appearance of guiding the clan down this path. Someone else had to be the first to come forward.

"I will follow you." Granlor stepped out of the crowd. Unsheathing his sword, he knelt before her, the point of the blade on the ground, his hand resting on the hilt. She had asked them to join her, not follow her, but that is precisely what he had just pledged to do. Two more young men came forward, close friends of Granlor's, and joined him.

And then there were others: a few older men, one of the leading women, and then Hierm and Rinala together. The sight of Hierm kneeling before her moved her deeply and strengthened her resolve. Next came Horgris, along with men she knew to be members of the Order of the Fox, a semi-secret society dedicated to the re-unification of Lothan. And when Horgris came forth, it was as if the dam had burst. Soon, she was ringed by members of the Hawk Hill Clan, all kneeling before her. Larris and Allyn stood over to the side, Larris smiling and Allyn looking at her dispassionately. Seeing the two of them side-by-side now, it was strange to remember that she had once preferred the standoffish archer to the gregarious prince.

Only a small knot of young people remained standing. Six young men and three young women, led by Arlus, a broad-chested young clansman with flowing auburn hair and a sparse beard that scarcely covered his face. He scowled at her, his face filled with contempt.

Horgris looked up and noticed those who had not joined them. "We would be having this unanimous. No division among the Hawk Hill. Join us, men of Monaghan."

Arlus shook his head. "She be an outlander and a woman at that. You hear her words. She be wanting peace with the Malgog, with the other clans. She would break bread with those who spill our blood. The Hawk Hill cowers before no one!" His companions nodded. "We be proud warriors of Monaghan, born to fight and die for clan and honor, no to be making nice with our enemies."

"Lothan has more enemies than it can count." Shanis wondered how Larris would receive what she was about to say. "Her borders are threatened by greedy neighbors who see the lack of unity as weakness. Every year her borders shrink." The elders gathered around her murmured in general agreement.

"And there are others. I have seen with my own eyes the creatures of the Ice King. I was there when brave men of the Hawk Hill clan slew such beasts."

Horgris stood up, fished around inside his tunic, and withdrew the silver-gray paw of an ice cat. He held it up for all to see. The people gradually stood again, and they stared at the paw in fascination. Had he never displayed it before?

"Grandmother's tales," Arlus scoffed. "Next you be scarin' us with tales of boggarts and buggins. I be saying it again. I will no bend knee to no outlander woman, and I will no make peace with the Malgog. Not ever." He turned and strode down the hill, the others following behind.

"Your clan be seeing it different, Arlus!" Horgris shouted.

"It be no clan of mine." He stripped off his tartan and hurled it to the ground. "We be of the clanless. And Hawk Hill be our enemy." The others followed his example, leaving their clan garb lying in the dirt as they departed.

Horgris looked as if he would go after them, but then he turned back to face Shanis.

"The Hawk Hill clan do pledge its swords and its honor to the cause of unity. May the bearer of the Silver Serpent be leading us to a united Lothan."

As the clan cheered, the men raised their swords in celebration. Shanis drew the Silver Serpent, and raised it overhead. The morning light shimmered golden on the blade. Was she bringing a shining light to this dark land, or was she starting a fire that would burn out of control? Time would tell.

CHAPTER 7

Aspin stoked the cookfire and set a pot of water on to boil. He had found a most satisfactory campsite at the edge of a deep pool nestled in a tiny valley. The autumn sun, cheery and warm, shone through a stand of birch trees. It was a fine morning.

It would have been even finer were he not completely baffled as to where to go next. He had pursued the Malan girl past the Ramsgate, but not long afterward, the sorcerous blast had happened. How long he had lain unconscious there was no way to know, but by the time he awoke, the world was somehow different. The sky was a richer hue of blue, the clouds thicker and puffier. All the life surrounding him seemed more vital. The entire world was... more alive.

What was even more puzzling was what he had come to think of as a magical residue arching across the sky back toward Lothan. It was as if some powerful work of sorcery had taken place somewhere far above. He could not say for certain, but he could sense that the trail started in the mountains and ended back to the east. With nothing else to go by, he had changed his course and headed in that direction.

He checked the lines he had set out the previous night and was pleased to find he had hooked two fat silver-sides. His water was boiling by the time he finished cleaning the fish. He skewered them and set them to broil. He sprinkled some tea leaves into the pot—a fine Diyonan leaf. He inhaled the sharp aroma and smiled. With a full belly and a few cups of tea in him, he would almost feel human. He would get back on the trail and hope he was moving in the right direction. He should probably report back to the prelate, but he was too stubborn to do so until he could tell him something definitive. He sighed as unwelcome thoughts of the citadel intruded on his peaceful morning.

Something caught his eye, chasing those thoughts from his mind as quickly as they had come. The surface of the pond rippled. What could it be? He strode to the edge and peered down, but he saw nothing. A fish? Or just his imagination?

He was about to turn away when he caught sight of bubbles floating up to the surface. A shadow appeared deep down in the water, growing larger and taking shape as it rose. Then a head broke the surface. It was a young man, his brown hair plastered to his face, sputtering and gasping as he treaded water. Behind him, a young woman surfaced, also sucking in air in huge gulps as she swam awkwardly for the shore.

Aspin prided himself on seldom being taken by surprise, but he was positively baffled as to how and why two young people could suddenly appear out of a mountain pond in which he was certain they had not been before. This was most unexpected, and it piqued his curiosity.

The boy shook the water from his eyes and searched out his companion. He took her by the arm and together they hauled themselves, weighed down by their sodden clothes, to shore. Once on dry land, they each dropped the bags they carried, and dropped to the ground.

The boy was the first to catch his breath, open his eyes. He looked up at the sky and let out a whoop of delight, raising his fists in triumph. The girl sat up, smiled, and hugged him, both of them laughing joyfully.

They still had not noticed him, so he waited until the laughter died down a bit before making his presence known.

"Good morning," he said. The pair started, scrambled to their feet, and gaped at him. "My name is Aspin. I am a sai-kur, or a seeker, if you prefer." They continued to stare, so he went on. "You are welcome to share breakfast with me. I have fresh fish and hot tea."

He turned his back to them and strode back to the fire, where he fished two extra tin cups from his pack, along with his tea strainer. He had poured three piping cups by the time the two joined him by the fire.

They accepted the tea with quiet thanks. The girl drank it down so quickly that Aspin feared she would scald herself. The young man drank his slowly with his eyes closed, savoring the drink. His big hands dwarfed the cup, and he held it close to his chest as if to hoard its warmth. They did not seem eager to talk, but Aspin was a patient man and comfortable with silence. It was not long before the young man spoke.

"My name is Oskar. This is Khalyndryn." He paused, seeming unsure how to continue. "We are lost." He looked down at the fire, seeming to have nothing more to add.

Aspin's heart hammered in his chest like an invader seeking to batter down a city gate. These two were part of the Malan girl's party. This proved he was at least headed in the right direction. But where were the other members of the party? And most important, where was the girl? Was Oskar being reticent, or had he simply had no reason to mention the others?

"I must confess my curiosity about how the two of you came to be in this pond."

Khalyndryn flashed a look of warning at Oskar. He grimaced as he spoke. "We were in the mountains, got lost, and fell into a river. It carried us to this place, and we found our way out."

So he was being reticent. Perhaps if Aspin took him by surprise, he could jar the truth from the boy.

"Tell me, Oskar. Where are Shanis Malan, Prince Larris and the others?" He smiled politely and lifted his cup to his lips, enjoying the boy's startled expression. Khalyndryn sat up straight and glanced at her friend.

"Understand," Aspin continued, "I mean them no harm. I have, in fact, been sent by Shanis Malan's father to find her." It was almost the truth, but it would suffice.

"You know Andric Malan?" Oskar asked, taking a sip of his tea and trying unsuccessfully to look casual.

"Colin Malan," Aspin corrected. "And yes, I know him. Clever of you, though."

"When did he send you?" Khalyndryn's voice was sharp

with suspicion.

"I visited your village some weeks ago— just a few days after you left, in fact. I spoke first with Mistress Van Derin, and then your village blacksmith, before speaking with Colin. He apprised me of the circumstances surrounding your departure."

"You met Hierm's mother?" The corners of Oskar's mouth turned up in a wry smile, and he chuckled. "No doubt the pleasure was all hers."

"Did you see my parents?" Khalyndryn interrupted. "Master and Mistress Serrill. My father is the innkeeper in town. If you stayed in town, I suppose you took a room at the inn. It is the only one, after all."

"I fear I did not stay the night." Aspin needed to be cautious here. He had not yet won their trust, and the news that he had left town upon discovering Yurg had been murdered would likely unsettle them. "But Colin did indicate that no one believes your virtue has been tainted in any way. They know the truth about what happened, and they are anxious for your safe return. Colin urged me to begin my search immediately, as he is very concerned about his daughter, as well."

"Why did he not come after her himself?" There was suspicion in Oskar's eyes, if not his voice.

If the lad was intimidated by Aspin, or by sai-kurs in general, it did not show. He seemed astute, but there was something more about him that Aspin could not quite identify. Oskar had an air about him that drew Aspin's attention. He did not yet know what it was, but it would come to him in time.

"No one was certain of the direction in which you had gone, how far you might have traveled, or when, if at all, you planned to return. Given the circumstances, Colin thought it likely you had not gone far. He assumed that Shanis would return once she was certain Lerryn had gone. He wanted to be there when she came home. He planned to continue making inquiries and searching the forests close to your home."

"Why are we important enough for a seeker to take the time looking for us?"

"You are not, but Shanis is. And I consider her father a friend." No harm in that lie. He respected Colin Malan, even if he had no regard for him beyond that.

"I began by following Lerryn's path, on a hunch more than anything else, but neither of us dreamed you would have ventured such a great distance."

Khalyndryn hung her head, gazed into her cup, and said nothing. Colin had described her as a delicate girl, like a flower, but she had an underlying hardness Aspin had not expected. She was lean and serious looking. Obviously, the months of travel had toughened her. Had it hardened her as well?

"You have not answered my question. Can you tell me where Shanis is? It is important to her father, to me, and to her own safety that I find her."

"We don't know where she is." Oskar met his eye with a resolute stare that held no lie. "We have not seen her in days... weeks. We seem to have lost track of time. No sunrises or sunsets underground."

"Tell me this, then," Aspin said, keeping his annoyance in check. He had hoped these two would prove the key to finding the girl. Perhaps they still would. "Did you find the Silver Serpent?"

Had the situation not been so grave, he would have found their reactions amusing. Khalyndryn gasped and dropped her cup. She sprang to her feet and wiped her cloak with her hands, despite the fact that she was still soaked from her swim. Oskar gaped, his eyes bugged out like a bullfrog.

"H... how... how did you know?" Oskar stammered.

"That does not matter right now." Aspin's voice was harsher than he had intended, but he was wearying of their reticence. "Do the two of you have any idea of the importance of the Silver Serpent?"

"Larris said that the fate of Galdora hinged on the Silver Serpent" Oskar shrugged.

"The fate of the royal family," Khalyndryn corrected. "He didn't actually say that Galdora itself was in danger."

"That is true." Oskar glanced at her. "But we have to consider the army Shanis and Allyn saw headed toward Galdora. Larris thought they might be a threat."

"It was not an army."

"It wasn't exactly a handful either," Oskar protested. "And Shanis said that they mentioned meeting up with others." The two of them had forgotten Aspin in their bickering. "In any case, Larris was sure..."

"Peace! Both of you." Aspin's head was abuzz with this new information. "What are the two of you talking about?" If troops of any size were massing near the borders of Lothan and Galdora, the Citadel would have to know about it. Or perhaps they were already aware. It was the price he paid for cutting off communication for so long. "What army?"

The youths stared at each other until Khalyndryn finally nodded at Oskar. "Go on. You tell it. Be sure to tell him about the ice cats and the Thandrylls too."

Aspin buried his head in his hands and groaned. "My young friends, I fear that I will need more tea before I am ready to hear your tale. Would you care for some fresh fish?"

By the time they had finished off the last of the fish and a second pot of tea, Oskar and Khalyndryn had told Aspin their story. It was fascinating, almost beyond belief, that they had come to be here. The things these simple village youth had seen, particularly beyond the Ramsgate, fascinated him. The village of Thandryll definitely merited study, but not by him and certainly not at this time.

"What do you think?" Oskar asked. "Khalyndryn and I do not really know what to do next. Of course, an hour ago we thought we were going to die under the mountains, so we haven't exactly had time to give it any real thought. I suppose we should look for Shanis and Hierm, but we don't know where we are, and even if we could find our way back to Murantha, we have almost no provisions. Besides, I doubt they would still be there. They might even have gone looking for us."

"What do I think?" Aspin echoed. "I think it is an ineluctable conclusion that the sword Shanis took from the statue is the Silver Serpent. That would explain the transformation Khalyndryn observed. It is obviously an artifact of tremendous sorcerous power, which would explain the blast that struck me down. It is the residue across the sky that puzzles me. I think we should fol-low it." He realized he had said "we" rather than "I." He had not yet invited them to join him. Of course, lacking supplies, they had little choice but to rely on his aid. If either of them noticed his choice of words, neither said so.

"Residue across the sky?" Oskar frowned.

"Sorcerous power leaves its mark behind. The greater the act, the more substantial the residual effect." With his index fin-ger, he drew a line across the sky from west to east. "Something happened very recently. It makes no sense, but it seems to have begun in the mountains and continued… across the sky, ending somewhere east of where we sit. Whatever it was, it was so po-werful that it rendered me unconscious for some time, though I do not know how long.

A look passed between Oskar and Khalyndryn that they did not bother to hide.

"Excuse me, but what exactly is sorcerous power? I've heard it talked about, but what is it. Magic?" Khalyndryn was obviously trying to redirect the subject, but Aspin let it pass. What had he said that had drawn such a reaction? Given enough time, he would find out.

"They are not precisely the same thing. They both come from the same source, through different pathways, if you will. Sorcerous power is the channelling of the life force that the gods imbued in the earth at the time of creation. The sorcerer acts as a vector for that power, drawing it in and directing it outward. A bit like a funnel. Magic is an appeal to one or more of the gods, asking that the gods perform a certain action."

"The person does not perform the magic?" She cocked her head as she waited for the answer.

"The person in question says the spell and, if done properly, the god performs the action."

"So, it is like a prayer?" Oskar scooted closer to Aspin, very interested in the conversation.

"It is more like a formula. If one says the correct words, in the proper manner, some reactions are automatic. It is almost as if magic is an unlocking of the rules that govern the universe. Strictly speaking, one is making an appeal to the gods, but it is unlikely that the god is even aware of that request, or making a conscious decision to fulfill that request."

A contemplative silence fell over them. The wind rustled in the treetops, and somewhere far away a hawk sounded its hunting cry. Despite his impatience, instinct told Aspin this was an important conversation. There was something about Oskar. The boy was important.

"What can you do with sorcery and magic?" The young man seemed very interested. "I have read that sorcerers accomplished great feats in the past, but that now they can do comparatively little."

"That is true. There are various theories as to why this is the case, but most believe that, just as strength and vitality leave our bodies as we age, the world's life force has diminished over time. No one can say for certain." Indeed, it was a quandary that vexed scholars. Sai-kurs today could not do one quarter of what their predecessors had been able to do centuries ago. They still knew the theories and the spells, but their effects were nowhere near as powerful as what was described in the records of previous sai-kurs.

"As far as what one might do with the power, that would depend on the amount of force available, and the person's ability to channel and direct that force. Just as some men are stronger, faster, brighter, or more talented than others, sorcerers have different capacities to take the power in. Our gifts with that power differ as well. Of the sorcerers with which I am acquainted, most use the power as a weapon, either for defense or attack. Some can touch the mind of another. Others can commune with animals. Rare sorcerers can shape metal or stone, and can imbue their creations with life force that keeps those creations whole, invulnerable to the elements. Magical abilities are much more varied. Some discover magical abilities on their own, while others study a particular branch of magic, seeking to master the particular spells of that discipline."

"Fascinating!" Oskar truly seemed to mean it. "How do you know..." He stopped in mid-sentence. "Nevermind. We are grateful for your help. If you do not think we will be too much of a burden, we will travel with you."

"You shall not be a burden at all. I would be glad for the company." He was surprised to realize that he meant it, though only a little bit. He preferred solitude, but he enjoyed talking with this bright, inquisitive young man. And the girl was not nearly so foolish as he had been led to believe. "With luck, we will find your friends soon."

CHAPTER 8

Lerryn reined his horse in at the edge of a murky, green lake. His eyes scanned the ominous, black clouds drawn across the sky like a thick blanket. They would need to find cover, and quickly. He raised his hand, signalling the others to halt.

"We will make camp here. Edrin and Hair, find a good place to make camp among the trees. If the storm that is coming is half as strong as I suspect, our tents will not be enough." The two dismounted and led their horses into the forest of red cypress that ringed the lake. The massive trees, their trunks two war-horses thick, with heavy, low-slung branches, would provide a measure of protection against the heaviest rain.

"Bull, take the horses back into the trees and tend to them." He dismounted and handed the reins to the muscular, barrell-chested youth. Bull made a cursory bow and accepted Kreege's reins. Lerryn grinned as he watched the lad walk away. His shoulders were so big and his neck so thick that when the young man attempted a bow, it looked like his head was bobbing in and out of his chest.

When the young men had gone, he helped Xaver dismount. His vizier had nearly recovered from whatever had struck him down days before, but he was still weak. The pace they set was tiring him out as well. They rose early, pushed their mounts as hard as they dared, and typically waited until near dark before making camp. Xaver was convinced that the Silver Serpent had been found, and that its recovery was the source of the sorcerous wave that had rendered him unconscious.

They walked together along the edge of the lake, scanning the area for potential threats. Marauding bands of Malgogs were common to this area. He did not truly expect to come across anyone, though. It seemed that every Malgog in Lothan was on the move. They had been forced to hide from five separate clans, all traveling to some unknown destination deep in the heart of Lothan.

Xaver's eyes were on the western skyline, which was now a roiling black cauldron on this stormy evening.

"Do you still feel it?" Lerryn asked. "The resonance, or whatever it is you call it?" Xaver insisted he could feel what he called the echo of a massive use of sorcery somewhere beyond Karkwall to the west. If he was correct, it meant that Lerryn and his party had gone in completely the wrong direction on their search for the Silver Serpent.

"Yes, but it is fading. Every day it grows weaker, but it is still there. I am certain we are headed in the right direction… this time." His voice was weak and despondent. The quest was his long before Lerryn became involved. A bleakness had set in, as though Xaver was now without purpose.

"Do you have any further thoughts as to why the clans are moving?" Lerryn grabbed Xaver's arm and pulled him back just before his booted fot trod upon a marsh frog. The speckled brown creature hissed and sprang into the water with a loud plop. "Have a care. Their meat is delicious, but they spit poison. Deadly if it gets into your eyes."

"In that case, I suppose I should keep my eyes on the path, rather than the sky." Xaver grimaced. "I am not ready just yet to pass on to the next world." He grinned, his white teeth seeming to glow in the dusky light. "As far as the clans are concerned, I do not know. Some of their witches might practice sorcery at some level, in which case they would have felt what I did. It is possible that they have interpreted this event in such a way as to cause this mass migration."

"Could the Monaghan be launching a massed invasion of Malgog lands?" Lerryn asked. In his mind, war was much easier to understand than sorcery. "I know it would be unlikely. The Monaghan fight one another as often as they fight the Malgog.

But what if they had a unified purpose? A campaign of genocide, perhaps?"

"Were that the case," Xaver's tone was skeptical, "I would imagine that the women and children might move east, but the clansmen would be moving to meet the threat. I have never known of a Lothan clansmen of either tribe to run from a fight, but the women take up arms only in the most desperate of times."

"True," Lerryn said. They had circled about a quarter of the way around the lake. He was satisfied that the thick tangles of vegetation hid no human threat, at least not in the immediate vicinity. The two retraced their steps back to where they left the other members of their party.

"Suppose you are correct, and the Silver Serpent has been found by the Monaghan?" The words were bitter on his lips. He despised the thought of his prize in the hands of the barbaric hillmen. It belonged to him… to Galdora! "Could that be a reason for what we have witnessed?"

"Their prophecies connect the Silver Serpent with the reunification of their lands, so it is possible. If that is the case, we have to consider what threat a united Lothan with the power of the serpent behind it might pose to Galdora, or to the rest of Gameryah for that matter. We do not know the exact nature of the serpent's power, but we can be sure it is prodigous."

Lerryn pondered the thought. He was so frustrated by his own personal failure that he had not considered the likelihood of another nation bearing the weapon. Galdora existed under the constant threat of a superior Kyrinian force. What if an army from the south, aided by a weapon of legendary power, were to ally with Galdora's enemy? His nation would truly sit between the hammer and the anvil then. His eyes caught movement up ahead, and he saw Hair hurrying toward them. He would have to learn the boy's name one of these days. He and Xaver stepped up their pace as the long-haired youth hurried toward them.

"Highness, we found a small village nearby. Few people remain. Only some elders and a mute. They invited us to stay with them if we like." His tight grimace and narrowed eyes said that he was not comfortable with the thought for some reason. Odd, the lad was usually quite gregarious.

"There is something you are not telling us. What is the matter?" Out of the corner of his eye he caught a flicker of distant lightning. The cool breeze was fast becoming a strong wind, and he smelled the rain, heavy in the air. He would much prefer to pass this night indoors.

"I don't know." Hair looked down at the ground, scuffing at the mud with the toe of his boot. "It was an uncomfortable place— all dark and muddy. The mute was a strange one, and one of the other men was… I don't know how to say it." He bit his lip and looked away.

"Come now. Out with it, before we are caught in the storm. Did someone threaten you? Did you spot anything that might pose a danger to us?"

"I don't like little people." Hair would not meet Lerryn's eye. "A showman once passed through our town when I was small, and he had with him a man only about three feet tall. He did flips and handstands, but he was ugly and told very crude jokes. He frightened me and…" He stopped and clamped his mouth shut. If it were not so close to dark, Lerryn was certain he'd see the young man's face the brightest shade of red it had ever been.

"I understand completely," he said, clapping a hand on Hair's shoulder. "If this little man gives you any trouble, I shall cut off your legs at the knee so that the two of you can see eye-to-eye. Will that be of comfort to you?"

Hair grinned and shook his head.

"Would it not be easier, highness, to simply find a stump or large stone upon which the man might stand?" Xaver mused. "I would hate to see you nick the blade of your sword." Lerryn and Hair stopped to stare at the vizier.

"Why, Xaver my friend, I do believe you just made an attempt at humor." Lerryn gaped in mock-incredulity. "Truly this is a momentous occasion."

"I forgot myself for a moment, Highness. I am surprised that I could make a jest at all, so saddened am I at the absence of our friend Master Karst." The irony that dripped from his voice deprived his words of their humorous effect. Karst had ridden away the moment they discovered their quest had failed. No one had seen him since, and no one missed him.

They collected their horses and made their way to the Malgog village, which was no more than a league from where they had stopped. It was located on high ground among a soupy patch of stingreeds and swamp moss, and surrounded by a stockade of sharpened cane pole. They waited outside the gates for someone to invite them in.

It was the mute who finally came to greet them. He was, as Hair had described him, strange. He was as tall as Lerryn, but he leaned to his left as he walked, giving him the appearance of being shorter than he was. His right arm and leg were muscular, but his left side was shriveled and weak. His left leg was skinny, twisted inward, and shorter by a hand than the right. His tiny left arm he held clutched to his side, his pitiful three-fingered hand grasping something Lerryn could not quite see.

Even the left side of his face had not been spared of the defect from which he suffered. The left corner of his mouth drooped, and his left eye wandered. Bits of moss and twigs clung to his close-cropped black curls. He was clean shaven, unlike most Malgog men. When Lerryn went through the ritual introduction and stating of business, the man merely grunted and motioned with his good hand for them to follow, before hobbling back through the gate.

The village itself was much as Hair had described it: small, muddy, and unattractive. Malgog architecture was limited only by imagination and the available supply of sticks and mud. Their dwellings looked like inverted bird nests on poles, caked with mud and packed with vegetation, giving the impression of hillocks floating above the soggy earth. Their common buildings adhered to no set pattern, and usually conformed to the shape of whatever dry land on which they could build. The central gathering place in this village was a multi-leveled treehouse set in the branches of a huge red cypress that rose majestically above the surrounding settlement.

Leaving their horses with two elders who were as silent as the mute, they climbed up a rope ladder and onto a solid deck of black oak, the dark, jagged grain giving it a sinister look. They were sheltered by a canopy of woven reeds. Smoky torches cast an unsteady light upon those gathered. Lerryn crinkled his nose at the foul smell that emanated from the torches. It was necessary in a land where it was said the insects could suck a man dry in a night, and leave him a bag of bones in the morning. He grinned at the memory of the old grandmother's tale.

"Thank you, Haff'un. That will be all." An old man in the typical baggy Malgog clothing dismissed the mute and turned to greet them. "Welcome to our village," he said, bowing low. "Your young companion has already identified you to us. We are humbled to welcome such esteemed guests. His eyes included Xaver in the compliment. "My name is Jakway. I speak for what remains of the Gray Lake Clan. May I invite you inside for food and shelter from the storm?"

"We would be most grateful for your kind and generous hospitality." Lerryn led the group into a room that was actually a small cave carved out of the giant trunk of the red cypress where it grew up through the deck. Two others waited at a round table that took up most of the space. Tapers set in carved niches cast a peaceful glow around the room. They waited as Jakway made introductions.

"This is Maralla." He indicated a lean old woman with black-streaked silver hair and a kind smile that dampened the effect of her homely face. She nodded politely. "And this is Heztus." Heztus was the dwarf of whom Hair had spoken.

"I'd stand up and bow to you, but I'm no taller standing than I am sitting." The fellow was much younger than the others, no more than thirty summers. His black hair was done in about two-dozen narrow braids. Snake bones at the end of each braid clacked together when he turned his head. His beard and moustache were neatly trimmed, contrary to Malgog fashion. "Please, sit down and be at ease. Our table is your table. And don't tell me my hospitality is greater than my stature, because that's not much of a compliment, is it now?

"Actually I was racking my brain to think of another ritual reply, but I fear my knowledge of your customs is limited." Lerryn held out his hand, and Bull passed him a full wineskin he had brought from among their supplies on Lerryn's orders. "I hope this will be a satisfactory guest gift. We have recently come from Diyonus, and I still have half a skin of Monavan Orange that I would be delighted to share."

The dwarf looked pleasantly surprised, and he stood up in his chair to get a better look. He grinned at the sight of the wine-skin and nodded.

"A princely gift indeed," he said. "I fear we have no clan chief or other person of worth with us to formally accept your gift, but I hope you will allow one so lowly as myself to serve in his stead."

"Of course." Lerryn handed the wine to the dwarf with only a mild pang of regret. Monavan Orange was the finest in the world. He motioned for the others to take their seats.

No sooner had they sat down when Heztus clapped twice, and a cluster of old men and women tottered in with plates of food. The dishes were mostly foreign to him, but the aromas were enticing, and his mouth watered in anticipation. Bull's stomach rumbled, the sound filling the confined space. Everyone shared a good laugh at the abashed-looking young man's expense. Lerryn reflected again on Bull's good nature, so contrary to his brawn and rough exterior.

Unlike formal meals, the bowls were passed around the table and everyone served himself. First came a dish of fish and swamp peppers that numbed his tongue, followed by a soup of sweet vegetables in a thin, red broth. The next bowl was filled with crispy fried frog legs. Lerryn had eaten frog legs before, and found them tasty, so he helped himself to several. The others were obviously uncertain what they were about to eat, but took some out of politeness. Mashed tubers with butter, tiny black beans, and a salad of swamp lettuce and carrots rounded out the meal. The Diyonusan wine was an odd companion to the Malgog fare, but it was a most satisfying repast.

When the food and polite conversation had dwindled, Lerryn asked the question that had been gnawing at him.

"Forgive me, but where is the rest of your village? There can't be more than twenty of you, and this village could comfortably be home to two-hundred. The buildings appear to be in good repair, so they cannot have been uninhabited for very long."

"Two days." Heztus's voice was slurred by wine. "They left two days ago. Those of us they believed would be unable to make the journey, they left behind. So here we are: the elders, the cripple and the dwarf."

"Of course, Heztus is a capable guide and traveler. In his case, the others find his company...' Maralla smiled as she searched for the word.

"Tedious?" Heztus offered.

"Infuriating is closer to the truth." Maralla continued to smile at him. "You can't resist demonstrating your superior intelligence every chance you get."

"I don't do it on purpose." Heztus put his hand on his chest and adopted a wounded expression. "My superior intellect simply flows out of me at all times. They should accept it rather than flee from it."

"Where did they go?" Lerryn asked. "We passed several clans headed toward central Lothan, but we cannot fathom what might be there for them."

"Something happened six days ago. Something momentous." Maralla spoke slowly here eyes flitting to the other Malgog at the table. "Not everyone could feel it, or understand it, but for those of us who are attuned to such things, it caused a powerful disturbance.'

"We are aware." Xaver's eyes met Maralla's and something seemed to pass between them. Finally they nodded, both apparently satisfied.

"Two days later, word reached us that the Silver Serpent has come again into the world. The bearer is uniting the clans of Malgog and will once again unify Lothan. The clans are called to Calmut."

"What is Calmut?" Lerryn hated feeling ignorant, but his desire to understand what was happening outweighed his ego.

"It is where the new leader will be chosen. 'Tis very strange, but the bone women tell us that the serpent is raised in the *east*. A great warrior there is uniting the Malgog, and he vows that the Monaghan shall be brought to their knees."

"But the disturbance..."

"Was in the west," the woman added. "The serpent has been

raised there by the Monaghan." She grimaced like she had just swallowed something bitter. "Two people claim to bear the serpent. The choice must be made at Calmut."

CHAPTER 9

The highlands were never going to end. The hills rose all around them like an endless sea of green. Oskar sighed as he stared out in to the sameness through which he had spent the better part of the last two days hiking. From atop Aspin's stallion, Khalyndryn gave him a sympathetic nod and reached down to pat him hard on the head.

"There's a good boy. You can do it."

"I am not your dog," he mutterd. Then he looked up at her and saw her grinning. He laughed and gave her hand a squeeze. Such a casual act was a measure of how their friendship had grown in such a short time. She was no longer the self-important girl who had left the village. Needless to say, he liked her much better this way.

Winding around what seemed like the thousandth hill, they disturbed a fox, who darted away in a blur of orange. The horse shied, but Aspin calmed him with a word. Oskar wondered if it was magic, or simply good training.

The sai-kur was an enigma. He rarely spoke unless spoken to. He also had a way of sometimes answering questions without actually giving any specific information, or so it seemed to Oskar. The man was unfailingly polite and serene to the point of annoyance. He seemed to harbor no ill intent toward Shanis, but Oskar felt that Aspin had not sufficiently explained his reasons for wanting to find her.

A faint rustling sound caught his ear. As they drew closer he recognized it as the sound of falling water. It was a pleasant, peaceful sound, though it reminded him of that dark underground stream in and along which they had spent too much of their time.

At the juncture where twin hills met, a tiny waterfall snaked between the rises, tumbling down into a peaceful pond. Its smooth jade surface beckoned to Oskar, as it apparently did to Khalyndryn. With a squeal of delight she slid down from her mount, handed him the reins, and hurried over to kneel in the soft grass at the water's edge.

Something about the pond struck Oskar as unnatural. The surface seemed especially smooth despite the water splashing down from above. The surrounding vegetation was unlike any he had ever seen, and it gave the place an alien quality that unsettled him.

Khalyndryn waved to him, holding a finger to her lips. When she had his attention, she pointed to a thick stand of aquatic plants on the far end of the pool where a scaly green snout poked out.

Careful not to make a sound, he guided the horse over to where she sat. They watched as the animal swam toward them. It reached the shallows and stood a few paces away, water dripping from its emerald body.

"It's a little horse," she whispered. And it was, after a fashion. The size of a small dog, it resembled a horse, but with green scales and a spiny fin along its neck where the mane should be. As it moved closer, it lifted a leg out of the water, revealing a webbed foot tipped with three black claws. Khalyndryn reached out a hand to it and made kissing sounds. The creature's eyes narrowed and it hissed. She jerked her hand back and the beast leapt at her. Khalyndryn screamed as it went for her throat with its razor teeth and needle-like claws.

Some invisible force struck the creature and sent it hurtling across the pond where it slammed into the bank and fell limp at the water's edge.

Oskar shuddered. He felt like someone had first dunked him in an icy river and then set him afire. He put his arm around Khalyndryn. She was trembling, and her face was white as a sheet. He leaned against her, letting her bear some of his weight. He was suddenly weak in the knees and did not understand why. The creature had surprised him, certainly, but that was all. It was nothing to make him feel ill.

"What was that thing?" Khalyndryn did not sound nearly as frightened as Oskar would have expected. "It was so cute, but it was...mean." She said the last with wonder and a note of judgment. Oskar was surprised at her calm. This was not her usual reaction to danger. "I was foolish to get close to it without knowing if it was dangerous."

"That you were." Aspin squatted down next to them. "The buggan is small, but it can do you serious harm. Those claws and fangs can be deadly if they get your throat, or some other vulnerable spot. Fortunately for you, I was here." It was not arrogance on his part—simply a statement of fact.

"You did that?" Khalyndryn pointed at the stunned creature. "Did you have to hurt it? You knocked it all the way over there." The buggan was coming to. It raised its head and looked around, still hissing. "I've heard stories of buggans, but I never believed they were real." She frowned as if a thought had occured to her, and grew quiet.

"I assure you, I had no intention of doing anything more than deflect it away from you." Aspin crinkled his brow. "I do not understand what happened. I cannot remember the last time I underestimated my power like that. I have not done that since I was a disciple." He leaned down to look Oskar in the eye. "Are you all right?"

"I am all right." The quaver in Oskar's voice betrayed him. He felt like he was going to sick up. "I was just frightened for Khalyndryn is all. That thing gave me a scare when it leapt at her."

"Of course." Aspin's eyes bored into him like a hawk circling its prey. After staring at Oskar for a few moments longer, he rose to his feet. "Follow me," he ordered, pacing over to a level space a few paces away. Oskar, still woozy, followed behind.

"Sit down here in front of me." Aspin sat cross-legged on the ground. He watched impassively as Oskar did as he was instructed. "Look me in the eye and hold my gaze; do not look away."

Oskar again did as he was told. As he looked at Aspin, the sai-kur's pupils seemed to expand into pools of inky blackness, filling Oksar's vision until they were all he could see. He was in a whirlpool, being drawn into the darkness.

"Take a deep breath, and exhale slowly." Aspin's voice softened. "Now take another deep breath; hold it." A lengthy pause. "Now release it slowly and let your shoulders fall as you breathe out." Oskar felt himself drifting away, his eyes still locked on Aspin's. "Now...tell me about the moment Shanis Malan took up the serpent."

"I don't remember." Oskar's voice seemed to come from far away. He wondered why Aspin was asking him this right now, but he was too detached to care. "She grabbed it, and I don't remember anything else."

"How did you feel in the moment she touched it?" Apsin's voice was so calm, so inviting, that Oskar found himself dying to give him an answer. His mind swam back to the cavern. He saw the flowing blue light of the seastone coffins. He saw the statue. He watched Shanis, desperately trying to fend off the attack of the giant snake, reach for the stone sword. Her fingers closed on the hilt, and he felt...

"I felt cold all over, and then hot at the same time. It was like a shock. And then everything went black." Something told him that the memory was significant, but he could not concern himself with that right now.

"Tell me about the moment after the lightning struck the golorak. How did you feel?"

"I felt hot and cold and..." Oskar clammed up. He was still trapped in the sai-kur's gaze, but now he was trying to resist. Something inside him did not want to remember this. He tried to shake free from Aspin's gaze, but he was held fast.

"It was not lightning that killed the golorak, was it Oskar?" There was no accusation in Aspin's voice. He was inviting Oskar to unburden himself. Perhaps he could tell Aspin. Maybe it would be all right.

"Who slew the golorak?" The question hung in the silence. Oskar fought the urge to fill the silence, but the longing to tell the truth was too strong.

"I did." He heard Khalyndryn gasp at his revelation. "I don't know what I did, but I know I killed it."

The words startled him out of the semi-trance in which Aspin had put him. His mind seemed to float upward toward full consciousness.

"I held out my staff and a bar of light shot out of it. It sliced right through the golorak. I don't know how it happened. I really don't."

Aspin smiled and nodded. "Tell me how you felt the moment before it happened. Try and remember precisely what you thought, what you felt, anything you can recall."

"I watched Larris trying to fight it." As if the revelation had unlocked a door in his mind, everything came back to him clearly. "His sword just bounced off its hide. All I had was my staff, and I knew I couldn't do anything to help. He told me to finish the quest without him. He was ready to die and I couldn't help him. My friend was about to be killed before my eyes and there was nothing I could do about it."

He hung his head. The memory was powerful and painful. His voice was thick as he spoke. "Something inside of me just gave up."

Aspin looked... pleased, as if this was the answer he had been hoping for.

"In order to channel life force, one must step aside, so to speak, and allow it to flow through. You cannot force it to happen; you must allow it to happen. For most of us, the first time we do it requires total and complete surrender, which is what happened to you. The ability has always been there within you, but you were not in a situation desperate enough for complete and utter surrender of control."

Aspin sounded triumphant, and his smile was broad and happy. It looked out of place on his face, which, with its raptor-like eyes and hooked nose, made him look more like an angry eagle than a man.

"And that is why you could not do it again in the chamber. You did not know that you had to surrender to the power. You were trying to make it happen, weren't you? You wanted to slay the serpent the way you slew the golorak."

Dumbstruck, Oskar could only nod his head. He knew what Aspin was saying, but it could not be true. Him? It was unthinkable.

"I don't understand," Khalyndryn whispered. "Aspin, what are you trying to tell us?"

"I am saying that your friend Oskar is a sorcerer."

CHAPTER 10

Jayla was tired and hungry, and she didn't want to hide in the bushes anymore. Her escape from the shape-changing cat man had left her terrified. She had spent the last two days going east as fast as she could. She had found the wagon track that villagers sometimes used, but every time she heard a strange noise she would scurry into the bushes and wait until she was certain it was safe. Her hands and knees, already banged up from her flight down the rocks, were now covered with fresh scrapes. She hurt all over, and she wanted to sleep, but nerves and hunger kept her from sleeping more than an hour or two at a time.

Food was a problem. There were all kinds of berries along the way, but Papa had taught her that many could kill you or make you sick. She did not know which ones were which, so she had only eaten the fat, black grapes with the tough, bitter skin and mushy sweet insides. She had eaten them husks and all, sometimes swallowing the seeds by accident. She ate whenever she found them, which was not often enough. She had come across a walnut tree, but the branches were bare and nearly all the walnuts on the ground were rotten. She ate the ones that were not too bad, but her stomach cried for more.

Now she was hunkered down beneath an itchy, sticky evergreen bush, watching the rider come down the track toward her. His was a tall, graceful mount with long, lean legs and sleek coat, so unlike the short, broad-chested work horses with which she was familiar. As horse and rider drew closer, she got her first good look at the man, and what she saw made her draw in her breath in surprise.

He was the biggest man she had ever seen. Papa was tall and strong from hard work. This man was as tall as Papa, and he was big all over. His arms were like other men's legs. She wondered how long it took his wife to sew his clothes. Mama always complained about having to sew such long tunics for Papa. How would she feel about sewing for this man? His chest was as wide as Jayla was tall. His bushy black beard and dark curly hair made him look like a wild man. Suddenly, he snapped his head around to look directly at her hiding place. His black eyes narrowed, then relaxed. He could not possibly have seen her, not from so far away. Could he? She held as still as she could as he trotted toward her.

He reined his horse in and dismounted just a few steps away. He tied the horse off to a nearby tree and let it crop at a clump of grass on the edge of the path while he dug through his saddlebag. He pulled out a bundle and sat down right next to her hiding place, where he unwrapped a loaf of bread. It looked delicious, and she hoped her empty belly would not growl and give her away. He tore off a small piece and ate it slowly, staring up into the branches of a nearby tree.

"You can come out, little one. It is all right." His voice was surprsingly gentle, nothing like his outward appearance. "I won't hurt you. I imagine you are hungry. I have bread, cheese and dried meat."

Could she trust this man? He did not seem to be like the bad men at her village, but how could she know for sure? He was coming from the east, which was the way she was headed. Maybe he was from one of the villages there. Maybe he could help her find Mama and Papa and Harvin.

But she was so afraid. What if he really was a bad man? She thought for a moment more. She probably could not run away from him right now if she wanted to. He was big and strong and there weren't any good places to hide around here; just trees and bushes. There was no point in hiding. If he wanted to catch her, he would. Slowly, her heart pounding, she crawled out.

He smiled and held out the bread. Jayla snatched it from his hand without so much as a thank-you and took a huge bite. Mama would have scolded her for her bad manners, but she was so hungry and the man didn't seem to mind. He nodded and unfolded another cloth that held the cheese and meat he had promised. He placed it on the ground between them, taking a small piece of jerked meat for himself. After she had eaten most of the bread and cheese, he offered her a waterskin. This time she remembered to thank him when she accepted it from his hand.

"What's your name?" She was uncomfortable with the lengthy silence and her own lack of courtesy.

"Colin," he said simply.

"I'm Jayla. What are you doing out here in the forest?" Mama had told her before that it was not polite to ask questions, but Jayla was inquisitive by nature, and grownups usually laughed at her interrogations. She didn't know why they found her questions funny, but they did.

"Actually, I am looking for my little girl." He frowned and glanced down at the ground for a moment.

"Is she lost?" Jayla, too, was lost, and she felt sorry for any little girl who found herself in the same situation. It was scary.

"I don't think so." That was a funny answer. "She left with some friends of hers. I keep hoping she will come back home, but I don't know if she will."

"Her mother must be very worried about her. Is she little, like me?"

"Her mother died a long time ago." He looked very sad now. "And no, my daughter is not so young as you. She is more than fifteen summers. I suppose she is a young lady now, but to me she will always be my little girl." He turned his gaze toward Jayla. "You are not from my village, and you are a long way from anywhere else. May I ask what you are doing hiding in the forest?"

She hung her head. It made her unhappy to think about what had happened, but this man was sad, too. Maybe, if he knew her story, he wouldn't feel so bad about losing his little girl. Besides, he might know how to find her family. Before long she had poured out her story. Anger flashed in his eyes when she told him about the bad men, but when she described the man who turned into a cat monster, his eyes grew big and he sprang to his feet, his hand on his sword.

"You are not safe in these woods." He reached down and picking her up like she weighed nothing. "But you will be safe in my village. Will you tell your story to the people there?" She nodded. "That's a brave girl. Have you ridden before?" She nodded again, and he hastily untied his horse and mounted, plopping her down in front of him. As the horse cantered back up the trail, a thought struck her.

"Colin, can I stay at your house? I mean, since your little girl isn't home right now, maybe there is room for me. Only until we find my family." She couldn't see his face, but his voice sounded funny, like he had something in his throat.

"I suppose you can, little one. At least until we find your family."

CHAPTER 11

"Close your eyes. Take a deep breath and exhale slowly." Aspin's voice flowed through him like a lazy river. "Be aware of the life force that is alive in your body. Feel it in your fingertips and the tips of your toes." Oskar's fingers and toes began to tingle. Was he feeling the energy, or was it merely the suggestion in Aspin's words?

"Imagine the energy flowing up through your arms and legs, along your spine, and finally pouring into your mind. Feel it flow throughout your body."

He tingled all over, like he was being pricked by a thousand hot needles and pelted with drops of icy rain. The feeling took his breath away.

"Feel it now gathering in the middle of your body, just below the center of your chest. Do you feel it?"

"Yes," Oskar whispered. He could somehow see it— a silver orb the size of his two fists spinning inside of him, its glowing surface surging, ebbing, and pulsing like a living creature.

"Now slowly open your eyes. Good. Now hold out your hand, palm up."

Oskar followed Aspin's directions without question. This was the step at which he always failed. He could sense the power, but could not make it flow. He kept his eyes on the center of his palm, partly because he knew that was the next step, but mostly because if he looked up, he was certain he would see his own lack of confidence mirrored in the seeker's eyes. If Aspin did not believe in him, he could never believe in himself.

"Concentrate on a spot in the center of your palm." Aspin's voice continued to wash over him. "Now be aware of a channel flowing between your center of energy and the spot in your palm."

Oskar focused his thoughts and concentrated. He tried to create a pipeline of sorts running from his center outward to his hand. He could actually see it grow, creeping slowly outward.

And then it stopped.

He wrinkled his brow and tried to force it to keep growing, but he could not do it.

"The connection is already there, Oskar." Aspin's voice was serene, but firm. "You need not recreate it. Simply be aware of its presence."

This was impossible. That time he channeled and killed the golorak had been a fluke. He let his shoulders sag and, with a discouraged sigh, gave up.

And suddenly it was there!

The power surged through him. His arm felt like it was on fire. The sensation made him gasp.

"Good." Aspin's eyes twinkled, but he otherwise remained calm. "Now I want you to raise your hand in the air. You are in control of the power. The channel is now closed, but you may open it again any time you wish. Focus again on the center of your palm and, in one controlled burst, release the power out into the air."

Suddenly fearful, Oskar raised his hand and envisioned the center of his palm opening. A white bar of light shot up straight up into the sky. He was so amazed that, for a moment, he forgot to make it stop. Regaining control of his thoughts, he commanded the power to cease. The bar of light vanished, leaving its golden imprint burned into his vision. He sat in silence, his heart racing. He had done it!

"Excellent!" Aspin gave Oskar's shoulder a squeeze. "A bit more intense than I had planned, but very well done. I sense great power in you. You will require training, of course, but I believe you are capable of great things."

"You were wonderful!" Khalyndryn wrapped her arms around him from behind and hugged him tight. "I am so proud of you. I cannot wait to find the others and tell them what you have done. They are going to be amazed."

Oskar did not know what to say. In a matter of seconds, he had just received the highest praise of his life. He was not sure which was more gratifying: Aspin's prediction, or Khalyndryn's declaration that she was proud of him. So much of this journey had been like a dream. Bigger, in fact, than his most far-fetched daydreams. And now, to discover within himself a legendary power. It was just too much to believe. He figured he might as well enjoy it before he awoke.

"So, what comes next?

"Next we will teach you to gather the power in from outside of yourself and to safely release it again. But no more tonight. You have already exceeded my expectations."

Oskar grinned. He was so excited that he scarecely noticed Khalyndryn's arms still around him. It was not too long ago that the very thought of her embrace would have sent shivers down his spine and given him an upset stomach.

Now that he came to think about it, he was, in fact, shivering. He was freezing. He wrapped his arms around himself and drew his legs to his chest, his body shaking.

"Are you ill?" Khalyndryn held him tighter, but he could not feel her warmth.

"That happens quite often when you first touch the power," Aspin said. "It is normal, and it will diminish as you grow accustomed to sorcery. For now, you might wish to put on a heavier cloak, if you have one, and sit close to the fire. It would not hurt for Khalyndryn to remain close to you as well." Aspin winked and Oskar felt his face grow hot. He wondered if she noticed, but it appeared she had not, for she was already rummaging through his pack where he kept the brown cloak the Thandrylls had given him. She draped it around his shoulders over the top of his lighter cloak, sat down next to him, and leaned against him.

Aspin did a double-take when he saw Oskar's brown cloak, but he did not say anything. Oskar looked down at it and realized that it was nearly the twin of Aspin's sai-kur cloak, save for the fact that Oskar's cloak was made for someone half a head shorter and half again as broad of shoulder as Aspin. Before he could say anything about it, he heard the sound of riders approaching, and climbed heavily to his feet.

Aspin raised his hand, signaling them to be quiet. He moved quickly to where his sword leaned against a tree and belted it on. Oskar picked up his staff and moved to stand next to Aspin. He looked back at Khalyndryn, and inclined his head toward the tent, indicating that she should go inside. She shook her head. *The fool girl!* Not knowing who these passers-by were, it would simplify things greatly if they did not have a beautiful girl drawing the attention of any unsavory men who might be in the group.

He thrust his finger toward the tent, and mouthed the words "Now! I mean it!" To his surprise, she retreated to the tent without further argument.

Men appeared all around them at the edges of the clearing in which they were camped. Swords gleamed in the twilight, and he saw at least two bows drawn. Aspin whispered something too soft to hear, and Oskar's skin tingled.

"You need not hide from us." Aspin's voice rang with authority. "We will do you no harm provided you have come in peace."

Angry murmurs sounded from all around, but one warrior sheathed his sword and stepped out of the woods, chuckling as he came. His scarlet beard was twined in a mass of tiny braids, as was his hair. His clan garb was similar to that of Horgris's clan, save the sash he wore across his chest, which was stitched with a chain of blue stags, and his headdress, which was adorned with a pair of antlers.

"You do be a brazen one, me friend," he said, walking toward them. "The light be bad. Had I been knowin' we had a seeker and disciple here, I would no have been so concerned about the lights in the sky."

Aspin glanced at Oskar before turning back to the newcomers. "I apologize for the disturbance. I was giving my young pupil a lesson."

"It be of no moment." The man stopped suddenly, a confused look on his face.

"My apologies." Aspin whispered and flicked his fingers. "I had to protect us until I was certain of your intentions."

Oskar felt that they still did not know the man's intentions, but he would have to rely on Aspin's judgment. Had it been up to him, whatever barrier Aspin had conjured would have remained up for a while longer.

"Come and sit by our fire. I have no skok to offer you, but I have wine."

"Wine do be most welcome." The man hunkered down next to their small fire. "My name be Culmatan of the Blue Stag Clan."

"I am Aspin. I am a Sai-kur, as you have already noted." The two nodded to one another. Apparently no further formalities were required, and Oskar did not merit an introduction. "Oskar, will you please retrieve the wineskin from my tent?"

Obvioulsy Aspin did not want Khalyndryn coming out, or he would have called for her to bring it out. When Oskar slipped inside the tent, she was sitting near the doorway holding a knife, but she appeared calm. She gave him an inquiring look, and he shrugged as he retrieved the wineskin. "I think it's going to be all right," he whispered, "but stay here for now." She nodded and relaxed the grip on her knife.

Back at the fire, the two men were engaged in quiet conversation. Culmatan's clansmen had stepped out of the trees and stood around the clearing. They had put away their weapons, but none of them looked comfortable.

"So your bone woman has been in contact with the Malgog?" Aspin was asking, surprise in his voice. "That seems unusual."

"No so unusual as all that." Culmatan tilted his hand from side-to-side. "The bone women, they no hold to the clan wars in the same way we do. They be loyal in their own way, but they say they be holdin' to a united Lothan, even though that do be a memory, at least for now." There was a distant look in his gray-green eyes as he accepted the wineskin from Aspin. He took a long drink and handed it back, nodding in approval. "That be no so bad for wine."

"So what do the bone women tell you?" Aspin took a drink and handed the skin back to Culmatan.

"They say someone be claiming to raise the Silver Serpent. They be rumors he use the power to heal many in one of the clans. I don' know which one. Maybe Bannif or Circle of Oaks, I no be sure."

Oskar took note of the man's use of the word *he*. Did Shanis no longer have the sword? Most likely she had given it to Larris. He was the one who was searching for it after all. What if she still had it, and the man was simply assuming that the bearer was a man? Some things never changed for Shanis. He smiled at the thought.

"The Malgog, though, they be tellin' us that someone be raisin' the serpent in the east. Whoever it is, he be stirring things up there. Been raidin' the borderlands near Diyonus and Galdora. Some of the young 'uns be flocking to his banner, but most of the clans no be sure what to think, so they do stay away. And then, when they hear of one in the west, they make their decision."

"What decision is that?" Aspin's look was intense and his voice sharp. Clearly the news of two people claiming to possess the Silver Serpent had taken him by surprise.

Culmatan's mouth twisted into a sour grimace. He spat on the ground between his feet. "Bah! They say a choice must be made. They call us to gather at Calmut." He shook his head. "Couldna' have come at a worse time. The Three Oaks have Badla, and they be close by. We be headed to raid them when the word come to us."

"Must you go to this Calmut place? Is it required?" Aspin asked. Oskar was surprised. He had always assumed that seekers knew almost everything. Apparently, there were gaps even in Aspin's knowledge.

"Aye. That we must. Honor requires it. 'Tis a place we all hold sacred. When the bone women do call us to Calmut, we must go or be cursed." He took another swig of wine and belched.

Oskar could not hold his tongue. "So the Monaghan and the Malgog will be at this place together? Is that a good idea?" Aspin looked annoyed at the interruption, but Oskar did not care. Culmatan might think he was Aspin's disciple, whatever that meant, but he was not under the man's command. Of course, he would need to be careful not to offend Aspin if he was going to continue his lessons.

"The peace of Calmut rules there. We can no lift so much as a finger while we be there. No against one another, nor against the ice-encrusted Malgog." He let out a stream of vile oaths that made Oskar's ears turn red. Aspin cleared his throat, and the clansman regained his composure. "Forgive me, Seeker. I forget myself."

"It is of no moment." Aspin waved his hand as if to brush the apology aside. "Pray tell, what happens when you reach Calmut? I assume you will confer with the other clan leaders and the bone women and choose which person to follow."

"It be something like that," Culmatan averred. "We must confer, aye, but there be more to the decision. Otherwise the Malgog most likely follow the man from the east and we follow the one from the west."

"So your clan will follow the bearer of the serpent?" Oskar's heart was pounding. He remembered from his talks with Larris that part of the serpent prophecies, at least the Lothan prophecies, was that the recovery of the Silver Serpent would signal the reunification of the clans, while a different, more obscure, prophecy spoke of the bearer actually leading the reunified nation. If that person was either Shanis or Larris, he was very interested in how things would unfold.

"If I be satisfied that this man do bear the true Silver Serpent, then I will follow. I be a member of the Order of the Fox, but I no suppose you know what that do mean." Oskar nodded that he understood. Culmatan raised his eyebrows in surprise and continued.

"I be certain that all of my clansmen who be members of the order will follow. Most of my clan be followin' as well by my say-so. The rest, who knows?" He shrugged and raised his hands. "If enough men no follow, we just trade one kind of war for another. I be hoping, though, that what we do at Calmut be enough."

"You said there was more to the decision." Aspin had forgotten the wine, and now he gazed intently at Culmatan. "What more is there?"

"Calmut do be a... special place. I can no tell you very

much, but I can tell you this. When the two who claim to be bearers of the Silver Serpent do come to Calmut, they will be submitting themselves to the Keeper of the Mists. One will be chosen, one will no come back again."

"What happens to the one who does not come back?" Oskar could hear the tremor of fear in his voice.

"I can no say. I only know that, of those who entered and did no come back, not one has been seen again."

CHAPTER 12

"The Three Oaks be just up ahead." Granlor reined in his horse and looked back over his shoulder at them. "I think their outriders be seeing me. Maybe they come, maybe not."

"They saw you." Allyn fixed him with a disapproving stare. Granlor grimaced, but did not reply. The two had been scouting together since they left the Hawk Hill settlement. Granlor was good, but Allyn was better, and Allyn let the young clansman know it every chance he got. He had changed so much from the young woodsman who had taken pleasure in tracking and hunting with Shanis not so long ago. "And now they will be coming."

"No need. We will go to them." Shanis hoped the tension she felt did not show. Speaking to the Hawk Hill clansmen had been difficult enough, but they had already witnessed her power and thus had reason to believe in her. The Three Oaks clansmen knew nothing of her. It would not be easy. "We mean them no harm, so there is no reason for them to fear us."

Horgris, riding to her left, leaned in close. "The outlanders should be movin' to the back. You, at least, look like a Monaghan. They'll no believe any of it if they see the prince or his man." He glanced over his shoulder. "And that be true of you as well, husband of me daughter."

Hierm grimaced and gave Shanis an apologetic look which she returned with a smile and a shrug. It comforted her to have friends close by, but she was not about to interfere with Hierm's new family. According to Monaghan tradition, Hierm must treat Horgris as he would his own father. If only they knew how well

Hierm got along with Lord Hiram.

"It will be as you say, father of my wife." Hierm wheeled his mount and rode toward the back of the clan, out of sight.

"Larris, will you and Allyn please join the rear clutch?" Larris did not answer, but he complied with her request, Allyn following behind. Allyn still rarely spoke directly to her and, at times, he seemed almost pained by her presence. Twice, she had tried to engage him in a private conversation, but each time he had remembered some errand or other and hurried away from her.

"I think only a small contingent should approach them," she continued. "We will look less like we are about to attack if only a few ride up, as opposed to bringing an entire raiding party down on them."

"It no matter now." Garmon, the oily little man who served as Horgris's tracker and messenger pointed ahead of them. A long line of men emerged from the woods. More than fifty clansmen armed with shortbows stood with arrows nocked and ready. A cluster of men on horseback rode out of the center. The man in front held their banner: three golden acorns on a field of dark green.

The riders drew to a halt halfway between the two lines. Shanis did not hesitate, but rode out to meet them. Her heart was in her throat as she approached.

Horgris cursed and hastily called out five names. He and the five he had called brought their horses up behind Shanis. The groups were of the same size, seven Hawk Hill and seven Three Oaks. She assumed there was some matter of honor involved. She would have to learn some of these traditions before she made too great a fool of herself.

When the two parties met, a man with a yellow-streaked gray beard and a headdress with oak branches jutting out like horns brought his horse forward a pace and looked first at her, then at Horgris with unmasked disdain.

"Gerrilaw." Horgris gave him a curt nod.

"Horgris." The other man inclined his head a fraction. "Before you be telling me your business, mayhap you be telling me when you did become a jokester. Or do you be meaning to insult my clan?"

"There be no insult here." Horgris's face was already flushed, and it appeared to be a struggle for him to remain polite. Obviously, most of his diplomatic expertise involved hacking at another man with his sword until the fellow saw things his way. "This be…"

"You be bringin' a woman as part of your seven!" A young man, his blond hair twisted into a knot with oak branches crossed through it, stood in his stirrups and pointed at her. "You be sayin' one of us be half a man?"

"Peace, Gendram." Gerrilaw motioned for the young man to sit.

"But Father, he…"

"You be calmin' yourself, my son, or I be sending you back to help your mother tend the young ones." Gerrilaw never took his eyes from Horgris, but the rebuke stung Gendram, who sat down hard in his saddle, shame evident in his reddening face. "We be talking about this insult later, Horgris. Now you tell me where he be."

"Where who be?" Horgris sounded both impatient and confused.

"The snow take you, Horgris! The bone woman been telling us that you got a man in yer clan be claiming to bear the Silver Serpent. They say he healed a girl who…" His voiced trailed away. Shanis assumed he was remembering that it was his own clan that had done the girl harm in the first place.

Hot anger raged inside of her. No matter where she went, people underestimated her, even ignored her, because she was a woman. Now she bore a talisman of prodigious power and she still gained neither respect nor regard. She reached back over her shoulder, took hold of the hilt, and drew the sword. It slid free with a serpentine hiss.

"I bear the Silver Serpent," she said in as loud a voice as she could manage without shouting, holding the blade aloft. The Three Oaks men drew back and gaped at the blade glinting in the sun. "And I bear its mark." She pulled down the neck of her tunic to reveal the serpent on her chest. She lowered the blade, but kept it out in plain sight.

"And who do you be?" Gerrilaw's voice was hoarse from shock.

"My name is Shanis Malan." She felt as though she should say more, but now did not seem the time to make her speech about the end of the clan wars.

"A woman," Gerrilaw replied. He did not sound scornful this time, but neither did he sound pleased. "And you claim that this be the Silver Serpent."

"No," she said. Horgris started to say something, but she spoke over him. "I claim nothing. This is the Silver Serpent. I have come to demonstrate its power, that you might know I am the one."

"This can no be." Gendram had forgotten his father's instruction to calm himself. "A woman must no bear the serpent. A woman can no lead the clans. Father, this be a waste of our time. Tell these Hawk Hills to leave us be and take their girl with them."

This time, Gerrilaw did not reprove his son. Instead, he turned and fixed Shanis with an expectant stare, waiting for her to continue.

"Have you forgotten whose corpse you carry so proudly?" Angry mutters from both sides told her they did not care for her choice of words, but she did not care. "Yes, we have heard. Your clan attacked innocent people, and nearly killed a little girl, because you thought they wanted to steal the dead body of the last warrior to lead a united Lothan." She raised her voice so the Three Oaks men who waited in a line behind their leader could hear her.

"And who is this leader, whom you all revere? Who is this great warrior, over whose memory you have shattered your kingdom?" Stone silence was her only reply, but she did not need their admission to know her words had struck home.

"Badla. A warrior queen. Did you hear that? *Queen!* A woman. Do you still believe a woman is too weak to lead? Because if you do, feel free to hand her body over to a clan who remembers her greatness, and still reveres her as a fighter and a leader. She deserves better than to be carried by those who are ashamed of her simply because she is a woman."

"You go too far, girl!" Gerrilaw gritted his yellow teeth.

"I will go much farther than this before I am finished." Once again her anger was getting the better of her. She could almost see Master Yurg shaking his head. "Your world is about to change, Gerrilaw. The sooner you accept that fact, the better it will be for you and your clan. Too many people have died fighting over a woman who is not coming back. The time has come to join together to fight as one. This," she hefted her sword again, "is the herald."

"If that do be the Silver Serpent, then we just take it from her and wield it ourselves." Gendram spurred his horse forward.

"Take it." Shanis reversed her grip on the sword and held it out hilt-first for the young clansman to take. The jeweled serpent's eye sparkled in the sun.

Gendram hesitated. He had thought to intimidate her, and her reaction was not what he expected. His eyes moved from Shanis to the sword, over to his father, and then back to the sword. His expression said he was weighing the possibility that this was a trick against the probability that he would look like a fool if he did not follow through on his words. He reached for the sword, but paused just before his fingertips touched the hilt.

"I wouldna' do it were I you," Horgris said. "No one be able to touch it but her. Many did try and all did fail. It do burn and freeze your hand at the same time. I no think you should, but you may try it if you like. We will no stop you."

Gendram remained frozen for an interminable instant before Gerrilaw waved him away. "Follow me," he said to Shanis. "We be seeing what you do be about."

The Three Oaks village looked much like that of the Hawk Hill. The structures were solid, but lacked an air of permanence. She wondered if the Lothans would ever live in true towns and cities again. As they rode, everyone they passed stopped and stared. What she saw in their eyes broke her heart. Despair and hopelessness lay heavy upon these people. But in a few eyes that met her own, she thought she saw a glimmer of hope. If some believed, then others could as well.

A group of older men were gathered in a round dirt area at the village's center. She dismounted and handed the reins over to Garmon, who scowled but said nothing. He had not liked her since their first encounter on the road so many months ago. She reflected that he really should not direct his anger toward her—it had been Allyn who put an arrow through Garmon's hat. Of course, he did not like Allyn either. She was not certain the man liked anyone very much.

"This woman claim to be the one." Gerrilaw climbed down from his mount. "What say the council?" The men exchanged looks, clearly unsettled by the revelation that the bearer was not a man.

"Can you be proving it?" A short, fat man, who was missing his front teeth, asked. "We hear you be doing remarkable things. Can you be showing us some demonstration of your power?" The others nodded. And the clan circled around, though they kept their distance.

Shanis was hardly confident in her abilities. Since the episode at Hawk Hill, she had practiced drawing the power from the sword and putting it back until she could do it almost all the time. Still, almost was a far cry from always, as Master Yurg used to say. She unsheathed the sword and held it out in front of her with both hands. She did not need to touch the sword to draw on it, but she hoped the sight of it would have an effect on the onlookers.

She was not disappointed. Many people gasped and backed away. Though the prophecy did not speak of what the serpent looked like, the sword was obviously something special. The fat man stepped forward for a closer look. His eyes followed the blade to its tip, then back down to the hilt and rested on the sparkling jewels. He gave an approving smile, satisfied with what he saw.

Gendram would not be persuaded so easily. "A fancy sword be no proof. Anyone can be carryin' a blade. Show us what you can do."

What would satisfy them? Something impressive. Her eyes fell upon a cluster of trees topping a nearby hill. Could she channel enough power to blow up the hilltop? That would show them something. She took a breath and prepared to draw the power when she realized the trees were oaks. Considering this was the Three Oaks clan she was trying to impress, destroying their namesake trees might be a grave insult.

A few of the onlookers were already growing impatient. A couple of the young men started to laugh. She needed to do something now. Her eyes fell on a boy only a few summers younger than her. His spine was twisted and he stood hunched over.

Can I do it?

Refusing to entertain thoughts of failure, she strode toward him, sheathing the sword as she walked. She took a long look at the faces of the laughing men, fixing every detail in her mind. One of them, a handsome fellow of below-average height, leered at her as she met his eye. The anger did not distract her, but fueled her determination.

The misshapen boy's jaw dropped when he realized she was coming to him, but he did not try to back away. A heavyset woman, probably his mother, started to protest, but her husband silenced her with a touch and a shake of his head.

She lifted the boy's chin so their eyes met, and she saw fear there. "It's all right," she whispered. Between practice with the power and the time she spent reflecting on her healing of the Hawk Hill girl, she had come to the conclusion that the power was not something she could pull into herself. She had to allow it to flow.

Focusing her thoughts, she opened herself to the energy, and felt it surge into her like a raging torrent. She directed the flow down her arms, through her hands, and into the young man. He gasped and jerked when the power poured into him. His mother whimpered and reached out for him, but her husband held her back.

Trying to repeat what she had done to the injured Hawk Hill girl, Shanis let her mind follow the flow of the power down his twisted spine. The power soaked into the muscles and tendons, loosening and stretching them. She felt him go limp, but she held him up with the energy of the serpent. The power encased his spine, turning and reshaping the bones. The boy grunted with each pop as the vertebra moved into place.

Finally, she was finished.

"Stand." She felt the muscles draw tight again, pulling him up to his feet. When she took her hands from his head, he looked down at his feet and then around at his clansmen, who were in an uproar. He took one tentative step, then another, and then hopped up and down. His mother burst into tears and embraced her son. His father dropped to his knee in front of Shanis.

"Thank you," he said. "You be the one. I do pledge to you my faithful service for all of my days." His wife and son joined him on their knees in front of Shanis. "I do pledge my family to your service as well."

"I accept your pledge." It felt inadequate, but she could think of nothing more to say. "Please stand," she added.

The young man was the first to rise. "My name be Olphair," he said. "I can no thank you enough for what you do for me. However I can repay you, I will."

"No thanks is necessary." The joy in his eyes was all the thanks she needed. This was what she was meant to do—make people whole again. Make a nation strong again.

A commotion arose behind her. While many of the villagers had dropped to a knee, bowing to her, Gendram had moved to stand with the elders, waving his arms and shouting.

"What is she going to do. Heal the Malgog into submission? A leader can no be a healer. A Monaghan leader must be a fighter. Must be one who can lead the clans to victory by the strength of the sword. Can this girl be doing that?" Many appeared to agree with him.

Too many.

"Gendram!" She shouted so that all could hear her. "I challenge you to prove yourself by strength of arms." She had no idea whether this was appropriate, but she remembered it from one of Oskar's stories, though it had not been a story of Lothan. She hoped he accepted. Right now, there was nothing she wanted more than to knock some sense into Gendram, and prove to everyone there that a woman could fight if she must.

Gendram stared dumbstruck at her. Many of the young men urged him on, but he stood rooted to the ground.

"You have been challenged." Gerrilaw looked gravely at his son. "Honor do require that you be answering that challenge."

"I can no fight someone with a magic sword," Gendram sputtered. "It do no be a fair fight."

Shanis unslung her sword and sheath and handed it to Ol-phair. "Hold it by the strap and do not touch the hilt." He accepted the sword from her, though he looked at it as if it were a live viper, and not a thing of steel.

"If someone will lend me a sword, I believe that will put us on even terms." She walked directly toward Gendram, forcing herself to keep a check on her anger. Now was not the time to lose her temper. She stopped less than a pace from the young Monaghan. He was only a hair taller than her, and she could look him in the eye with ease.

"I will no fight a woman," he protested.

"Does someone have a skirt for Gendram to wear?" she called out. His face reddened as laughter rang out all around. She did not push it farther. She remembered Pedric Karst and the way he had baited Natin by doing insult to their entire village. Most likely, she had already made a lifelong enemy of Gendram, but she was here to heal, not to divide. She would not offend the Three Oaks. "I know this is a proud clan of strong warriors," she said, turning around to address all of those assembled. "If this man will not cross blades with me, perhaps someone else will?" No one stepped forward.

"I will try you, girl." Gendram drew his sword. "And may Dagdar guide my blade and have mercy on your soul."

Granlor hurried over to her. For a moment, she thought he was going to try to interfere, but he offered her his sword.

"I hope you do know what you be doing."

She tested the sword weight and balance and found it satis-factory. It was longer and heavier than the sword she had grown up using, but she was as tall and strong as most men, and it was not too much for her. She took a couple of practice cuts before making ready. She glanced at Horgris and saw a concerned look in his eyes. His clan had thrown their lot in with her, but they had never seen her fight. She would not let them down.

She nodded to Gendram, who raised his sword and leapt

foward, a ferocious roar rising from his lips.

She turned his first stroke with ease and countered with a slash that he beat away almost contemptuously. He drove forward, hacking at her like a woodsman at his work. She kept her thoughts and feelings focused on the blade, just as Master Yurg had taught her. She turned away each stroke, giving ground as Gendram came at her. Many of the onlookers interpreted her retreat as a sign that she was in trouble, and cheered Gendram on. Gerrilaw and some of the others, however, were already looking worried.

Gendram's attack slowed, and his technique became sloppy. He had expended too much of his energy in his aggressive attack. Sweat poured from his brow, and he was breathing through his mouth.

Now it was her turn.

She sprang forward, striking first high, then low. His defense was clumsy and, when she gave a thrust to his midsection, he scarcely turned it aside. Two overhand strokes in quick succession drew his guard up high. She feinted low, and struck high. Slowed by fatigue, he could not get his blade up in time, and she sliced open his left cheek.

Spewing vile curses, he swung at her head with a broad, reckless swipe that she easily ducked. She pivoted and swept her foot out, catching his ankle and dropping him to the ground. He landed hard on his back and his sword fell from his grip. He looked up at her, wondering what she would do next.

She did not know why she did it, but she tossed Granlor's sword aside, and beckoned for Gendram to come at her again.

He clambered to his feet, teeth gritted and hands curled like claws. He did not come charging at her like before, but circled, standing on the balls of his feet, tensed to spring. She took a similar stance, and they moved in lock-step, each looking for an opening.

The Three Oaks shouted encouragement to both combatants. Her skill with the blade had swayed a few more supporters to her cause. Gendram struck at her face, but she twisted to the side, making him miss. She repaid him with a kick to the shin and a jab to the jaw that did no damage. He grabbed her wrist, but she twisted her arm and jerked back, pulling free. Gendram struck her hard in the ribs with his left hand. She grunted and grasped his tunic, yanking him toward her as she drove her forehead into his nose. The sound was sickening and her forehead stung from the blow. He staggered backward, blood pouring from his ruined nose. He ignored the injury and kept his hands at the ready.

Shanis feinted with her left hand, then followed with a kick aimed at his knee. He managed to grab her ankle, but before he could pull her off balance, she sprang up and kicked him square in the chin with the heel of her free foot.

Gendram wobbled, took a step backward, and crumpled to the ground.

The onlookers cheered. She knelt and laid her hands on his head. After healing Olphair, it was a simple task to repair Gendram's nose and bring him back to consciousness.

He sat up shivering, eyes wide. He looked at her with a blank expression on his face. Finally he nodded.

"So that be it, then." She stood and offered her hand, which he clasped, and she heaved him to his feet. Loud enough for those around them to hear, he said, "I do believe you be the one, and I do accept you as leader." He did not take a knee as others had done, but the words were more than she had hoped for.

A long journey lay before her, but she had taken another step.

CHAPTER 13

"Are you certain this is the way we must go?" Lerryn gazed at the tangle of vines and creepers that blocked their way. They had been fighting through the growth for what seemed like half the day.

"Please." Heztus sneered. "I am the guide, remember?" The dwarf turned and hacked at the thick foliage with a long, flat knife that looked like a short sword in his hand. Two swings and the vines came down, revealing an overgrown pathway. "And here we are. Follow me, but not too closely. There are certain stinging vines you don't want to touch. They are rare, but sometimes we find them in this area. I shall warn you if I see any." He started forward again, continuing his battle with the dense vegetation. "By the way, if you should see any snakes, don't pick them up, all right?"

Lerryn chuckled and followed behind the dwarf. He held Kreege's reins in one hand and his long knife in the other. He still could not believe he had agreed to let the little man join them. Then again, the fellow knew the shortest, safest route to Calmut, or at least he said that he did. If that was where the Silver Serpent was headed, Lerryn wanted to be there.

He was not certain how the Malgog would receive an outlander in one of their most sacred places, but he was determined to go regardless. He stole a glance behind them to confirm that the others were still following behind. Xaver looked disgusted by the mud and the mess, while the three young men wore dazed, wearied expressions. He wondered at how their worlds had changed since they entered his tournament. When this was all over and they were students at the Academy, they were going to find themselves blessedly bored.

"Are you sure our horses will be able to make it through?" Hair called to Heztus. The way had grown ever more precarious, and some of the paths they had most recently trod were quagmires the consistency of thick porridge.

"Young man, if I am going to have to answer each of your questions three times or more, it is going to make for some exceedingly boring conversation."

Lerryn could not resist the opportunity to needle Heztus. "I suppose this is a bad time to ask you if you are certain that moving due north is the best plan, given that Calmut lies northwest of your village?"

Heztus looked back, rolled his eyes at the prince, and muttered something about "swimming in quakewater" before returning to the task of hacking his way down the path with renewed vigor. Doubtless, he was taking out his frustrations on the surrounding plant life.

Lerryn laughed. He rather enjoyed Heztus' good-natured insolence, so unlike Pedric Karst's sour disposition. It occured to him that, once again, they were a group of six. Perhaps this time the six would bring them luck.

The sun had disappeared behind the trees when they stopped to make camp on a sand bar in the middle of a blackwater swamp where a lone cypress spread its limbs across the width of the bar and out into the water. They tied their mounts in the shelter of the tree and tended to them before settling down for the evening.

Heztus lit a smoky fire to keep the insects away, and they dined on dried meat and some tasty raw tubers the dwarf had brought along. Heztus and Hair each took turns teaching the others drinking songs of their respective countries while they passed around a skin of the sourest wine Lerryn had tasted in years, though he drank his share. By the time they turned in, the wine was gone and Lerryn was feeling better than he had in some time. All in all, it had been a good day. He did not know what lay ahead of them, but he finally knew where he was going, and that was a good feeling.

A frightened cry jolted him from sleep. He bolted up, his hand instinctively going to his sword. The cry came again. Rather, it was a pained scream.

"Bull!" Lerryn shouted. "What is happening?" The young man had taken the first watch, all the while insisting that it was folly to believe they might be attacked here in the middle of the swamp.

A torch blossomed in the darkness and Heztus scrambled out from under a low branch. "Leeches! Huge, poisonous leeches. Do not let them spit in your eyes."

"I've got to help Bull. Which way..."

"He's already dead. I'm going to get the horses. The leeches consume flesh of any kind." He scurried off into the darkness, and Lerryn followed.

The news about Bull pained him, but he was a trained warrior and had lost men before. There would be time enough for grief later. He grabbed a flaming brand from the fire and followed the dwarf. Up ahead, one of the horses whinnied in fright, and then another. He heard men shouting, and suddenly an intense white light blossomed up above them, bathing the sand bar in an ethereal glow.

Two of the horses were on the ground, twitching in their death throes. Black, pulsing masses like creeping sacks of mud crept toward the remaining men and horses.

Xaver held one hand aloft, keeping the light burning in the sky. With the other hand, he pointed one-by-one at the slugs. Each time he pointed a finger, one of the slugs burst into blue flame. The fire did not deter the other slugs. They gave the fires a wide berth, but kept coming. Edrin was putting arrows in the air as fast as he could, but his and Xaver's combined efforts would not be enough. There were too many of the things. Hair stood holding the reins of the horses that remained alive. He looked to be on the verge of panic. Heztus had bound a strip of cloth around his eyes and was trying to fend off a slug half his size with a torch and short sword.

Ignoring the dwarf's earlier warnings, Lerryn leapt into the fray, cleaving a slug in two, then turned to look for another victim. Two more of the slimy monstrosities oozed toward him. Shielding his eyes with his left arm, he dashed toward them. He heard a wet hiss, and felt something spatter all over his forearm. It seared his flesh and he cried out in anger. Before one of the slugs could spit at him again, he leapt over them, twisted in mid-air, and came down behind them. With a vicious stroke, he cleaved them both in two.

"Follow me!" Heztus, the cloth now stripped from his eyes, darted past him. Keeping the light aloft, Xaver brushed by with the others close behind. Lerryn relieved Hair of Kreege's reins and took the rear.

It was like one of his worst nightmares come to life as he stumbled through the darkness. Creepers reached out to ensnare his legs, and with every step, the sand gave way beneath his feet, making him feel that he was running in place. Another slug slid out of the undergrowth, and he skewered it on his sword.

Suddenly, he was out of the sand and on firm ground. He heard a cry up ahead and saw Edrin clutching his arm. Lerryn slashed the slug that had spat poison at Edrin, and then helped the young man along. The slugs were slow, but they were everywhere.

They ran for a league or more through mud, sand and water before Heztus finally called them to a stop.

"We are well clear of the swamp." He dropped to the ground and sat with his forehead in his palms. "I do not know what to say. I have never seen them out this late in the year, and at no time in memory have they come up out of the water after their prey. I do not understand."

"Much has changed in the world in a very short time." Xaver was examining Edrin's arm. "There is no blame to be placed here. Right now, I could use your assistance in tending to this boy's arm."

Heztus told Xaver which herbs made the best poultice to counter the effects of the poison on the skin.

"His Highness will need a poultice as well." Heztus indicated Lerryn's injured forearm. In the fight and flight, he had completely forgotten about the injury.

"Am I poisoned? It hurts, but otherwise I feel strong."

"It only burns the skin," Heztus explained. "If it gets in your eyes, it can blind you. If you are bitten, however, you will die very quickly. That is what happened to your man."

"We should go back for Bull's body when it is daylight," Hair said, "and give him a proper burial."

"He is gone." Heztus looked at the young man with genuine regret. "I am sorry, boy. There is no delicate way to tell you this, and even if there were, I doubt I would bother. The leeches were dragging his body into the water to feed. I imagine he and the horses will be nothing but bone by morning.

Hair shuddered, but accepted the dwarf's words.

Lerryn could think of nothing to say that would bring comfort to the others. He was angry at the needless loss of life, but he held no animosity toward the dwarf. It was an unfortunate tragedy, nothing more. His mood was now black as the mud beneath his boots. Somehow he would make things right.

CHAPTER 14

Karst had never seen so pitiful a group of people as those who stood before him right now. They were all that remained in this mudhole the Malgog called a village. Most of their number had already fled his coming. The cowards. These had not even bothered to put up a fight when he and his men rode into the village, but instead looked up at him in resignation and waited for him to state his business. It was getting too easy.

"You follow me now." He called out so that anyone who might be hiding in one of the mud huts would hear him. "I am the bearer of the Silver Serpent." He pushed back the sleeve of his tunic and raised his arm, revealing the silver armband that snaked around his wrist and forearm. He felt a thrill of delight. This was his favorite part.

"Behold my power!" He pointed at a nearby hut, and it erupted in flame.

"Grandfather!" A woman ran screaming toward the burning dwelling, but by the time she got there, the flames had already reduced it to cinder. Power was a marvelous thing and could be an effective tool in the proper circumstances.

"Get her away from there." Padin and Danlar obeyed instantly, taking the woman by the elbows and dragging her away. He paid no attention to where they were going with her. Instead, he turned to continue addressing the villagers.

"My terms are simple. You will give me and my men a tithe from your stores and a portion of any coin or other valuables you might have. You will swear fealty to me, and all able-bodied men will join me on my quest to unite the clans of Malgog. The rest of you will remain here, continue on with your lives, and await my return."

"Do we have a choice?" A wizened old man looked up at him, the defiance in his tone matched by that in his eyes.

"As a matter of fact, you do." He guided his horse over to where the man stood. Too stupid to know what was about to happen to him, the old man stared up at him, unafraid. In one swift movement, Karst drew his sword and slashed him through the heart. He heard gasps and a few moans, but everyone was too shocked to scream. He once again addressed the villagers.

"Your other choice is death."

Feeling that was as strong an ending as he was likely to have, he dismounted, gave his horse over to one of his men, and made his way to the central hut.

Malaithus waited inside.

"Another fine job, Lord Pedric. Your father will be pleased to hear of your progress."

"I expect he will." Karst dropped into a chair facing Malaithus. "That was nicely done with the hut."

Malaithus waved the compliment away. "It is a simple thing, and they never take notice of me, dressed as I am. They think it is all your doing."

"Yes, they do." Karst propped his feet up on the table and rocked back in his chair, folding his hands across his chest. He was not sure what to make of Malaithus. The man had found him in a tavern, drowning his frustrations after abandoning Lerryn and his failed quest. He came bearing a message from Karst's father. Duke Rimmic Karst had grand plans for his son, and Malaithus was to serve and advise Pedric as he put those plans into action.

He remembered the letter from his father.

The forces of ice have captured the Silver Serpent. Someone must fulfill the prophecy and unite the clans to oppose the next frostmarch. You must be that someone. It was your destiny to bear the serpent. You must reclaim that destiny. If they will not bend to your will, you must bend them.

The next thing Karst knew, he was wearing a snake-shaped silver armband and traveling from village to village in northeastern Malgog, proclaiming himself as the bearer of the serpent and calling upon them to follow him.

The first village had been a challenge. They had scoffed at his claim, until he and Malaithus had given them a display of power. After that, the demonstration was always the first response to any hint of resistance.

Not everyone had to be bent to his will. Many had flocked to his banner, mostly young men eager for adventure, or bitter older men who wanted payment for what they believed were the wrongs life had done them. Some were violent by nature and viewed following Karst as an opportunity to oppress and abuse others without fear of retribution. His ranks quickly swelled, and he had taken to sending small raiding parties into Diyonus where they raided farms, vineyards and villages. This not only afforded them more provisions, but sated the appetites of the more unsavory of his men.

Of late he was finding the villages almost deserted. No one told him why, and he did not ask. He refused to appear ignorant in front of these primitives. His men believed the able-bodied villagers were fleeing in fright, and that explanation was good enough for Karst.

He now had a respectable force at his back, and virtually all of western Lothan had sworn fealty to him. The Mud Snake clan had forsaken their chieftain and elders, and had sent emissaries to Karst, pledging their support and acknowledging him as the bearer of the Silver Serpent. Padin and Danlar were Mud Snakes, and bloodthirsty raiders. They sometimes went a touch farther in their depredations than Karst would have preferred, but he appreciated their enthusiasm. They were eager for Karst to lead an invasion of the lands of the Black Mangrove clan. That would come in good time, but right now, Pedric Karst was the lord of what amounted to a small nation.

"Something is on your mind." Malaithus interrupted his thoughts. "What is it?"

"How does my father know the fate of the Silver Serpent, and why does he want me to be the one who unites Malgog?" There. It was out, and the snows take him if Malaithus did not like the question.

"I wondered when you would ask." Malaithus chuckled, and the sound was like a gurgle deep in his throat. He stretched, yawned, and shifted in his seat before answering. "Let us say I have a special window into certain events. I may not say more, but the time will come when I can tell you all."

Karst thought about that. A window into events. Was it Xaver? Malaithus was a sorcerer. Perhaps the two were in league. It was the only explanation that made sense. He smiled at the thought of that drunken fool Lerryn being too blind to see that his most trusted adviser was the spy in his midst.

"As for why he chose you, I think that should be obvious. Malgog borders your family's duchy of Kurnsbur. With a Karst in control of those lands, King Allar can no longer dismiss Kurnsbur and Duke Rimmic as inconsequential. It might even mean an Earldom and a favorable marriage for you."

And no one could ever call me a pig farmer again. Though he enjoyed the thought of his family gaining power and honor, something bothered him.

"So, this is not truly about making ready for the next frost-march?"

Malaithus met his gaze with a level stare of his own.

"Does it matter, Lord Pedric? Given the choice, would you choose any other path? What difference does it make if the fear of another frostmarch is merely a tool to aid you in conquest? The end result is the same, is it not?"

Behind him, someone cleared his throat. Karst turned to see Padin standing in the doorway.

"My Lord Karst." The young Malgog stood straight, trying to look like a proper soldier. "There is a bone woman here who begs an audience with you. Will you see her?"

An old woman bustled through the door, shoving Padin aside. Padin looked at her in bemused surprise and did not try to stop her.

"I don't beg nothing of nobody." She scowled at Padin, as if daring him to interfere. Satisfied, she gave him a curt not and joined Karst and Malaithus at the table.

"I have a message for you," she said without preamble. "You have been summoned."

Karst exchanged glances with Malaithus, who looked as baffled as he felt.

"I have been summoned," he repeated, recovering from the surprise and gathering his thoughts." Very well. By whom, and to where?"

"Another claims to bear the Silver Serpent. The clans call the both of you to meet at Calmut, where you will face the Keeper of the Mists. There will the choice be made, and there the clans will swear their allegiance to the true bearer."

"It is a lie!" Malaithus's face tightened. "The Silver Serpent is in the possession of the ice."

The old woman moved her head from side to side, as if to say, *perhaps, but perhaps not.* "All the same, you have been summoned."

"But I already have the allegiance of every village in eastern Malgog from the border of Galdora down to the lands of the Black Mangrove clan."

The woman laughed.

"The clans have gone, boy. Haven't you noticed? Save the Mud Snakes, they have all gone to Calmut. You have the allegiance of a few villagers—the old and the infirm, and an army of troublemakers, but you do not have the clans. Go to Calmut, submit to the Keeper of the Mists and, if you are the bearer, then you will truly rule the clans."

"What is this Keeper of the Mists?" Karst was annoyed at being called *boy*, and his voice was harsh.

"It is a myth. A product of superstition." Malaithus scowled at the bone woman while he spoke to Karst. "They gather in a ruined city. The leaders enter a cave, inhale some steam, come back out, and do whatever it was they were already planning on doing long before they arrived at Calmut."

Now he addressed the bone woman. "Tell your sisters to pass this message along to the clan chiefs; the bearer will not lower himself to participate in your demeaning, primitive rituals. They will bend knee to him or pay the price."

The woman was unfazed. She turned to look at Karst. Her eyes bored into him, making him feel dizzy.

"Does he speak for you, or have you a mind of your own?"

"You tell them this." He bolted up out of the chair, sending it clattering to the floor. "You tell them Pedric Karst is no man's lapdog. Pedric Karst does not come when an old woman calls." He gripped the table, his body quivering with rage. "Now get out of here."

The woman looked from him to Malaithus and back again. One corner of her thin, dry mouth turned up in a sneer.

"So be it then, bearer. The call comes only once. The clans gather in Calmut should you come to your senses." She strode from the room with the same sense of determination with which she had entered.

Karst watched her go, rage boiling in him like a seething cauldron. With great effort, he regained control of his emotions.

"So much for the foolishness of old women. If the clans have gone to Calmut, this is a perfect time to move our forces south."

CHAPTER 15

"There be riders ahead." The Blue Stag outrider brought his horse to a halt. "It do look like a full clan, maybe two."

"Do they be moving in the direction of Calmut?" Culmatan took off his headdress and ran a hand through his braided hair. "Most likely they be meaning us no more harm than we be meaning them, no?"

"That do seem to be the way of it." The rider squinted at the distant riders. "I do see some Hawk Hill down there, if I no be mistaken."

"Hawk Hill is Horgris's clan, is it not?" Aspin asked. Culmatan nodded. "Horgris and I are on good terms. I think I should like to ride on ahead and speak with him. Oskar, you and Khalyndryn have met Horgris and his clansmen. Would you care to join me?"

"I suppose." Oskar shrugged. He had no particular desire to see Horgris again, but it might make for a nice change of scenery after traveling with the Blue Stags for three days. They were a standoffish lot, perhaps because he was traveling with a seeker. In any case, he was going to stay close to Aspin. Khalyndryn, who was mounted up behind him, agreed as well.

"I be going with you, then." Culmatan settled his headdress back on his head and put his heels to his his horse. "I must give them my greetings and speak of the news."

The four of them followed the outrider along the dirt road that twisted through a thin scattering of trees. The highlands were starting to level out a bit as they made their way down out of

Monaghan territory. They emerged from the sparse forest at the top of a long, sloping hill.

A long line of clansmen and women stretched out below them. As they trotted their mounts down the hill, a few of the Hawk Hill men broke off from the main body and rode out to meet them. They made no effort to hide their suspicion of Culmatan, but Aspin's presence piqued their curiosity. After questioning the seeker, the men escorted them to the front of the Hawk Hill column.

As they drew close, Oskar spotted Horgris riding in the lead alongside a tall red-haired clanswoman. There was something familiar about her. Suddenly, he realized who it was.

"Shanis!" Oskar cried. "Shanis!" He spurred his horse to a gallop, and almost fell from his saddle as he bounced along.

"Careful! Don't take me down with you." Khalyndryn clung to him as they rode along. "Is it really Shanis?"

"Yes. She's with Horgris."

Up ahead, Shanis heard her name and turned around. Her eyes fell on Oskar and Khalyndryn and she immediately turned her horse and galloped toward them. Two more riders followed, and now Oskar recognized Larris and Hierm.

It was a joyful reunion. In his eagerness to dismount, Oskar tangled his foot in the stirrup and landed flat on his back. Laughing uproariously, Larris and Hierm piled on him. When they unpiled, he was surprised and pleased to see Khalyndryn and Shanis hugging. Not to be left out, he rushed over and caught them both up in a crushing embrace.

"I am so sorry." Shanis's voice was pleading. "I tried, but I couldn't save you. And I didn't mean to leave you. I still don't know how we got out of the mountains. The sword brought us here."

"What happened to you?" Larris asked. "How did you get here?"

"It is a long story best told over several ales. I imagine you have much to tell us as well."

"That we do." Larris grinned at Hierm, who looked abashed. Seeing Oskar's confused expression, Larris clapped a hand on his back. "Don't mind us. Come and let Hierm introduce you to his wife."

Oskar was amazed by all that had changed in such a short period of time. Shanis had the power of sorcery as well, it seemed, though unlike Oskar, she actually had an idea of how to use it, at least in the aspect of healing. And the path she had chosen was a daunting one, but he admired her for her choice. He had always been able to look past her faults, but this act of selfless surrender for the good of a nation not her own was remarkable. He tried to imagine her leading an army, but could not form the image in his mind.

Truth be told, he had not given much thought to the future of anyone other than himself. In a very general way, he had assumed Shanis would find a way to use that sword of hers, perhaps working for Lord Hiram guarding his wagons or some such thing. He had never truly believed she would become a real soldier, though even now he would not say that to her face. It was just too much to believe.

He caught a glimpse of Larris across the fire. He was so happy to see his friend again. The evening had been consumed by catching one another up on happenings, but he looked forward to renewing their conversations about books and history and the like. He had already made up his mind that the best way he could help Shanis would be to research serpent lore and Lothan history and tradition. How exactly to go about that he was not entirely certain, but it seemed like putting his scholarly gifts to work to help his friend was the wise course.

Larris had an odd expression on his face that had nothing to do with the wine. He and Shanis kept exchanging glances when they thought no one was looking. Had Shanis finally come around? The young royal's regard for her had been obvious to anyone with eyes, but she had either ignored or rejected all of his overtures. Of course, that relationship would be fraught with difficulties, but who was to say what could or could not happen anymore? It was not too long ago he had been a starry-eyed farmboy. And now he was… something more, though what exactly his path would be was still to be determined.

"You are awfully quiet, Khalyndryn." Hierm lay propped on one elbow next to his wife Rinala. His marriage was not as improbable as Shanis bearing the Silver Serpent, but it was very much a surprise. What was more, he truly seemed to care for the girl, which was a feat since they had known one another such a short time.

"I'm just enjoying listening to the stories. It is all so hard to believe." A few of the young women whom she had befriended in their previous visit with the Hawk Hill clan had sought her out when they learned of her arrival, but she had politely declined their invitation to walk about, choosing instead to remain with her friends. Since then, she and Rinala had engaged in quiet conversation while listening to the stories.

"Where did Allyn go?" Oskar had noted Allyn's absence and thought it strange.

"He went out." Larris let his gaze fall. "He spends little time around people anymore. I fear that our experience has affected him in some way I do not understand." His eyes held a sadness Oskar had never before seen in the young man. "I regret bringing him with us."

"You did not force him to go with you." Shanis took Larris's hand and gave it a squeeze. "He wanted to. He did it because he is your friend."

"He was my friend, you mean. He hardly speaks to me anymore, and he never wants to be around us. You saw how uncomfortable he was tonight. He didn't even finish one drink before he left." He lay down on his back with his head in Shanis's lap. If the subject at hand was not so somber, Oskar would have laughed at the sight, especially when Shanis began stroking Larris' hair. "In any case, he came because of our friendship, which is precisely why it is my fault."

"I have come to understand," Khalyndryn said, her voice grave, "that acts of friendship are gifts given without price or obligation. I was the reason we left our village in the first place." Her pained expression made Oskar's heart ache. "For a long time I felt guilty about that. But when Oskar and I were lost under the mountains, and all I could think of was keeping him alive, I realized that I was doing it because I wanted to. I was never much of a friend to anyone before, and it felt good to be needed, and to do something to help a friend. As difficult and frightening as it was, I still count it among my fondest memories." A stray tear trickled down her cheek. "None of this makes much sense, I suppose. What I'm trying to say is, if you don't accept someone's gift of friendship, you are robbing them of something very precious."

"I think that be one of the wisest things anyone ever be saying," Rinala whispered, reaching out to take Khalyndryn's hand. Even Shanis appeared moved by her words, and she gave Larris a sad smile.

"I would not trade it either." Shanis looked around at her friends. "This is what we were all meant to do, isn't it? Me, Oskar, Hierm…"

"I still do not know what is intended for me." Khalyndryn forced a laugh. "Perhaps I'll be a guide through underground caverns."

"If it makes you feel any better, I spent most of my childhood and youth fully convinced that my destiny was to bear the Silver Serpent and save my people." Larris made a mocking face at Shanis that elicited laughter from everyone gathered around the fire.

"Shanis, I've been wondering," Oskar said, "how you will learn to use this power you have."

"I don't know." She shrugged. "I suppose I shall just keep figuring it out on my own. It's worked so far, and I don't know any other way to do it."

"Aspin, the seeker, has been teaching me. I believe he would be willing to help you if you like. He was actually searching for you when he found us."

"Was he?" Shanis sat up straight, her voice cold and her expression uncertain. She glanced down at Larris, who looked thoughtful. "Did he happen to say why?"

The memory struck Oskar like a blow to the head, and he could not believe he had forgotten to say something before now. "Actually, he says he knows your father." Her eyes widened when he mentioned Colin. "He came to our village, and your father asked him to help search for us. Your father believed we had not gone far and would return soon, but he asked Aspin to look for us as well."

"That does not make sense." Larris sat up. "What reason did he give for coming to your village in the first place? And why would he travel so far? In fact, how did he know where to look for us?"

The same questions had occurred to Oskar, and Aspin's answers had been sorely lacking in detail, but he had not wanted to offend the sai-kur by pressing him too hard, especially now that they were traveling companions. Now Oskar's training in sorcery added another layer of complication.

"The only thing he told us was that Shanis is important somehow. I don't know any more than that, but if you were to ask him, I think he would tell us the truth."

"I don't like it." Larris stood and began pacing back and forth. "You should watch yourself around him, Shanis."

"So now you're giving me orders?" She grinned and gestured for him to sit back down, but he shook his head.

"I am serious. He had better have some very good reasons for pursuing us like he did. And even if he does have reasons, I won't trust him until he proves himself."

Allyn chose that moment to reappear. No one noticed his silent approach, and they all looked up, startled, when he interrupted their conversation.

"Oskar, may I have a word with you?" His tone was cordial, but his face was set in a mask of discomfort, as if being close to his friends made him ill.

When they were out of earshot of the others, Allyn finally spoke.

"Can you feel it? The magic, I mean. Can you feel the way it pulses and pounds? It's like my head is the anvil and..." He pressed his hands to his temples and groaned. The groan soon increased in pitch until it became a snarl of pain and frustration.

"I don't feel it." Oskar took a step back. "Well, not really. I do seem to... sense something when I'm near the sword, but that is all." What was Allyn trying to tell him? Was Allyn a sorcerer too? Or was it as Larris had said? Had the entire adventure damaged the young man in some way?

"I cannot stand to be close to her for very long. She must think I hate her. Larris looks at me like I am mad. They don't understand. But if they knew…" He sucked in his breath and stared up at the moon. "I am not going crazy, Oskar."

"No one believes that." In spite of his words, he could not help but wonder if, in fact, Allyn was losing his mind. Why had the sword affected him that way, but had not done the same to anyone else in their group?

"My ears are sharper than you think. I know what Larris says about me. He suspects I have been damaged in some way." His expression suddenly changed. Terror filled his eyes, and his breath came in gasps. He grasped Oskar's shoulders with trembling hands. "I have been damaged, Oskar." His voice was strident and filled with desperation. "I am trying to get out. Help me get out!"

"But Shanis can heal people now. Let her try and help you. Better yet, there is a seeker with me…"

Allyn snarled and struck him across the jaw, sending him stumbling back. "Tell no one!" The fear was gone from his voice, and he now spoke in a tone like a primordial growl. "Do not betray me, *friend*. I only need more time!" He turned his back and dashed away into the night.

CHAPTER 16

"Do you think we have done enough?" Hiram Van Derin's voice had an odd ring to it. Deferring to his hired man was obviously uncomfortable for him. "I wonder at the wisdom of remaining here at all, so far from the larger towns and the military outposts. Perhaps I should send more riders for help?"

"To whom would you send them?" Colin's attention was still focused on the boys who were feathering shafts under the close supervision of Nelrid Hendon. Galsbur had no fletcher, and most of the locals were self-reliant enough to make the few arrows they needed for hunting. Nelrid had a particular aptitude for the task, so Colin had set him to training some of the boys who were too young to fight. "We have sent men everywhere I know to send them. In any event, much help is not likely to arrive ahead of the enemy."

"Bah! It chills me when you talk like that." Hiram scuffed the ground with the heel of his boot and stared down. "An army marching toward Galsbur. Who would have believed it?"

"Believe it," Colin said. "Everyone who has fled from them tells the same story: wild ones, exiles, and mercenaries led by coldhearts and shifters." He found it difficult not to shiver at the thought of the latter.

"I'll believe in shifters when I see them," Hiram said in an overloud voice, glancing toward the boys who had ceased their work on the arrows and were listening intently. "No need to frighten them with grandmother's tales come-to-life," he said in a softer voice. "It will be trouble enough without them fearing the monsters of their nightmares."

"Perhaps." Colin had never truly understood children. Consequently, he raised Shanis like he would a young man. There had been other compelling reasons for such an upbringing, but it had left him woefully lacking in empathy for young people. "But what happens when they finally see one face-to-face?"

"Likely the enemy will put enough fear in them that not much will scare 'em any worse." Nelrid left his charges and joined the conversation. "I've only been in two battles in my life. Soiled myself the first time, but the second time I just didn't think about nothing but fighting. War is frightening enough all by itself, don't you think?"

Colin nodded, his eyes still on the young men who were now back at work. How many of them would live to see next year? Or even next week?

"The shafts aren't going to be dried properly. You know that, don't you?" Nelrid indicated the arrows on which the young men were working. "Not enough time to do an adequate job of it."

"All you can do is your best," Colin assured him. "I am certain that your worst arrow is a far better one than I could ever make."

"That's kind of you to say." An embarrassed grin seeped across Nelrid's face. "So tell me, Malan, where did you see fighting?"

Colin was spared the difficult answer by Faun Van Derin, who chose that exact moment to intrude, along with her elder son, Laman, who stood behind her, his angular face and intense eyes the mirror of his father.

"We are going now, Hiram." Faun's face, usually so severe, drooped like a sodden sheet on the line, and her voice was gentle, almost pleading. "I truly wish you would let me remain behind with you. It will be so dangerous here."

Colin glanced at the cluster of mounted escorts, the carriage, and the heavily laden wagon containing so many of Faun's prized possessions, and knew her words to be false, though the feelings behind them actually seemed sincere. Hiram probably knew it as well. He loved the woman, but he was no lackwit.

"Which is precisely why you must go, my dear." Hiram took her by the hand and pulled her close to him. "I could not bear the thought of you in harm's way. Besides, your regard for our capital city is no secret." His smile did not reach his eyes, but Faun beamed at him.

"At least let *me* stay with you, Father," Laman said. "I know I am not much with a sword, but I can do my part. I am not afraid."

"I know you are not afraid." Hiram took his eldest son by the shoulder and fixed him with a grave look. "That is precisely why I trust you to see your mother safely away, and to defend her if the need should arise. Should anything happen to me, you will be the man in the family." He looked up at the sky. "Besides," his voice grew hoarse, "I might have already lost one son. I do not intend to lose another."

Faun gave a little cry and fell against her husband's chest. Hiram enveloped her in his arms and pulled her close, pressing his face into her silken hair. It was the most affection Colin had ever seen between the two of them.

"He is all right." Hiram whispered and stroked her head. "Hierm can take care of himself. Wherever he is, it must be safer than home right now."

"I just want him to come back to us." Her voice was muffled as she pressed her face into his chest. "You don't truly believe we've lost him?"

"No," he soothed, "but I'll not take any chances with Laman. The two of you had better get going now." With obvious reluctance, he drew away from his wife, clasped hands with his son, and escorted them to the waiting carriage.

Colin turned away, looking up at the sky. He tried not to think about Shanis. There was naught that he could do, and ruminating on it did not make things any better. He was certain she was alive, though. Most likely her destiny had finally caught up with her no matter his wishes. But enough of such thoughts. He had a responsibility to these people to keep them alive if at all possible.

A rustling in the nearby trees drew his attention, and one of the local youth who had been dispatched as a scout appeared from the foliage. Behind him walked a man and woman with their young son.

"These folks have just found their way here," he said. "They say trouble's not too far behind." He shook his head. "Still can't believe it."

"Nor can I." Colin turned his attention to the new arrivals. "You did well to make it here in one piece. I daresay you'll find a few of your townspeople among us. I'll show you to the inn. You'll be fed and given some clean clothes, and then we'll see about a place for you to stay."

"I intend to work for my keep, Sir," the man said. "We don't want nothing just given to us."

"When the invaders arrive, there will be plenty of work for you to do, I assure you."

Colin led them into town and across the green, which was now populated by tents and temporary shelters for those who had fled from the invaders, as well as some locals who had reluctantly abandoned their outlying farms for the relative safety of town.

They passed Mardin Clehn and his sons, who were sharpening stakes to be set in the ground to build a defensive wall. Mardin nodded, but did not greet Colin. The Clehns seemed to blame Shanis for Oskar's decision to leave town. If they had taken any time at all to get to know their eldest son, they would have known the wanderlust was strong in him.

The front porch of the inn was crowded with people exchanging gossip, which they called "news." A few children played in the grass nearby, kicking around a rag ball. Though they were engaged in common, everyday activities, there was an eerie quiet about the scene. Everyone was afraid.

"Papa! Mama!" A familiar voice shrieked. "Harvin! It is really you!"

"Jayla?" the woman whispered, her face pale and her eyes wide with disbelief. She turned around and was nearly bowled over as Jayla leapt into her arms. She swept the little girl up and held her close, as if fearful she would get away again. "I can't believe it."

Almost instantly, the family was locked together in a knot,

squeezing each other tight. Jayla told them of her escape, and how Colin had found and looked after her. Her parents sobbed and laughed and recounted how they had searched for her near their town until they dared not wait any longer.

Colin chose that moment to slip quietly away. He did not wish to intrude upon their joy, and he had things to which he must attend. While he was pleased to see the family reunited, it also served to remind him of his own broken family. First his wife, then Shanis. Now Jayla would no longer brighten his home with her smiles and laughter. Sadly, he was growing accustomed to losing girls.

Chapter 17

Aspin was far enough now from the encampment that he could be reasonably assured of privacy. He found an open spot in a dense stand of the stunted, twisted oaks that choked the road-ways of central Lothan. He cleared a space for a fire, scooping out a trench to contain the flames, crumpled dry leaves, added bits of twigs and tinder, and continued adding increasingly larger sticks until he had a modest fire lay. Now it was time to cheat. He whispered, and then a cheery flame engulfed the wood.

He could not suppress a grin. Not only had his sorcerous abilities grown stronger, but his magic was more consistent now, and the responses to his spells were more immediate, effective, and dependable. He had pondered the source, but had drawn no firm conclusion.

He took a pinch of ground aciash root from the soft leather pouch at his belt and sprinkled it over the flames. The result was immediate. Thick, white smoke smelling vaguely of pine and ce-dar roiled upward in a dense, twisting pillar. But when the smoke reached head-high, it ceased climbing, and held there, boiling in an angry mass.

A figure appeared in the smoke: first a vague outline, then a solid shape. It was one of the younger men— one who had fol-lowed the clerical path. Aspin had never bothered to learn his name. He looked at Aspin beneath lowered eyelids, as if he was half-asleep.

"May I help you?"

"You may bring the prelate immediately."

The man's eyes snapped open. "Aspin," he whispered. "Wait. I shall fetch him straightaway." The young man vanished from the smoke and was soon replaced by Denrill. The prelate's expression was one of relief mixed with a strong dose of annoyance.

"I shall not ask where you have been," he said. "The foremost question in my mind at the moment is— Do you have the Malan girl?"

"I am with her," Aspin said. It was the truth. He could not honestly say he *had* the girl, she was not the sort one could control with ease, but he was certainly with her." We are in central Lothan, moving toward the Malgog border."

"What? Your orders were to bring her to us so we could prepare her! She cannot possibly be ready. Doubtless Colin and Yurg taught her to fight, but there is so much more she must learn before she can lead." Denrill clenched his fist as if he were going to shake it at Aspin. "Why," he asked, his puffed chest deflating like a stuck bladder, "would you deviate from a plan that has been so long in the making?"

"I did not deviate from it, Denrill." Aspin was perhaps the only sai-kur who dared address the prelate by his first name. "She chose this path before I found her, and she will not be deterred." In truth, he had failed to even engage her in anything other than casual conversation. She would not talk with him alone, and abruptly ended the conversation any time he tried to discuss her plans.

"I don't understand any of this." Denrill's voice was tight with exasperation. "You are telling me that she had already set off to reunite the clans when you found her?"

"That is... accurate, though it is an oversimplification," Aspin took a bit of perverse pleasure in Denrill's frustration. "There is too much for me to tell you at this time. Suffice it to say I am with her, and she has chosen her path—one for which she is woefully unprepared, but I assure you, I will do all I can to help her succeed."

"I hope the time will come soon that you can explain this all to me. I assume you experienced the recent *event?*"

"The event..."

"Freeze you, Aspin! Do not toy with me. I am speaking of the wave of sorcerous energy that, according to our reports, shook all of Gameryah. I assume you did not miss that? Some of us felt it, even at this great distance."

"Certainly not, Prelate. In fact, I was so close to the source that it rendered me unconscious for the better part of a day or more."

"So you know the cause?" Denrill's voice grew soft and he leaned forward, as if Aspin could whisper in the ear of the smoky spectre that hung before him.

"I assume it happened when Shanis Malan took up the Silver Serpent."

The reply had the expected effect. Denrill, who was taking a sip of wine, choked and began hacking. Aspin reached out to clap him on the back before remembering it was only Denrill's image in the smoke. Denrill glared at Aspin while he recovered his breath.

"I declare," Denrill wheezed, "I have half a mind to send as many men as it takes to drag you back here and have you horse-whipped. To the ice with you and your arrogance! You will tell me what I need to know and tell me quickly before your smoke dissipates."

Aspin gave a quick recounting of his pursuit of the Malan girl, her connection with Larris Van Altman, and her recovery of the Silver Serpent. He also told Denrill of Prince Lerryn's similar, albeit failed, search.

"That allays one of my concerns," Denrill said. "You cannot imagine the uproar over both princes of Galdora vanishing during a time of war."

"A time of war?" Aspin sat up straight.

"I see it is my turn to surprise you." Denrill paused, savoring Aspin's surprise. "The news is not good. Kyrin has invaded Galdora. They have not penetrated deep, but are holding the territory they have taken. Much of northeast Galdora is now under Kyrinian control."

Aspin cursed, but did not interrupt the prelate.

"The duchy of Kurnsbur in southeastern Galdora has declared its independence. We have little information at the moment, but the Duke of Kurnsbur is somehow connected to a group of marauding Malgogs who are terrorizing eastern Lothan. The Diyonans have mobilized to protect their border and are threatening to take a hand. And surprise of surprises, what passes for the Lothan army has moved across the border into Galdora. They are doing little more than burning a few barns, but it is the first time Orbrad has shown any sand. The Galdorans are occupied on the Kyrininan front, and are unable to deal with Kurnsbur or the Lothans. King Allar needs his best captain in the field, yet Lerryn is off on a failed treasure hunt."

"I fear I can only add worse news." Aspin grimaced. "I have reason to believe a large force is moving out of the mountains and into western Galdora. I found signs of its passing through the mountains, and Prince Larris confirms that he and his companions actually saw one detachment of the same army. We do not know for certain that they are headed to Galdora, but that is the direction in which they were headed."

"I do not know where I need you the most," Denrill said. "No one is better qualified than you to intercede between Kyrin and Galdora. Do not bother to argue." Denrill held up his hand to quell Aspin's protest. "But if the Malan girl can unite the clans, perhaps that will take some of the pressure off of the south and we can focus on Kyrin."

"As well as whoever or whatever is coming in from the southwest," Aspin added.

"Yes. And that as well." Denrill's eyes took on a faraway cast, but he quickly recovered. "Send Larris home. I don't know what help he will be, but it is something. He needs to be in Archstone right now. We need to find Lerryn. Let us hope your paths cross again."

"Larris will not want to leave. He appears to be quite taken with Shanis Malan."

"His nation is being invaded from all sides. He will see reason." Denrill stood, the top half of his head vanishing from the block of smoke. It would have been amusing were the circumstances not so dire. "The clans must be reunited. See to it that it happens with all due haste."

"I will, as always, do all that I can," Aspin said.

"Aspin." Denrill's voice was like stone. "Be assured, if you ever again wait this long to report to me, you will surrender your cloak. Am I understood?"

"Perfectly." He did not go on because, just then, a commotion was rising from the direction of the camp, drawing his attention. "I must go, Prelate. Forgive me." Without waiting to be dismissed, he sprang to his feet, kicked dirt over the small fire, and dashed back to the encampment.

He had not gone far when a group of riders galloped past him, steel bared and eyes aflame. As he hurried on, he passed more armed men, all running around and shouting confused questions.

Someone kicked the anthill, Aspin mused.

A group of men ringed Shanis's tent, but they made way for him as he strode into their midst. He ducked inside to see Khalyndryn covered in blood, lying on a blanket. Her tunic had been ripped open at the chest. An arrow shaft had pierced her just above the breast. He had seen more than his share of battle wounds, and this was a grave injury.

Rinala lookd up from where she knelt, cleaning the flesh around the arrow, and shook her head. The meaning was clear. Her mother and sister were there as well, each holding one of Khalyndryn's hands.

"It did pierce her heart," Rinala whispered. "She did live only a short while. We have no told Shanis yet. She is no in her right mind, I think."

Shanis sat cross-legged a few paces away, with Larris on her right and Hierm on her left. Her ashen face glowed in the dim light. "I couldn't find it," she mumbled. "I tried and it just wouldn't come. Why couldn't I find it?"

Larris caught sight of Aspin. "We were attacked," he explained. "Raided would be more accurate. Arlus has apparently been gathering other disenchanted young men to join him. One of them managed to slip in among us, and when the raid began, he used the moment of confusion to take a shot at Shanis. Khalyndryn saw him and put herself in the arrow's path." He looked at Shanis, who continued to stare straight ahead.

"I couldn't heal her," she whispered. "Sometimes the power

just flows through me, but this time…" She shrugged and then her entire body sagged, and she let her head fall onto Larris's shoulder. "Do you know what she said to me? She was lying there in my lap, and there was blood and that… arrow just sticking out of her, and she said, 'I finally found my purpose.' Like saving me from that arrow was her entire reason for being born. And now, when I think about the way I've treated her all these years…"

"You must be strong," Larris said. "You are going to rule the clans, and a ruler may only show weakness in private."

"We're private enough at the moment," Hierm said. "It is only us and my… family." Rinala turned and gave him a wan smile. "I am not quite accustomed to having new relations," he whispered. "So strange."

Aspin knelt in front of Shanis, drawing her gaze to his. "Listen to me. Healing is a difficult thing to master. It requires knowledge and experience that you do not yet have. You cannot do it alone. Please let me help you." Aspin had rarely said 'please' to anyone, but it was imperative that he make a connection with this girl.

She stared into his eyes, that implacable gaze so reminiscent of her father. "For right now, you must help Khalyndryn, if you can." Her voice was desolate, as if she already knew his efforts would be futile. "We will talk later."

"I am sorry, but she can no longer be helped. She is gone." He expected Shanis to break into grief-racked sobs, fall back onto Larris's shoulder, but instead she met his gaze with a blank stare, her eyes void of emotion. "There is, however, something you and Larris must know. I have word from…"

"Not now! I can't…" She sprang to her feet. "Later." She waved away the protest that was forming on his lips. "Larris, I need you." She took the prince by the hand and led him out of the tent.

Aspin watched her go, resisting the urge to follow her. He had never been one to mourn the dead. People lived and people died, and the world did not stop for every minor tragedy. The snows take Shanis and her Malan stubbornness! Of course, she came by it honest, but that did not help matters right now. He needed to tell them about his conversation with Denrill, and he needed to find a way to persuade Larris to return home. That was obviously not going to be easy.

CHAPTER 18

"Are we almost out of the swamp?" Lerryn scraped the last of the gooey, black mud from the bottom of his boot. The last rays of the setting sun had disappeared over the horizon, and they would soon have to bed down for the night. He would prefer to do it outside this accursed bog, if at all possible. They had not encountered anything else as bad as the leeches, but the need to constantly be on watch during the day for quakewater, poisonous reptiles, and the myriad of other potential perils had put him in a foul temper, and lack of sleep thanks to the biting insects had only made it worse.

"What is that you say?" Heztus looked up at him, mock surprise painted across his face. "Surely you are not in a hurry to leave the hospitality of my lovely home."

"If it is all the same with you, I will be pleased to reach dry land, as it were. I feel damp all the way through. Dry land, a fire, and a bottle of wine will suit me nicely."

"Good news then, Highness. The road to Calmut is just beyond that thicket. We will not precisely be out of the swamp, but the land here is a mix of lakes and swamplands, and not so dangerous as that through which we have just passed. And the road is, as you say, dry. A good place to pass the night. After that, Calmut is not too far."

"That is good news," Hair said. "I…" He stopped as Heztus held up a hand.

The dwarf cocked his ear and frowned in concentration. "Riders are coming."

Lerryn rested his hand on the hilt of his sword. Hair and Edrin moved to flank him while Xaver and Heztus stepped back. As they watched, a squad of Monaghan riders appeared around the corner, reining in at a distance and frowning at Lerryn's party.

"Good evening," Lerryn greeted them in a firm but courteous voice. No reason to be impolite, after all. "Do you travel to Calmut?"

"Aye," the man in the lead replied. He was a long, angular fellow with a braided, red beard. "We be escorting the bearer of the Silver Serpent." His back straightened a little as he said the last, and his voice resonated with pride.

"Do you, now?" Lerryn's emotions were a mix of curiosity, jealousy, and suspicion. He wanted to see this person who had claimed what should have been his. "I should like to meet him." At that, the Monaghan men smirked. "Did I say something amusing?"

"You be seeing for yourself." Another of the men, a young fellow with scarcely any chin whiskers of which to speak, grinned at him. "You come with us." His voice gave the words a sense of both invitation and command. In any case, Lerryn was not about to pass up the opportunity to meet the man who had claimed his prize.

The warriors led them into a crowded encampment. It appeared that the Monaghan had brought everyone: men, women, children, even their elders. Most paid Lerryn and his party no mind, but a few spared curious glances for them as they passed through, doubtless most of them staring at the dwarf Heztus, who ignored them all.

Lerryn took everything in, his eyes searching for the bearer of the serpent. His gaze fell upon a young man seated by a campfire. Lerryn froze at the sight of him.

"Larris," he whispered. What in the gods' names? "Larris!" He shouted. His brother jerked his head around and his face fell as he he stared at Lerryn with a stupefied expression. He mumbled something to the person seated next to him, a familiar-looking young woman with red hair. The two of them stood, Larris looking sheepish, and the young woman looking defiant.

"Brother," Larris greeted him, standing up much straighter

than courtesy dictated.

"Brother." He folded his arms across his chest and waited for Larris to explain himself. Larris appeared to be using the same strategy, because they waited in silence for one another for an uncomfortably long time. Xaver joined them and stood off to the side, his expression of mild amusement out of place on his normally serious face.

The girl ran out of patience before either of them did. "This is ridiculous. Larris, if you're not going to explain things to him, then I will."

Lerryn remembered her now. The Malan girl— the one who should have faced Karst in the finals of the tournament. The girl who, by rights, had not been defeated.

"The Victor," Xaver murmured. He cleared his throat and raised his voice. "Tell us girl, where is the Silver Serpent?"

She answered him with a defiant grimace, reached over her shoulder, and drew a gleaming sword. The image of a serpent was etched in the blade, and the hilt and guard were crafted in the shape of a coiled, open-mouthed serpent.

Just by looking at it, Lerryn could feel its magnificence. It should have been his. "How?" he whispered, involuntarily reaching out for it.

"I wouldn't." The girl sounded friendly, and not the least bit defensive. "You're welcome to try, but so far no one but me has been able to hold it."

Lerryn pulled his hand back and looked over the group that had now assembled.

"Royal Blood," he said, looking at Larris. "The Victor." That would be Shanis— he believed that was her name. Behind her, a broad-shouldered youth rose to his feet. "The Bull." Another young man rose and strode over to stand next to the Malan girl. It was the Van Derin boy, a fair-haired youth with deep blue eyes. "The Eyes of Sky." He looked around. "I suppose Allyn is here somewhere?"

"And he would be the Archer," Xaver said. "But where is the Golden Mane?"

"What are you talking about?" Shanis's face flushed.

"He is talking about the prophecy." Larris's words came

slowly, like the first raindrops in a summer storm. "Despite my skepticism, if not outright disbelief, it seems we have inadvertently managed to fulfill the prophecy." He turned to Lerryn. "Our friend, Khalyndryn, must have been the Golden Mane. She died today."

Lerryn supposed he should offer words of sympathy, but he did not care. He had failed.

"Highness," Xaver began, "I suppose we can take some consolation in the fact that we were correct, at least about the Six."

"But we were the wrong Six." Lerryn shook his head and then looked again at Larris. "I do not suppose you would care to tell me why you chose to embark upon *my* quest?"

Larris's eyes flitted toward Xaver, then hardened.

"Allyn and I embarked upon our own quest because, as you know, I do not trust Xaver. And, forgive me brother, I had concerns about you bearing the Silver Serpent, considering your..."

"You did not want it in the hands of a drunkard." Icy fury swept over Lerryn, but it melted almost instantly because he knew his brother's words were true. He wanted to protest that he was gaining control over his need for wine, but he knew how pitiful that would sound. Though the words words pained him, he knew Larris was right.

"That is not the word I would have chosen. You are far from a drunkard, Lerryn, but you cannot be counted upon to be sober when you are needed the most."

"Says the boy who ran away from home to go on an adventure."

"Says the man who succeeded," Shanis snapped. Her eyes blazed and she looked like she was about to strike Lerryn. "You should have stayed home and let him go on the quest."

"Let it go," Larris said, touching Shanis' arm in a familiar way.

The gesture did not go unnoticed. There was obviously something between the two of them. His noble brother had fallen for a commoner? Their father would be apopleptic.

"As I was about to say, I wanted to find the serpent first. I did not, however, believe in the prophecy. I gathered all the stories and legends I could find, and we set out on our search. Along the way, we joined with Shanis and her companions, and became the Six without ever realizing it. Every time we seemed on the verge of failure, providence nudged us back onto the path. The prophecy was real after all."

"A small comfort to me." Lerryn's mouth was dry. He wanted wine, but he would not give in to the urge—at least not where the others could see him. "So where does this leave us?"

He directed the next question to Shanis. "The prophecy says the Silver Serpent will save the royal line of Galdora. You are a subject of Galdora, yet your current path indicates that you plan to forsake your country in an attempt to become leader of this…" He could not properly call the clans of Malgog and Monaghan a 'nation,' at least not in any true sense of the word.

"There is more than one prophecy." She sounded uncertain for the first time. "The finding of the Silver Serpent also heralds the reuniting of the clans. Too many here have died. Someone must bring them together."

"There is more." A man in a brown robe spoke up from where he sat in deep shadow just beyond the firelight.

Lerryn searched him out. A sai-kur! How had he not noticed the man until now? He truly was slipping.

"My name is Aspin. As you have doubtless noticed, I am a sai-kur. I must say, Highness, it is providential that we meet at this time. There is news of which all of you are unaware. I was just about to apprise the others of this when you arrived."

"What do you mean?" Suspicion crept into Lerryn's mind. Sai-kurs were often of great service, it was true, but they always had their own agendas.

"There are many things of which you are not aware. Please sit down." Aspin motioned for everyone to return to the campfire.

Lerryn motioned for Xaver to join the group at the fireside and instructed the remainder of his company to find a place to bed down for the night. He moved closer to the fire but did not take a seat. Instead, he stood waiting impatiently for Aspin's news.

"I have received word from my prelate, and the news is

grave. Your nation is at war. Kyrin has invaded from the north. Meanwhile, Orbrad is making noise along the border, and at least one of your southern duchies is in full revolt. This rebellion might or might not be connected to a pretender in the east who claims to be the true bearer of the Silver Serpent." He paused to let the news sink in.

Lerryn's neck grew hot. Though a matter of concern, war with Kyrin was not a surprise. That particular threat was what had led him to seek out the Silver Serpent in the first place. His stomach sank as he thought again of his failure, but he pushed the thought away. He had more pressing matters now. A rebellion in the southwest? It was unthinkable.

"There is more," Aspin said. "The western border of your kingdom, it is rumored, is also under attack."

"The army we saw in the mountains," Larris breathed. "I'll wager that is who it is." He turned to Lerryn. "While we were in the mountains, we came upon a sizable force of armed men. They did not appear to be particularly well-organized, but there were plenty of them. We debated whether or not we should try to head back to the east and deliver a warning, but… we decided to continue on our quest." He stole a quick glance at Shanis before looking back at Lerryn.

"We have no reliable information," Aspin said, "but if the rumors are true, the army is headed directly toward Galsbur." This elicited surprised comments from Shanis, the Van Derin lad, and the large boy who had not yet been introduced.

Aspin looked meaningfully from Lerryn to Larris. "I am sure you both understand that this is not a good time for Galdora to be without both of its princes.

Lerryn clenched his fists, drew in a breath, then relaxed. It was a simple exercise that at least permitted him to appear as if his emotions were under his control. "I shall return to Galdora on the morrow. Larris, you shall come with me." He turned to Hierm. "Master Van Derin, I remember you from the tournament. You are a fine swordsman and, if you wish it, I can offer you a place at the academy. In any case, you shall return with me as well."

Shanis and Larris exchanged glances. Lerryn gave it no

mind. Obviously, his brother fancied the girl, but that did not matter. Larris had a a higher calling upon his life that superseded the desires of the flesh. He was a prince of Galdora, and he would fulfill the obligations of his station.

"And you, Miss Malan. I thank you for recovering the Silver Serpent. As you know, it is prophesied that the serpent and the fate of Galdora are bound together. You shall return with me as well. I know it is unorthodox, but you may have your place at my academy until we determine how and when the Serpent shall come into play."

"She no be going anywhere." Horgris, the clan chief had joined them. Lerryn had met him years before, and he had changed little. He was still a bear of a man. He stood with his hand on the pommel of his sword. "She do be our leader, and she be leading us to Calmut."

"She is a subject of Galdora." It was only with great difficulty that Lerryn kept his temper in check. "She is my subject. Her liege demands her obeisance."

Shanis sprang to her feet and moved to face him. She was tall for a woman, and Lerryn needed only to look down slightly to meet her eye. She stood nose-to-nose with him, glaring at him with an intensity that caught him off guard.

"I am my own person. I go where I choose, and I do as I please."

"And what will you do if I insist?" Lerryn's voice was soft, but she could not miss his meaning. He was suddenly itching for a fight, and this jumped-up girl would do for the moment.

"You no want to try and take her out of here against her will." Horgris sounded like a father counseling an impudent child. "Fine soldier you may be, Your Highness, but you no can best my entire clan."

He was right. Lerryn took another calming breath and forced himself to speak in a reasonable tone, despite his urge to strike her down for her temerity. "Your home is under attack. Your nation is threatened from all sides, and you hold its salvation in your hand. What shall you do? Hide in the jungle and pretend to be a clanswoman?"

For a moment he thought, even hoped, she might draw her

sword. Instead, she flashed him a look of pure hatred and stalked off into the forest.

"I will go after her," Larris said. He vanished just as quickly without sparing a glance at Lerryn.

Lerryn turned to Aspin. "Can you not talk sense into her, Sai-kur? She is obviously too stubborn to listen to me."

"Even if I could, I am not certain which is the most sensible path. The Silver Serpent…"

"Belongs in Galdora. The prophecies say…"

"The prophecies are vague. And of all the prophecies, only one suggests a connection with Galdora. In fact, it actually says that the Silver Serpent…"

"Will mend the broken crown of Galdora. I am quite familiar with that passage. In any case, our nation is broken. We must have the Serpent.

"And what of our own prophecies?" Horgris growled. "Those of Lothan. We do have been at war for all my life. Galdora, what, a few days? Our prophecies do say the Silver Serpent be going to heal us all. Will bind us together as one. Do my people no deserve peace as much as yours?"

"She is a subject of the crown."

"And she be of our blood." Horgris rose to his feet, quaking with anger. Was everyone going to confront Lerryn today? "And if things do go as I expect, very soon she may wear a crown of her own."

"Your Highness," Xaver interjected. "Forgive me, but unless you intend to capture the girl and take her back in chains, the only thing that matters is what she believes. Perhaps your brother can convince her. He seems to have, shall we say, forged a special connection with her."

Lerryn did not like it. His instinct was to use the power of his station, and force of arms, if necessary, to get what he wanted. But, in this instance, Xaver spoke sense. He looked down at Van Derin and the other boy, who met his gaze with uncertain looks

"Tell Allyn, Shanis, and my brother this— All members of Larris's party who remain loyal subjects of Galdora will leave with me in the morning. I shall leave each of you to the consequences of your choice."

He motioned to Xaver, and together they left the gathering. Finding the spot where Hair, Edrin, and Heztus had made camp, he accepted a cup of wine and a bit of bread and cheese before retiring to his tent. He had a long, sleepless night ahead of him.

CHAPTER 19

"What are you going to do?" There was no challenge in Larris's voice, only sympathy.

"I don't know," she sighed. "It seems that whatever I choose, it will be wrong." Shanis sat on a fallen log, her head resting in her hands. She had been so certain that reuniting the clans of Lothan was the proper things to do, but now she was not certain. Galdora obviously need her. But how could she leave now? Forgetting for a moment that she had vowed to bring the clans together, there remained the fact that so many people were suffering in Lothan. Children were dying. How could she not try to stop if she had the power?

Larris sat down next to her and put his arm around her. His soothing presence relaxed her.

"What about you? Are you going to go with your brother?" She braced herself for the answer she knew was coming.

"I have no choice. As prince, I am honor- and duty-bound to serve my king and country. I am ashamed of the way I left, and I will not add to my disgrace by failing to be there when my country needs me the most."

Shanis had expected nothing less, though it pained her to think of him leaving her now. She felt tired, confused, and so very alone. All of her life, she had been surrounded by friends and family upon whom she could rely. But she had left her father and Master Yurg behind, and was now losing her friends one after the other. Hierm was now married, Oskar spent most of his time with Aspin, Allyn had become a recluse, and Khalyndryn was dead. Larris was all she had left, and now he was leaving her.

"You could come with me," he whispered.

She tried to imagine going back to Galdora with Larris. Before all of this started, she would have loved nothing more than to gain a spot at the academy. Now, that seemed such a childish dream. She realized she had been playing at the sword all her life. Now she was part of something real. And what sort of life could she and Larris have anyway? She was a commoner.

Putting aside her selfish desires, how could she abandon the Lothans? They had followed her based on her promise that she would make them whole again. They were willing to make her their leader. Would it matter to them that the only home she had ever known was in danger, when danger was all they had known their entire lives? She certainly could not tell them she was abandoning them in order to be with Larris.

A memory came unbidden to the forefront of her thoughts, and she remembered the words whispered to her by the serpent as it fought her. It had tried to break her will by making her question herself. *Selfish*, it had called her, and it had replayed for her a lifetime of choices that benefited none but herself. And how had she defeated it? By affirming to herself that what she now did was not done out of a selfish desire for power, but from a desire to help others, and to do the right thing.

"I am not selfish," she whispered. "Larris, I started out on this course knowing that I was doing the right thing for the right reasons. That has not changed. But if I go with you, I could not be certain if my decision was made out of a desire to help those in Galdora who are in danger, or out of a selfish desire to be with you.

"I have to finish what I have begun here. It is the only way I can know for certain I am acting selflessly. I might regret my choice, but I know in my heart that there is no selfishness in it." She stood, took his hand, and pulled him up next to her. "I don't know much about the power, but I am almost certain that it will never answer to my selfish whims. That probably makes no sense to you, but I need you to trust me."

Larris enfolded her in his arms and drew her close. She laid her head on his shoulder, allowing herself a moment of weakness.

A solitary tear fell from her cheek and melted into his cloak. For just a moment, she wanted him to argue with her—to convince her she was wrong. Make her go along with him. It would be so much easier than the path she had chosen. But that was precisely why she could not go with him.

"I cannot fault your decision." His voice was choked with pain. "My heart tells me to stay with you, but what I want and what is right are seldom one and the same."

They stood there in the darkness for a long time, holding each other close, and dreading sunrise.

"You will be safer with your family." Hierm saw skepticism in Rinala's eyes, if not outright defiance, and he hurried on before she had the chance to interrupt. "I do not know what dangers we will meet on the road, and I have no idea when I might see combat." It had all happened so fast. A few hours earlier, they were on their way to Calmut with Shanis, all thoughts of Galdora and the life he had left behind were buried in the deepest parts of his mind. Now he was on his way home. Not just home, but to the prince's academy, then to the army. After that, who knew?

"What do you be talking about?" Rinala stood with her hands on her hips, staring at him as if he were a fool on a festival day.

"You cannot go with me. You are with child. It would be wrong to take you into the middle of a war." He secretly thought it would be a relief to be away from Rinala for a short while, at least. His marriage was another thing that had happened too fast. He was unaccustomed to the constant close presence of another person in his life. He no longer enjoyed any sort of privacy. Besides, the girl was mule headed, outspoken, and much too certain of the value of her own opinions. Then again, he sort of liked those things about her. She reminded him of Shanis. In fact, he had grown quite fond of Rinala. Still...

"Oh, do that be so?" He had heard this tone of voice from women before. It usually preceded bouts of screaming and hurling breakable objects. "You no want me to ride into a war zone? And what do you think I been doing all of my life, Hierm Van

Derin?"

She had a point. The girl lived in a society that was constantly at war. And if he should leave her behind, she would still be a woman with child traveling into dangerous territory.

"Don't you want to be with your mother and your family when our child comes?"

"You do be my family now." She moved in close until their bodies almost touched, her expression softening as she reached up to stroke his cheek. She really was quite lovely, if a bit rough around the edges. "A woman of Monaghan do make her home at the side of her husband, wherever that be." Tears glowed in her eyes, and he could see that an unasked question waited there. He rarely understood women, but this time he thought he knew what she was thinking.

"I do want you to come with me." It was an easy admission to make, though he was surprised to realize how much he meant it. "I want to be there when our child is born…"

"You mean when your son do be born!" Horgris, apparently considering this to be sufficient notice of his presence and intent to enter their tent, stepped inside. Another man might have at least apologized for the interruption, but that was not the way of Hierm's new father in-law. Hierm still found his presence intimidating.

"I tried to get her to stay with you," Hierm said. The big clan chief surely would not want his daughter to stray so far from home, especially when he was so eagerly anticipating the birth of his first grandchild.

"No. There be none of that now. Rinala do be a clan chief's daughter, and she know her duty. She do be a strong girl, and you will be needing her at your side." His voice grew husky and he grimaced. "That do be our way."

He did not know what to say. Rinala fell into her father's arms, sobbing. Hierm felt like he was intruding on a private moment between father and daughter. Finally they broke the embrace, and Horgris held her in arms length.

"You do bring my grandson back to see me soon as you can. And remember how proud your mother and I do be of you. Always."

Rinala smiled and nodded. She gave her father's hand a squeeze and said, "We do be having things to get ready, but I will come to see you and mother shortly."

Horgris nodded and took his leave.

Rinala turned, grabbed Hierm by the back of the neck, pulled his head down, and kissed him soundly. When she let him go, he felt dizzy, but pleasantly warm. She was something.

"I can no wait to see your home and meet your family." Her voice trembled and her eyes sparkled with excitement.

Hierm's stomach sank like a stone dropped into a well. What, he wondered, was his mother going to think of his new bride?

CHAPTER 20

"Shanis, you must come now!" Larris's voice quavered and his face was pale. He trembled as he reached out to take her hand. "It's…" Words failed him, and his face twisted in… pain, nausea, she did not know what. He let his hand fall to his side, and he turned and hurried away. Surprised and confused, she dropped the last of her breakfast of bread and cheese onto the ground and hurried along behind him.

A crowd milled around an unfamiliar tent. A worried-looking Hierm was there, along with Rinala. Prince Lerryn stood in the center of the group, his arms folded across his chest, looking as though he might, at any moment, cut off someone's head. His traveling companions stood behind him, all save the purple-eyed man whom Larris had told her was a sorcerer and Lerryn's adviser. She could not remember his name, but she recalled his unsettling eyes and aloof manner.

"This is Xaver's tent," Larris said, his voice hoarse. "I think you should see this, but I warn you, it is a grim sight. Steel yourself before you go inside."

Granlor stood at the front of the tent, his expression grave. As Shanis approached, he drew the flap aside and stepped out of the way. The smell that emanated from the tent told her what she would find before she even looked inside—blood and death.

Xaver lay sprawled on the floor, his arms and legs askew like a grotesque parody of a discarded rag doll. His clothing was shredded and his body torn. It was the most revolting thing she had ever seen. His throat was ripped open in an uneven gash, and deep cuts crisscrossed his chest. His palms were sliced as well. All around him was blood: on the floor, on the walls of the tent, on the upended chair. It was positively horrific. She stepped back from the tent, marshalling all her willpower to keep from retching. It was important that she appear strong and resolute in front of the Lothans.

"We think he knew his attacker," Larris said. "Xaver always took… steps to protect himself and his tent at night. He also was capable of defending himself with sorcery if need be, but obviously…" No further explanation was needed.

"So Xaver must have been comfortable enough with whoever it was to let him come close enough to…" she swallowed the bile rising in her throat, "…to kill him. But who could it have been? He knew so few people in the camp."

"We will find the murderer," Lerryn said, pushing through the throng of Monaghan milling about, "and I will deal with him personally. You and your… *people* will not interfere. I want your word."

"You no be giving orders here!" Granlor stepped toward Lerryn, his hand on his sword. Before the prince could reply, the sound of hoofbeats broke the silence, and shouts arose from all around.

"They be back!"

"They have someone!"

"We be catchin' him!"

A shiver ran down Shanis' back. If the killer had truly been caught, might she now be asked to administer justice? Despite Lerryn's vow to see to the killer himself, he held no power here. Did the Lothans already view her as a leader? Would it fall to her to decide how they would deal with the perpetrator? This was much more complicated than healing, or even fighting. This would involve her deciding someone's life based solely on her judgment. Could she do it?

The crowd gave way as the riders, led by Aspin, cantered up to where she stood. They dismounted and handed their horses over to three young men who led the mounts away. Now she could see whom they had captured.

Allyn, bound and gagged, sat astride a horse, with a Monaghan clansman on either side, half supporting him, half holding him in place. His eyes were wild with crazed fury, and he snarled and twisted against his ropes and his captors. His clothing was caked with dried blood, and spatters of blood marred his battered face and pale hair.

"He killed Hamor!" one of the warriors shouted. "Put an arrow right through his heart, he did. Had it no been for the thick forest, I do think he would have killed more of us before the seeker be puttin' up his magic shield or whatever it was." He shivered at the thought. "He is no one of the clan, so we be bringin' him to you for justice, my lady."

Shanis's heart fell. This was going to be complicated no matter what she decided. Allyn was Lerryn's subject, and Larris' friend. He was *her* friend, for that matter, and Oskar's. If his captors were to be believed, he had killed Lerryn's vizier, which gave Lerryn the right to dispense justice upon him, but he had also killed a Monaghan, and this was not Galdora.

"It cannot be," Larris whispered, moving toward his friend. "Allyn, tell me what has happened." He reached out to his friend, but Allyn twisted away, still snarling like a feral beast. The Monaghan men wrestled him down from atop the horse and frogmarched him to where Shanis stood. As one warrior knelt to bind Allyn's feet, Lerryn stepped forward, his fists clenched.

"No, brother!" Larris shouted, stepping in front of the larger man and trying to push him back. Lerryn stood stock-still, gazing with hate-filled eyes at Allyn. "Think!" Larris pleaded. "You have known Allyn for nearly all of his life. There must be an explanation!"

"I *thought* I knew Allyn. We shall hear what he has to say, and then I shall kill him."

"Doesn't seem to have much to say, other than growling." Heztus was trimming his fingernails with his dagger. "I doubt you will learn anything from him. He looks insane to me."

"Perhaps I can help with that." Aspin strode through the crowd. Those who had pressed in close now gave way to him as if touching a seeker was taboo. Oskar, looking like he was about to sick up, followed a few paces behind. Shanis felt for Oskar. He and Allyn had been close. She also did not like that he spent so much time in Aspin's company. He even wore the brown cloak the Thandrylls had given him, making him look like a young seeker himself.

"Hold him tight," Aspin instructed the men who were struggling to keep Allyn from squirming loose, though, bound as he was, he would not go far in any case. "Oskar, do you remember the calming spell I taught you?"

"What?" Oskar looked like he had been wakened from a nightmare. "Oh, yes I do."

"Very good. I want you to use that spell to settle him down so I can question him. Do not stop the spell until I say so. Do you understand?"

"Yes, Sai-kur," Oskar said, more formally than Shanis had ever heard him speak. He positioned himself directly in front of Allyn and began whispering. Shanis did not recognize the words, but she felt their power. The air around them grew warm, and the serpent mark on her breast burned. Oskar continued the spell and, as his voice grew softer, Allyn's struggles diminished. Finally, he stood calmly, almost in a daze.

Aspin touched Oskar's shoulder, and the young man stepped to the side, still whispering his spell. The seeker took Allyn's head in his hands and gazed into his eyes. His incantation was harsher, more guttural than Oskar's, delivered at a primordial cadence that made Shanis want to squirm away. All around them, everyone had gone silent, watching in rapt attention.

Aspin's raptor-like eyes widened, and sweat beaded on his forehead. "Speak your name," he whispered.

"Which name shall I speak?" The voice that came from Allyn's mouth was not his own but was instead a low, throaty snarl. "Mine or that of the other?"

"Speak *your* name," Aspin commanded with greater force.

"I shall not," the voice growled. "If you harm this body, you harm only the boy."

"There are other ways of doing harm." Aspin took a deep breath and Shanis felt him drawing power into himself. It was as if a strong wind blew at her back, flowing toward the seeker. As the drawing grew stronger, the air crackled with energy as life force gathered all around.

Shanis was sweating profusely, and her skin tingled. She looked around and saw that no one else seemed to be affected. Just when she thought the very air would shatter from the sheer force of the gathered power, Aspin ceased drawing in. His eyes bulged and his gaze intensified.

"It hurts! Take it away!" Allyn screamed, and this time it was his own voice. "Larris! Make him take it away!"

Larris took a step toward him, but Shanis held him back.

"Tell me your name," Aspin ordered.

"My name is Allyn," he sobbed. "Please kill me. I am evil and should die. Kill me!" He wailed in agony.

"I shall not kill this boy, thereby setting you free. Tell me *your* name."

"Take it away!" The sinister voice was back. "Take it away and I will tell you my name."

Aspin did not relent, but continued to bear down on Allyn, his eyes burning with intensity.

"Aaaaah!" The voice was weakening. "My name," it croaked, "is Takkas."

"Takkas, by your name you will obey me!"

"I will." The coarse voice sounded resentful, but cowed.

"When did you take possession of the boy?"

"Time holds no meaning for me. I possessed a human named Moggs. I grew weary of him and left his body."

"In the dungeon at Karkwall," Shanis whispered. "All this time Allyn has been under this... thing's control?"

"The boy is stubborn. Even now I reside within him, but I cannot always control him."

"Why did you kill Xaver?" Aspin quavered, but Shanis could tell by his demeanor and posture that it was not from fear, but rage.

"The boy went to him for help in getting rid of me. I regained control of him in time to kill the sorcerer before he discovered the truth."

"Why did Tichris unleash you upon the world?" At the sound of the ice king's name, a collective shiver ran through those assembled.

"You know nothing. Tichris is nothing."

Angry mutters ran through the crowd. Shanis heard whispers of, "Seeker's tricks," and "Devil boy."

"Release me and I will spare the boy. But if you force me from him, I shall destroy him."

"You have not the power," Aspin said. "You gave me your name."

"But what shall you do with me? I am a mere shadow… mist… I shall fly away on the wind. Or perhaps I will take control of this boy," Allyn's eyes locked on Oskar, who blanched but did not falter in his incantation. "He has power and I have knowledge. I shall claim his body and then I shall destroy you. Or better, I shall claim his body and destroy these others. And when you kill me, I shall fly away again."

There was a commotion on the other side of the circle and Magla, the bone woman of the Blue Stag clan, scurried forward, clutching a bleached skull.

"Your Honor," she whispered to Aspin, and held up the skull. Aspin looked startled, but then he smiled and nodded to the woman.

Magla grasped the top of the skull and twisted. A circle of bone popped out like a cork, and she held the grinning skull directly in front of Allyn's face. He shied away, and Takkas's voice became high-pitched as he blathered incoherently.

"Takkas," Aspin said, his voice filled with an air of command that would have been the envy of any king. "In the names of the seven gods, I abjure your control over this man and order you by your own name to come forth."

Allyn and Takkas screamed. Allyn's features blurred, and then it was as if he was being split in two. A corporeal form of roiling gray mist was rent, bit by bit, from his body. Shanis could feel the agony as Takkas was drawn out with excruciating slowness. With a final shriek of rage, Takkas burst forth, floating above Allyn's body which had gone limp. His smoky form was that of a muscular man with the head of a cat. He laid his head back and screamed like a mountain lion. The men holding Allyn leapt back, letting him fall unconscious to the ground.

"By the earth of Dagdar I summon you," Magla spoke. Takkas' smoky form wavered for a heartbeat, and then broke apart and was sucked into the skull, which Magla hastily capped with the circle of bone.

Aspin staggered to the side, and Oskar hastily moved to steady him. Shanis suddenly found herself supporting Aspin on his other side, and together she and Oskar guided him to a stump where he sat down heavily and let his head rest in his hands.

She was overwhelmed by the feat this man had just performed, and the power it had required. There was no longer any doubt. She had to let him teach her.

"What was that?" she whispered.

"A cogarra," Aspin said. "It is a spirit creature of the ice king. There are blessed few in recorded history. They can possess a man almost at will. One who is predisposed to violence or inflicting pain upon others is easily taken. A strong person like Allyn can fight it, but he will always lose in the end. Now we know why he has been keeping his distance since my arrival. I had no idea that was what was wrong with him, but I sensed its presence almost as soon as I delved into his mind."

"And that thing is trapped inside the skull?"

"It is," Aspin replied. "I do not know what we shall do with it, but at least Takkas is contained for the time being." He drew long, controlled breaths, visibly weary. "Allyn will need sleep, and he may be confused when he wakes, but he should make a full recovery."

"Perhaps…" Shanis bit her lip. "Perhaps when you are rested, you can begin teaching me?"

For a moment, the weariness drained from Aspin's face, and he smiled. "I shall be delighted," he said. "But first, as you say, I must rest, or I will be no good to anyone." He laid a hand on Oskar's shoulder, and the young man helped the seeker walk on shaky legs back to his tent.

Shanis felt a pang of jealousy at the sight. Oskar had changed. Aspin had claimed some part of her friend, and there was now a subtle distance between them. A feeling of remorse bit at the back of her throat, and she suddenly longed for everything to be as it had been. She wanted them all to be farm children again. The cares she had once thought so great seemed small compared to what she now faced. She missed…

She cut off that line of thinking with a firm shake of her head and returned her attention to Allyn, who still lay unconscious. Larris knelt beside him, holding his friend's head in his lap, his face awash in disbelief. Lerryn stood over them for what seemed no more than a heartbeat's time, then spun on his heel and strode away.

"I cannot believe we could spend so much time with him and not…" Larris's voice trailed away.

"We knew something was wrong," Shanis whispered. "He was not himself."

"Truth be told, I thought he was jealous of you and me. I never dreamed he was… possessed."

"It does not matter now," she said. "The demon is gone now."

Someone nearby cleared his throat. It was Heztus, the Malgog dwarf who accompanied Lerryn. "I have some herbs in my pouch that will let him sleep, and keep away dark dreams. I can fetch them if you like."

"My thanks," Larris said, nodding to the dwarf, who gave a quick bow and hurried away.

They laid Allyn on a soft bed of furs in Larris's tent. Heztus appeared soon thereafter with a pot of boiling water. He rummaged in his pouch and drew out a pinch of some tiny, green leaves. He crushed them and let them fall into the water. They gave off a minty aroma. He held the pot close to Allyn's head and fanned the smoke toward his face.

"With some herbs," he explained in a soft voice, "I would make a tent over the patient's head in order to concentrate the vapor. This herb is much…" He cupped his hand and appeared to scoop a handful of vapor into Allyn's nose. "… more…" He fanned the mist toward Allyn's mouth. "…delicate." He fanned once more, and then hastily drew the pot away.

Allyn snorted and, for a moment, his entire body quaked. Just as suddenly as the tremors had started, they ceased. His body relaxed, and his breathing became deep and regular, and his face relaxed in a peaceful mask of sleep.

"He should sleep all day and through the night, and his dreams will not trouble him." Heztus bowed again, and before they could thank him, he disappeared from the tent.

Shanis gave Larris's shoulder a squeeze, and he smiled a tired smile. "You stay with Allyn," she whispered. "I have some thinking to do."

Chapter 21

The air in the tent reeked of stale wine, dirt, and sweat. Lerryn lay sprawled on the ground, an empty bottle lying next to his open hand. The bedding that had been set out for him lay ignored in the corner.

Shanis grimaced at the sight. Larris had told her about his brother's... problem, but she had never known a drunkard before. Jamin Rhys back home had come home one night too drunk to walk straight, and his wife had dunked his head in the rain barrel until he begged for forgiveness. The women in Galsbur tolerated the occasional overindulgence on the part of their menfolk, but that was all. In any case, a man too deep into his cups would be hard pressed to keep up with the hard life of a Galsburan farmer.

She sighed as she looked down at the prince of Galdora. By all counts, his drinking notwithstanding, he was a great warrior and leader of men. No matter how desperately Shanis wanted to go back to Galsbur, to stand beside her father and defend her home, she knew in her heart she could not. Her destiny lay here. Someone else had to defend her homeland.

She had thought on it all morning. She could return home and possibly help save the people of her village. At worst, she could heal the injured during the battle to come. Or, she could remain here and possibly heal a nation. If she could stop the clan war, how many more lives would be saved? It was the right thing to do. It was the unselfish thing to do.

Now she needed Lerryn.

"Wake up!" She nudged him with her foot. He groaned, but did not otherwise stir. "Get up!" She put her foot on his shoulder and pushed with all her strength.

With unexpected speed and strength, Lerryn grasped her ankle and yanked, dropping her hard onto her backside.

"What do you want?" he grumbled, sitting up slowly and casting a bleary gaze on her. "I was trying to sleep, in case you had not noticed."

"I need you. Your people need you. Have you forgotten the war?"

"They don't need me." He shielded his eyes from the paltry sliver of sunlight that trickled into the tent. "I have made a botch of everything. I am an utter failure."

"Stop feeling sorry for yourself." She had a vague idea that speaking in this manner to a royal was a bad idea, if not outright dangerous, but her temper and Lerryn's current state combined to embolden her. Besides, something told her that what he needed right now was not sympathy. "Yes, you failed in your quest. Yes, you allowed drink to take over your life. Now, what do you plan to do about it?"

"Do about it?" He regarded her in slack-jawed amazement, as if she was a raving lunatic. "What can I do about it? Xaver is dead. You have the Serpent. It is over."

"Nothing is over. Well, Xaver's life is…" She winced. Her mouth sometimes ran faster than her thoughts. "What you can do about it is stand up and fight. I have always heard that you are a fearsome warrior, no matter the drink. There are men outside waiting for you to lead them in defense of our homeland. Forget what is past. Lead them today." She felt as if she was babbling, but something seemed to have gotten through to him. He now wore a thoughtful expression as he fingered the stubble on his cheek. A glimmer of hope sparked inside her, but it was immediately snuffed out as Lerryn sighed and let his chin drop to his chest.

"I need a drink," he muttered, feeling for the wine bottle that he obviously did not know was empty.

Shanis wanted to throttle him. This was her prince? Her supposed liege? She reached for him to give him a good shake, but as she touched him, something deep within her… spoke to her. Her skin tingled, and she suddenly saw Lerryn as if through a tunnel of fog—everything in her field of vision was cloudy except his face.

Guided by this unseen… instinct, or whatever it was, she placed her trembling hands on his temples. He tried to pull away, but a torrent of icy cold rolled through her, coursing down her arms and into Lerryn. He gasped and went rigid.

Shanis felt the connection between the two of them. Her consciousness flowed into him, and she was suddenly aware of his body. All of his physical hurts, his inner workings, even an awareness of his very thoughts, was open to her. It was the deepest connection to another human being she had ever felt, almost indecent in its intimacy. She knew she should probably be frightened, but overwhelmed as she was by the force that guided her, she simply allowed it to be.

Lerryn seemed… sour on the inside, as if something were fouling his body. The power gathered in his center and slowly expanded, an irresistible wall of something beyond understanding. Lerryn groaned and twisted, but he did not resist. Cold sweat dripped from every pore in his body; his eyes and nose ran, and the air was suddenly filled with the foul odor of his bladder and bowels letting loose.

Shanis was dimly aware of a frightened part of herself that screamed for her to let go of this power before she killed him, but a deep, abiding sense of peace calmed her fear, assuring her that all was well.

Now something else oozed forth from him—a viscous, yellow substance that stank like nothing Shanis had ever smelled. She grimaced, but still did not draw away. She sensed that something important remained yet to be done.

She let her thoughts flow again, searching his entire being. His body felt… purified. The foulness was gone, yet something about him remained incomplete. The body was whole, but the spirit…

There was something there. Rather, there was an absence of something. In a way which thoroughly baffled her, she understood Lerryn completely, yet his inner self was beyond her comprehension. What she *did* understand, however, was that in the midst of his soul was a void. It spun like a whirlpool, draining him of his spirit. She could not even fathom what this was, much less what to do about it, but that was a good thing, because the force that had been guiding her simply took over.

The power poured into the void, spinning counter to its relentless depletion of Lerryn's very soul. Lerryn grabbed her wrists and thrashed about in silent agony, but she held on. The power seemed to solidify, filling the empty space. Gradually, the spinning slowed, and finally ceased.

And somehow, she knew Lerryn had been made whole.

Shanis released him and backed away. She knelt there, afraid to move further, afraid to break the silence.

Lerryn did not open his eyes. He inhaled deeply, like a released prisoner breathing the air of freedom for the first time. A trace of a smile grew on his face as he exhaled.

"If you would be so kind as to bring me water and soapstone," he finally said, his eyes still closed, "I should like to make myself presentable before my departure."

"Of course." Standing, she turned and pushed back the tent flap. Clean air filled her nostrils, and the midday sun seemed somehow brighter.

"Shanis!" Lerryn spoke in a firm voice.

She jumped, startled at hearing him call her by her first name. She turned to face him. His eyes were open now, and they radiated strength and something more profound.

"Yes, Highness?"

"I don't know what you did, but thank you."

It was a somber farewell as Lerryn's party departed for Galdora. Rinala exchanged tearful hugs with her family, and even Horgris looked as if he might cry, though he maintained his gruff exterior. Hierm sat astride his horse, looking as perplexed as he had almost every moment since his marriage. He had shared with Shanis his worries about how Mistress Faun would receive her daughter-in-law. She wished she could be there to see it. Faun was going to be apopleptic. The thought raised her spirits and helped numb the pain of Larris's departure. He bade her goodbye with a long, passionate kiss. She had never let him kiss her in front of the others before, and her friends wisely pretended not to notice. Allyn was pale and visibly weak after his ordeal, but he managed one of his roguish smiles as he said his goodbyes. For the first time in months, she saw flashes of the young man she had met so long ago, and was glad. Hair and Edrin, the only remaining members of Lerryn's original six, were returning with him as well.

Oscar had chosen to stay behind, more so that he could continue studying with Aspin than out of any desire to stay with Shanis, she suspected. Heztus had chosen to join them on the journey to Calmut where, she supposed, he would rejoin his clan.

Hierm had promised to get word to Shanis's father, as well as Oskar's and Khalyndryn's families. Her heart fell as she thought about Khalyndryn. Shanis was certain the Serrils would blame her for taking their daughter away. She hoped her own father, at least, would forgive her for the choices she had made.

Lerryn sat his horse with poise and dignity, exuding a powerful sense of strength and self-assuredness. The healing she had performed upon him seemed to have done more than merely sober him up. She did not know how to explain it, but she had filled a hole in his spirit, and the result was what she saw before her now. Their eyes met. Lerryn gave her a military salute, touched his heels to his horse's flanks, and led his party away.

Shanis watched until they vanished behind the trees, wondering if she would ever see any of them again.

CHAPTER 22

Karst hated these meetings with his father. The man treated him as if he were still a child, and not the feared leader he was fast becoming in eastern Lothan. As disenchanted Malgogs continued to swell his ranks, and frightened villagers bent the knee, his plan gained momentum. He hated having to slow down for anyone—especially Rimmic Karst.

The guards outside his father's tent were both familiar to him, having watched him grow up. They bowed to him, though not as respectfully as he thought he deserved. Karst ignored them, pushed back the flap, and entered the tent, followed by Jakom, a disgruntled Malgog whom he had appointed his body-guard.

Duke Rimmic Karst sat poring over a map spread out on a table in the center of his tent. Without looking up, he motioned for his son to take a seat. After a long wait, he finally raised his head.

"You have not reported to me in some time," Rimmic said, before returning his attention to the map, "which is why I felt it necessary to come to you. I expect that you will not let it happen again."

Jakom tensed and inhaled sharply at what he obviously per-ceived to be an insult to his leader. A dismissive wave from Karst settled him.

"I have sent messengers every week, Father. If some did not get through..." He shrugged. It was a lie, but he did not care if his father believed it or not. He would need his father a while longer yet, but not forever.

"So give me the report now," his father said, finally giving him his full attention. His stare was as hard as granite.

"I estimate that we control half of the Malgog lands- the equivalent of the eastern quarter of Lothan." Of course, that control had not been too difficult to achieve, as most of the able-bodied Malgog had gone to some place called Calmut.

"And the Diyonan border?"

"Stable at the moment. We have had a few skirmishes, but nothing to speak of. Now that they know we are here to stay, and have no intention of leaving, they seem content to let us do as we please, provided we do not cross into their lands. They patrol the border, but no longer cross over into our territory."

"That is satisfactory for our purposes," Rimmic said. "And the river?"

"We control almost all of the Igiranin." Karst continued on as his father arched an eyebrow at the word 'almost.' "As we go farther south, and thus closer to the sea, the way grows more difficult. It is a dense jungle, and we are finding it nearly impossible to root out the Malgog there. They know the land better than we do. They can hide with ease and ambush us without warning."

"Then do not try to root them out. Bring them into the fold instead."

Pedric frowned. "It amounts to the same thing."

"It most certainly does not." Rimmic folded his fingers together and looked at his son with an expression of exaggerated patience. "It is the difference between taming an animal and breaking it. Until you understand that, you will not be an effective leader."

Karst bit his lip, reminding himself again that he needed his father's support and resources. The lectures and chastisements would not be forever. He did, however, regret letting Jakom come along. Letting one of his followers witness him being lectured by his father did not strengthen his standing. Of course, Jakom had been one of his first volunteers, and the man was one of his most devoted followers.

"I suppose we could build rafts and send men downriver to negotiate with the Malgog who live there. Perhaps we could purchase right of passage on the river and then proceed from there. I will need gold for that, though."

"Gold? Bah! Think, boy! What use do the Malgog have for gold? Their cities are abandoned and fallen to ruin. They have no commerce, save barter. Give them the things they need: food, tools, blankets. Show them that their lives will be better if they are with us than against us."

"And if that is not successful?" Karst understood the wisdom in his father's advice, but he could not bring himself to admit it.

"Unless you make a complete botch of it, I have every confidence that our efforts will bear fruit. I realize some of your followers are... zealous, and follow us only because we offer them an opportunity to exercise their more... animalistic tendencies at times. They will not do for this job, so choose your envoys with care. Once the river is ours to safely travel, we can establish ourselves and work on extending our control. Now, how stands the west?"

"We have met with little resistance. So many of the clans have traveled to this Calmut that few remain to resist us. We could march all the way to Calmut virtually unopposed if we wished, but what would be the point? We have what we want—firm control of the Igiranin River and the land surrounding it." In fact, Karst now controlled an area larger than his home duchy of Kurnsbur. "We do not have sufficient manpower to risk overextending ourselves, so I have chosen the most defensible positions and established a western border of sorts. Of late, I have been focusing on maintaining order and making incursions to the south."

"The incursions shall cease," his father said, "in favor of negotiations. You were wise, however, to establish a definite, sound border. We have all the land we need, save the southern stretch of the river. Access to the sea will be important for commerce."

Karst hated that a compliment from his father lifted his spirits. So much of his life he had received nothing but criticism from the man, and he had not entirely broken the habit of trying to please him.

"At long last, Kurnsbur shall once again be a free land."

Rimmic stared off into the distance, as if seeing that land before his eyes. "As it should be."

Karst was about to take his leave when Rimmic's eyes refocused, and his gaze snapped back to Karst.

"One other thing." He took a folded piece of parchment from the table and handed it to his son. Karst noted the family seal stamped into a wax circle. "Give these instructions to Malaithus. He is to be High Priest of Kurnsbur. Along with restoring order, we shall be instituting a new religion."

"What? You want to bring the Galdoran way of worship into…"

"Wrong. The people of Kurnsbur once worshiped Arthos, the god of the hunt. We shall reinstate that worship. You have in your hand instructions for basic prayers, rituals, and items for worship. Begin with those most loyal to you, and proceed from there." He paused, looking Karst in the eye. "It is of the utmost importance that you do this. Do you understand?"

"I understand." In fact, Karst did not understand at all. Well, he understood what he was to do, but the point of it was beyond him. He supposed it did not matter. Let the people mumble a few prayers and sacrifice the occasional animal. He had greater concerns. "Is that all?"

"That is all. You are dismissed."

Karst bowed, hoping his father did not notice his reddened cheeks. Dismissing him like a common servant! He maintained his composure as he left the tent, returned to his horse, and rode away. His time would come.

CHAPTER 23

"Tell me again about the way in which you heal people." Aspin was supposed to be teaching Shanis about sorcery and magic, but it seemed he was spending more time trying to understand her than teach her.

"I do not know how I do it," she said. "Sometimes it does not work." She paused, thinking. "The times it does work, I sort of reach my mind into the sword, and it is like a channel opens. What is inside the sword flows through me and into the person I am healing. Sometimes I know exactly what needs to be done, although I don't know how I know that, and I guide the power. Other times, the sword seems to know what to do on its own, and I am merely the vessel. That is what happened with Lerryn. I don't think I had anything to do with it at all, save being the one who transferred the power into him."

"And what do you actually do to someone when you heal him or her?"

"I don't know how to explain it exactly. I search them, understand them somehow, and the power... does what it needs to do."

"No, that is not how it works." Aspin shook his head. "You describe opening a channel; that is how sorcery works. The sorcerer opens himself to the power drawn from the life force all around him. Power flows through him, and he redirects and releases it."

"So, you are saying the Silver Serpent is a vessel for sorcerous power?"

"In principle, there is no such thing as sorcerous power. We are merely vectors for the energy that exists in all life." He raised his hand to cut off her protest. "I understand your question, though. I first believed the sword to be such a repository, but what you have told me indicates that I am mistaken. The sorcerer merely gathers life force and exerts it against an object. It can move things, even destroy them, but it cannot heal."

"But you can heal. I saw you."

"Yes, but healing is done by magic, not by sorcery. It is a thing of the gods."

"I thought it was all the same."

Aspin sighed. "I am sorry. I am usually a much more patient teacher." Sitting on the other side of the fire, Oskar snickered, but the sai-kur ignored him. "I grow frustrated when I am unable to comprehend something." He also had been teaching Oskar for some time now, and he occasionally forgot what he had taught Oskar, but had not yet taught Shanis. More than once he had chastised her for forgetting something he believed he had already told her, only to realize he had taught it to Oscar. Rather than being put out, however, it seemed to be of comfort to her to realize that seekers, as she still called them, were not as perfect as many made them out to be.

"All magic is prayer. You do know what prayer is?" Shanis rolled her eyes, so he continued. "A spell is merely a personal plea to the gods, which the gods answer. The result is what we call magic." He raised his hand again, cutting off another potential interruption. "There are many ways to draw the gods' attention: prayers, sacrifices, rituals. You make your request and the gods grant it. Only their power and… tractability limit what can be done. But gods are whimsical beings, oh yes. Priests might pray all day and not get an answer, while someone else says a short prayer and gets an immediate response."

"So how can you make sure your magic works? If it is all subject to their whims?"

"That truly is the question, is it not? Somewhere along the way, no one can say how long ago, someone noticed certain prayers, always said with precisely the same words and in the exact same way, always drew a like response. Some wise cleric wrote the prayers down and they became the first magic spells. Over time, our knowledge of spells has increased. Some sai-kurs devote their entire lives to gathering spells from other lands and cultures. So you see, magic is essentially nothing more than reciting a prayer which we know will get a response.

"Why do some prayers always get a response?" Shanis was an inquisitive student, though she argued more frequently than he would have liked.

"As to that, we can only speculate. But I feel confident of the answer. Imagine you are a god. You have access to the prayers of all of your adherents. In fact, you hear every prayer uttered by each and every one of your worshipers." He smiled as Shanis shuddered at the thought. "Exactly. You would spend all of your time answering prayers. It would consume every moment of your existence and you likely still could not answer all of them. But you cannot simply ignore prayers, or your worshipers lose faith in you, and a god's worshipers are his power."

Shanis exchanged glances with Oskar, who made a placating gesture and inclined his head toward Aspin. Her inquisitiveness had the unfortunate effect of drawing Aspin off of the subject at hand if he and Okar did not rein her in.

"That is another lesson for another time," Aspin said. "At any rate, it is believed that the gods have, if you will, effectively closed their ears to most prayers. In the case of certain spells, though, it appears that humans have found the precise wording and cadence to speak to the gods on a subconscious level. That is why a spell must be spoken perfectly, not only in wording, but in pacing, pitch, and cadence. Of course, one cannot perform great feats through spells; for that you need to draw the immediate attention of the god. But the properly trained magician can work wonders. You see, while sorcery is truly little more than hurling energy at a target, to do magic is to do the work of a god. That is why sorcery can only destroy, but magic can make whole."

"You told me before that not everyone has the ability to be a sorcerer. Can anyone be a magician?"

"Theoretically, yes. Anyone with a disciplined mind who can learn and perfectly recite the spell can perform magic."

"But I don't know any spells," she protested. "How did I

heal when I don't know magic?"

"Could you have learned some sort of healing spell when you were very young and, buried it in your memory?" Oskar suggested, though he sounded doubtful. "Or perhaps there are spells stored inside the sword?"

"That is not possible." Aspin shook his head. "Power, raw energy, those can be stored if you have the proper vessel. Spells are words, not powers to be stored. Shanis is drawing power in the manner of a sorcerer, but the power she is drawing works in the manner of magic. It is most confounding.

"If healing is of the gods, and the sword allows me to heal, then might it be possible that the gods made the sword for that purpose?"

"I cannot say," Aspin replied truthfully. "I simply do not know."

They made camp early that evening. Heztus had advised Shanis that the land ahead was marshy, and adequate places for an encampment would be difficult to find until they reached Calmut. The distance was not far, he assured her, but the going would be slow.

She could not decide if this was good news. On the one hand, she was eager to get to Calmut and face whatever challenge lay ahead. On the other hand, everything had happened too fast. She now wondered if her vows to unite the clans and stop the killing were merely another product of her rash nature. She still knew little about what she could do, and absolutely nothing about why she was able to do it. What if she was not ready for the challenge she would face at Calmut?

Her slumber was fitful, as it so often had been. The darkness pressed in upon her, embracing her in its sinister arms and dragging her down into disturbing dreams. She struggled against its irresistible force, fighting to escape its clutches.

The dreams carried her along dark tunnels of stone that seemed vaguely familiar. She was dressed in fine silks and escorted by a grave-faced young man who would not meet her eye. In a room of pulsating blue light, she knelt before a stone altar.

She mouthed words, and she could almost understand what she was saying, but the meaning slipped away. She raised her head and all was pain. She felt her sword ripped away from her…

…No! That was not part of the dream! She sat bolt upright, her eyes searching the darkness. Silhouetted against a faint slice of starlit forest, a figure loomed above her, a knife clutched in his upraised hand. She cried out and twisted to the side as he struck. The knife pierced the blanket where her head had lain only a moment before. Her legs were tangled in her blanket, but she struck out with her fist, catching her assailant in the temple. He grunted and stumbled back a few steps before regaining his balance. She frantically struggled to extricate herself from her tangled bedding, all the while waiting for him to strike again with the knife.

Instead, the man ducked down, grabbed something, and sprang from the tent. She finally pulled the last of her blankets away and leapt to her feet. She was now aware of noises outside of her tent: sounds of combat, cries of alarm, orders being shouted, and the clatter of hoofbeats.

She reached for her sword, which she kept by her bedside, but she could not find it. Kicking aside the blankets she had flung on the floor, she searched with her hands across the dark floor – nothing. As her eyes adjusted to the dim light, a feeling of cold resignation spread through her. The light streaming through the slice in the canvas at the back of her tent revealed what she feared to be true—the man had stolen the Silver Serpent.

She freed her belt knife from its sheath and hurtled through the hole in her tent. She was determined that someone would pay.

The night air was cool on her sweaty skin. Her bare feet seemed scarcely to touch the ground as she dashed into the middle of camp. Already the fighting seemed to have abated, and the faint sound of receding hoofbeats told her she was too late.

"Do Shanis be all right?" Horgris called from somewhere up ahead.

"I'm fine," she called back, not trying to keep the bitterness from her voice. She let her hands fall to her sides as she moved toward the sound of his voice. The big Monaghan chief emerged from the darkness, followed by a cluster of angry-looking warriors.

"Who was it?" she snapped.

"It was Arlus and some of the others who abandoned us when we did make you leader," Horgris growled, his head swiveling as if he might spot some new foe upon which to vent his rage.

"Clanless," Granlor muttered. He spat on the ground as if to get the foul taste of the word out of his mouth.

"How did they get through?" Shanis demanded.

"No one did get through." Granlor frowned and cocked his head. "They did try to get to our horses down on the far end of the camp, but they no succeeded.

"One man got through," she said. "The attack was a diversion. He came into my tent."

"But he no hurt you, did he?" Horgris stepped closer and peered intently at her.

"No," she said, "I am fine. But he stole my sword."

CHAPTER 24

Her frustration grew with every day they spent in pursuit. *Three days,* she thought, *wasted.* The Hawk Hill and Three Oaks clans had each provided one of their finest trackers: Granlor from Hawk Hill, and Gendram from Three Oaks. Heztus, Aspin, and Oskar had come along as well. They were six again, for good or ill, and she hoped that number would again lead them along the proper path.

Unable to track in the dark, they had been forced to give their quarry a night's head start, though travel in this tangled land was so difficult that Arlus and his followers could not have gained much of a lead. Nonetheless, she feared they were not gaining much ground at all.

The trail they followed divided, with some of their quarry heading north in the direction of Galdora, and the remainder turning east. Though reluctant to split up their group of six, she set Granlor and Gendram to following the northern trail, while she, Oskar, Aspin, and Heztus continued east. She was pleased to discover that Heztus was as good a tracker as she was—perhaps better, given his familiarity with the land.

She believed they were on the right track. The men who had headed north had made no effort to hide their passage. The trail she followed was not so obvious. Already they had come across places where the men had either ridden up streams, or dismounted and changed direction, leading their horses across hard-packed ground in order to throw off pursuit. They had also laid false trails and sometimes simply erased their tracks. She did not mind. She was certain that the time the men had spent trying to hide their passage far exceeded the time it took her and Heztus to pick up the path again whenever it vanished.

She *had* to recover the sword. It would be of no use to anyone other than her, but she needed it not only for the power it provided, but because of what it symbolized. Now, she had only the serpent branded over her breast to identify her as the one chosen to unite the clans; that would not convince anyone.

"Where do you think they are taking it?" Oskar asked.

"To the pretender, most likely," Aspin said. "What better way to prop up a false claim than to carry with him the very proof people expect?"

"I suppose the pretender could wear it, as long as he is careful not to touch the hilt," Oskar mused. "Perhaps that would be enough. He only needs people to believe he is the rightful one. In any case, keeping it away from Shanis helps the pretender's cause."

"I must confess, I never thought someone would try to take it." Shanis still could not believe it was gone. A part of her wondered if she ought not be relieved—no sword, no burden. She could return home to be with her father, and perhaps with Larris. But she knew that to be her own selfish nature rearing its ugly head. And even if she was tempted to give up and go home, her anger at the thieves' temerity and her desire for retribution overwhelmed any desire she had to go her own way.

Oskar turned to Heztus. "You are a Malgog. Do you know anything about this pretender?"

"A man. An outlander like yourself," Heztus said. "He has gained many followers among my people. At first it was discontented young men, troublemakers mostly. As he grew in power, some villages bent knee for safety's sake. Others actually believe he is the one. Of course, with most of Malgog headed to Calmut, he has faced little resistance. He now controls nearly all the eastern portion of the kingdom—everything north of the Black Mangrove Clan's lands from the Igiranin River east to the Diyonan border. Of course, that tells you nothing about the man, only the circumstance. In any case, he seems to draw the vilest and most sadistic to his cause. I have no sympathy for the traitors who have bent knee to him."

"People are starved for peace," Shanis muttered. "I cannot fault them for that."

"But if he gets the Silver Serpent, he could cement his hold on the east." Heztus said. "Does that not bother you? Your destiny is to unite the clans"

Shanis sighed. "I don't care about destiny. The only reason I haven't thrown that frost-blighted sword into the nearest lake and gone my own way is that I want to put an end to the suffering." She turned to meet Heztus's eye. If this pretender, whoever he is, helps bring peace, it would not be the worst thing to ever happened to the Malgog, would it?"

Heztus hesitated. "Of course not, but in order to bring peace to the rest of the land, the clans must believe that you are the chosen one. Without the sword…"

"But they have to believe her!" Oskar clenched the reins of his horse in a white-knuckled grip. "Clan chiefs have seen her with the sword. They know who she is and what she is."

"But others have not seen her." Aspin's voice was serene, but his eyes were flinty. "And there is little, if any trust in Lothan. If Shanis appears in Calmut without the Silver Serpent, the kingdom could remain fragmented. In fact, the east might be the only stable region in the entire realm."

"I fear that it could be worse," Heztus said. "We Malgog have fought one another just as fiercely as we have fought the Monaghan, and the same is true of them. Now, the Monaghan appear to be uniting behind Shanis. If the Malgog unite under this pretender…"

"It will no longer be skirmishes between clans, but an all-out war between two tribes," Aspin finished. "Meanwhile, Orbrad sits back and watches his kingdom bleed." His face was unreadable, but cold certainty filled his voice. "You have a good mind, Heztus. I am glad you have come with us."

The dwarf said nothing, but Shanis thought she saw a shadow of a smile on his face…

Shanis bit her lip, feeling her frustration turn to rage. It roiled inside her. How had she come to this point? All her life, she had wanted to be a soldier, to use the sword as she had been taught. But seeing the effects of war upon the clans of Lothan had changed that. She did not want to fight; she wanted to heal. And now, despite her best efforts, she found herself far from home in vain pursuit of the one thing that might help her fulfill what she now believed to be her destiny. But even if she did manage to recover the sword, she still did not know how to use it. Not properly, anyway. What if she did recover the sword, only to fail when called upon to use it?

"I should have gone home," she muttered.

"Shanis…" Oskar began.

"I should have gone home to help protect our families. I am neither a healer nor a leader. I am a fighter, though the thought of war turns my stomach. At home, at least, there is a clear right and wrong. Our families are in danger, and here we are riding through the gods-know-where, chasing after a sword I'm not sure I can use. I should let this pretender unite the clans. The end result would be the same, would it not? That is all that matters."

A reflective silence hung in the air as everyone took in her words.

"You truly mean it, don't you?" Heztus looked taken aback. "You don't want to conquer Lothan."

"Of course not." Shanis could not keep a touch of scorn from her voice. "All of this… everything happened by accident. I am no one special, and I have no great ambition in life, save to never again have to look upon the face of a dying child."

"So tell me who you were before you became the great hope of Lothan." This was the most interest Heztus had shown in her since they had met.

Shanis smiled despite herself. "A farm girl who wanted to be a soldier."

"You have come to the right place, then. There is plenty of fighting to be done here, and sometimes the women even fight."

"I have done very little fighting since I left home, yet I already want no more of it. Learning the sword, dueling, I realize now it was all a game to me. A duel was a contest of skill rather than preparation for harming another person."

"Putting a blade through someone is much more personal." Aspin looked away as soon as he said the words, but there was something in his face that led Shanis to believe that perhaps the seeker's comment went much deeper than the subject at hand.

"Well, there's no putting the milk back into the goat." Heztus regarded her with keen interest. "You have come too far to turn away now. You realize that, do you not?"

Shanis nodded. "I tend to say what is on my mind…"

"And only later does she actually think about whether or not what is on her mind is a good idea or bad," Oskar added.

She did not have to look at Oskar to know he was smiling. She could hear it in his voice. A touch of her friend's banter was a welcome comfort in this desolate place.

"If you are not abandoning us," Heztus said, "then what is your plan for bringing us together?"

"Nothing firm," she admitted. Since leaving home, everything that had happened to her had happened by chance. She had taken for granted, she supposed, that everything would continue to do so. The theft of the sword had taught her differently. "I need to understand your people before I can help them." Out of the corner of her eye, she thought she saw Aspin nod in approval. "Can you teach me about them?"

Heztus chuckled. "How much time do you have?"

"As much time as it takes."

CHAPTER 25

"My Lord," Danlar said. "There are some Monaghan here who wish to see you."

"Monaghan?" Karst sat up straight. "What do they want with me?"

"They say they come in peace. They have encamped at a respectable distance, no effort to hide their presence, and sent only three men. They are all unarmed except for... well, you will have to see."

"Fine. Bring them to me." Karst waved him out and exhaled deeply. What could Monaghan want from him? His efforts to gain control of the last remaining stretch of river had not been entirely rebuffed, but neither had they been particularly successful. The Black Mangrove clan, which made its home in the southern salt swamps seemed to prefer isolation. Karst's promises, sent through envoys, of peace and prosperity had made little impression upon them. They also seemed to place little value on material possessions, so trade or bribery was ineffective. They wanted nothing more than to be left to their own devices. Perhaps his father was wrong, and they would have to resort to force. If so, it would be a difficult, if not impossible, task to root out those human swamp rats.

He gazed out through the open window at the ruins of what had once been a Malgog city called Salgo. He had taken for his headquarters one of the few structures that remained standing. Located near the westernmost edge of the territory that was now under his control, Salgo had become his center of operations. He had put many of his new subjects to work clearing away two generations worth of uncontrolled jungle growth. Soon they would begin rebuilding the crumbling wall that had once surrounded this place. What better way to solidify his control than to set up a permanent capital? When the wall was rebuilt, this place would be as defensible a location as he could want.

He caught sight of the Monaghan men approaching under close guard. They did not wear the odd clothing with crisscrossed lines that identified their respective clans, and their beards had been trimmed short in the Galdoran style. As they entered the room, their eyes fell on Karst, and each gave a bob of the head that passed for a bow, but only barely. No more respect than what was necessary to meet the requirements of basic courtesy. He gritted his teeth, but returned the nods with one even less perceptible.

"Your Lordship." The speaker was a tall young man. His golden hair did not quite hide the scar that ran from mouth to earlobe on the left side of his face. "My name be Arlus. Once of the Monaghan, but now clanless. We be bringing you a gift." He produced a long, narrow object wrapped in a saddle blanket.

"What is that?" His voice was more severe than he intended. He did not care about being rude to these men, but he did not like sounding as though he had been taken by surprise.

The man tugged back the edge of the blanket to reveal an exquisite sword hilt. It resembled the head of a snake. A shaft of sunlight twinkled in its sinister jeweled eyes.

"This do be the Silver Serpent. We did steal it right out from under her nose."

Karst reached out to touch the hilt, but Arlus's words suddenly registered. "Did you say *her*?"

"Aye. Disgraceful how our clans have taken to following an outlander woman. Shanis Malan be her name."

The name was familiar. Where had he heard it before? And then it struck him. The girl from the tournament back in Galdora! The one who had shown him such disrespect, and whose disappearing act just before the final match had deprived him of a portion of the glory that was rightfully his. How had he forgotten that name even for a moment?

Karst's head swam. He could not keep his thoughts in the moment. Images burst forth one after the other. The image of the big, red-haired girl was as clear as if it had been only days since she had confronted him when he had beaten that fool farm boy in a fair fight. She had the audacity to want to fight him. He could not forget the challenging looks she had thrown his way throughout the tournament. And then she had fled before he could put her in her place.

"My Lord? Are you well?" Danlar reached out a hand as if to steady him.

"I am fine." Karst pushed the man's hand away. "I know this Shanis Malan." He turned his attention back to Arlus. "And she claims to be the bearer of the Silver Serpent?"

"Aye. She did arrive at the Hawk Hill settlement with this sword and a mark upon her breast. They believe she do be the one."

"And you do not?"

Arlus shook his head. "She do have the mark, and she did heal some, but we hear she do have a seeker with her. Could he not have done the magic? Maybe she do his bidding. And if she do be the one, how is it that we took the sword so easily?"

Karst had little idea what a seeker could or could not do, but he kept his silence. Arlus's objections, whether true or not, could be very useful.

"What exactly do you want from me?"

"I did hope you were a Lothan, but no matter. We do want to join you. We will no be ruled by an outlander girl, and certainly no by a seeker's puppet. I do no believe that the clans will accept her without the sword. If you go to Calmut bearing the Silver Serpent, and she do arrive with no more than a mark on her chest and a seeker pulling her strings…"

"What happens at Calmut?" He hated asking the question. He never liked revealing that he did not know something, but curiosity got the better of him.

"It do be where kings are crowned. They do submit to the Keeper of the Mists, and be accepted or no."

"So if this Keeper of the Mists accepts Shanis Malan, what happens then?" His heart was racing now.

Arlus shrugged. "Most will follow her, but some are no superstitious enough to believe in the clan witches' tales. We will no follow her."

Karst nodded. Yes! This could be the answer. He could get his revenge against Shanis Malan and gain control of all Lothan in one blow.

"Danlar, how far is it to Calmut from here?"

"A day's hard ride, perhaps. But, meaning no disrespect, your father said…"

"Well, you *have* given disrespect whether you intended to or not. My father is not here. In any case, he would not want me to pass upon the opportunity to take control of all of Lothan. Give me that." He reached for the sword.

"I would no…" Arlus said, stepping back.

Fire and ice filled his veins the moment his hand closed around the hilt. He gasped and staggered back, releasing his grip on the sword.

"I did try to warn you," Arlus said. "One can no touch it, save the girl. Anyone else tries to take hold of it, and…" He held his hands out, palms upraised.

"What good is it to me, then?" he snapped. "It is useless to me if I cannot even hold it."

"I would not say that, M'Lord." He had not noticed Malaithus join their group. "It is still a symbol of power— your power if you are the one who bears it. You may leave it in its scabbard and wear it slung over your shoulder where everyone can see and recognize it. The girl can hardly call herself the bearer of the Silver Serpent when you possess it."

"I suppose that is something." Karst pursed his lips. "Why are you smiling?"

Malaithus was grinning like a wolf in the sheepfold. "I was thinking. I have traveled far and wide, and learned many a story and song, and I have heard tell of many a magical artifact that will answer only to its rightful owner… until," his eyes gleamed, "that owner dies."

Karst grinned. "I think we should find out if you are correct, Malaithus." He now lifted the sword by its sheath and slung it across his back. It felt almost weightless, or perhaps it was buoyed by his happiness. "You will guide me to this place?"

Arlus nodded.

"Very well. Danlar, assemble my guard. We are going to Calmut."

CHAPTER 26

"Do you think we are safe in returning to the road?" Allyn whispered, peering off into the foggy hills. His personality had been slowly coming to the fore since he had been cleansed of the spirit that possessed him, but he was still decidedly jumpy and much more suspicious than he had been before.

"I believe so." Lerryn stroked his chin. "We are well past Karkwall, and rumors of raiding parties notwithstanding, I doubt Orbrad has extended his reach much beyond what it once was. Likely he raised his gates and armed his city walls the moment word reached him that the bearer was gathering the clans." The troops' absence, as well as that of the clans who had gone to the gathering, had made for a fast return trip. Nonetheless, he had insisted on giving Karkwall a wide berth as they made their way back to Galdora.

The muted thuds of hoofbeats on soft earth drew his attention as Hair came riding out of the forest up ahead, where he had been scouting. His eyes were wide and his face strained.

"Highness, there are soldiers ahead."

"How many?" Lerryn was already considering their options. They were too small a group to make fighting a prudent choice, though a part of him itched for combat. Since Shanis had… *cleansed* him, he supposed it should be called, all of his instincts were sharper, his mind clearer. He was eager to face an opponent and see what this newly-whole body could do.

"Forty that I saw, but they likely…"

"Have already sent out scouts," Larris interjected. He rode

behind Lerryn, along with Hierm, Edrin, and Rinala."

"You do not think we can slip around them?" Lerryn asked, turning his attention to his brother.

"Considering one of them just spotted us, I would say no." Larris indicated with a nod of his head a lone figure approaching them on horseback.

Before anyone else could react, Allyn had drawn back his bow and was taking aim.

"Stop!" Lerryn shouted. "I know this man!" He put heels to his horse and trotted toward the rider, who raised a hand in greeting. When they met, they clasped hands.

"Korlan, what are you doing here?" Lerryn was stunned to see one of the White Fang, his elite unit, in northern Lothan.

"Looking for you, Highness. Your father sent us personally. Told us not to come back at all if we did not find you." He then spotted Larris and his eyes widened. "And Prince Larris! This is most unexpected."

"Our father did not send anyone looking for me?" Larris's voice was unreadable.

"We… we did not know you were missing. You have not been at court, but your father told everyone you were away on his orders."

"Doubtless he did not want it known that both princes of Galdora had disappeared. I can think of a few relatives who might have tried to take advantage of that situation." Lerryn still felt foolish to have gone off on his quest, and Larris had admitted to feeling the same way. "What can you tell me of the situation at home?"

"Captain Tabars is the only one who knows the full of it. Let us join him, and I shall tell you what I can as we ride." Korlan led them on a winding route down through the forested hills, talking as they rode. "Kyrin has invaded in the northeast. They control two duchies and the war stands at a stalemate. It is taking all we have to fight on that front, since no other nations have come to our aid."

"So we have heard." Lerryn muttered.

In the southeast, Duke Rimmic has declared Kurnsbur to be its own nation. He has…"

"Rimmic Karst?" Lerryn could not believe what he was hearing. Aspin had told him about a revolt in a southern duchy, but if he had mentioned Karst, it had slipped Lerryn's wine-addled brain.

"Karst?" Hierm frowned. "Do you mean…"

"Pedric Karst's father. I curse the day I ever met that useless boy." If Lerryn had been eager for a fight earlier, now he truly wanted to take out his frustrations on someone. "So, the Duke of Swine is founding a nation of pigs. Doubtless they shall become the leading nation in Gameryah, what with the lack of adequate farmland and trade routes."

"Your father apparently feels the same way. He is content to let Rimmic play king until the other wars are over."

They topped a rise and below them saw a cluster of riders. In the center rode a blocky soldier with dark hair sprinkled with gray. He wore three silver bands around his forearm.

"Tabars!" Lerryn called. The man looked up at him and, for a moment did not seem to recognize him. Then a broad grin split his face and he hailed his prince. The other soldiers recognized Lerryn as well, and a cry went up that drew the men who had been scouting back from the forest.

Lerryn rode to his officer's side, where they clasped hands in greeting. Tabars stared into Lerryn's eyes, his brow furrowed. "Is something amiss?"

"No, Highness, but you look different somehow. I can't put a finger on it."

Lerryn knew exactly what the difference was, and he was pleased to hear it, but he was not going to proclaim before these men that a girl from Galsbur had cleansed him of drink. Let them discover on their own that he no longer had a taste for the stuff. In fact, the mere thought of wine, ale, or anything stronger, turned his stomach. He wondered if he would be able to take so much as a swallow again, but he doubted it.

Tabars then caught sight of Larris. "Your Highness." He inclined his head in respect.

"You need not be any more formal with me than with Lerryn." Larris rode forward and clasped hands with Tabars. Tabars remembered Hierm, Edrin, and Hair from the tournament in

Galsbur. He raised his eyebrows when Larris introduced Rinala as Van Derin's wife, but he greeted her with as much courtesy as a career soldier could muster. Soon they were on the road north to Galdora. They set a fast pace, having sufficient remounts so as not to overtax their horses.

"Korlan has told me of the situations in the northeast and southeast," Lerryn said. "What of the west?"

"His Majesty sent us to find you as soon as word reached Archstone about the force moving in from the west, thus little was known at the time we left. We do not know their numbers, or how well armed they might be. Some of the rumors claim they are accompanied by shifters and ice cats, but that is just backwoods superstition."

Lerryn and his brother exchanged tight glances, but let Tabars keep talking.

"They do not appear to be a proper army, but more of a large marauding force. They are moving in from the mountains, sacking mining towns and fur trader's encampments. Their progress is slow, but they are moving in a direct line toward Galdora. Specifically toward Galsbur." His eyes flitted to Van Derin, who said nothing, but made no effort to hide the fact that he was hanging on every word. "Your father cannot spare many troops from the war with Kyrin. He sent a small force as soon as he heard the news, and will send more as he is able. Our orders are to find you and accompany you to the western front, where you will take command of the defenses."

"Why can the king no spare more troops for my husband's home?" Rinala demanded. Rather than being offended, Lerryn rather found the girl's aggressive demeanor amusing.

"The duchies in the northeast are perhaps the richest farmland in all of Gameryah, with few natural barriers to aid its defense," Larris explained.

"And Galsbur is just a name on a map." Hierm's voice was bitter. "We are expendable." No one disagreed with him.

They traveled unmolested across the countryside, stopping where opportunity arose to graze the horses, or to buy or trade for feed for them. It seemed Lerryn had been correct in his assessment of the state of things in Lothan, and southern Galdora was much the same. People were keeping to their homes and going about their business. Larris observed that even this was a bad thing. Commerce, he said, was critical to the kingdom's well-being, and the empty roads indicated that goods were not flowing from place-to-place as they should. The young man would make a fine ruler some day. By contrast, Lerryn lived for the moment, and the immediate resolution of conflict. Larris saw the breadth and depth of things. He was wise in ways Lerryn had no desire to be.

On the third morning after meeting up with Tabars and the men, just as they were ready to depart, Lerryn called everyone together. His heart was pounding. The decision to which he had come had not been an easy one to make, but he knew it was the right thing to do.

"We shall part company today. Larris, you will take Van Derin, his wife, Hair, and Edrin north to Archstone." The protests began at once.

"But brother, I..."

"But my home..."

"We want to stay with you, Highness!"

"Enough!" Lerryn shouted. "I will hear not a word." He was a bit surprised that they all obeyed immediately—even Larris. "You three," he looked at Van Derin, Edrin, and Hair, "are not yet soldiers. Two of you took an oath to enter my service and train at my academy. You will better serve the kingdom when you are trained soldiers.

"Van Derin, you have taken no oath, but your liege commands your obedience. I understand you want to fight for your home, but you now have a family of your own to care for. Take your wife and unborn child to safety. Larris will see to it that she has safe quarters and is cared for." Lerryn realized that, in a way, he envied Van Derin. He regretted that he would never know the love of a family of his own. An image came unbidden to his mind of eyes that sparkled like emeralds. He forced it from his thoughts. Now would be the hardest part. He took Larris by the arm and pulled him close so they would not be heard.

"Father needs you. The kingdom needs you. I am a soldier. I

am of no use for any other purpose." He waved off his brother's protest and continued. "If you come with me, you will be another sword and nothing more. You are worth more than your sword. You will be a great ruler some day."

"What do you mean?" Realization dawned on Larris's face, and he was momentarily rendered speechless.

Lerryn seized the opportunity. He raised his voice so that all could hear. "I, Lerryn Van Altman, First Prince of the Sword to King Allar Van Altman of Galdora, declare before these witnesses that I hereby abdicate my crown and my birthright to my brother, Larris Van Altman."

Shocked silence hung like fog in the air. He did not wait for them to argue.

"Captain Tabars, do you witness this?" Tabars, rendered dumbstruck, merely nodded. Lerryn shook his head. "You must speak."

"I do witness this." Tabars' voice was dull and his expression sullen.

Lerryn now turned to the tall soldier with a pockmarked face who stood alongside Tabars. "Squad leader Khattre, do you witness?"

Khattre's face was beet red, and his eyes watery. "I do witness this."

"Hierm Van Derin, do you witness?"

The young man flinched as his name was called, but he immediately recovered from his surprise. "I... do witness, Highness."

"Make your mark on this," Lerryn drew from beneath his cloak the document he had prepared the night before, "and you shall no longer have to address me with that title." He drew his dagger, and each witness pricked his finger and signed in blood. He was pleasantly surprised and pleased to see that each knew how to sign his own name. When they were finished, he handed the parchment to Larris and dropped to one knee.

"All hail Larris, First Prince of the Sword!" Everyone present, save Rinala, dropped to one knee, and bowed. Each soldier placed his right fist over his heart.

"You may rise." Larris's voice was as bitter as Lerryn had

ever heard. He turned to Lerryn. "Come with me. We shall speak of this."

Lerryn's first instinct was to chastise his younger brother for addressing him in such a manner, but then he remembered he was no longer a prince, and Larris was now his liege. In other circumstances this would have taken some growing accustomed to, but in this case, it did not matter. They moved away from the others so they could talk without being overheard.

"Congratulations, Brother." Larris scowled down at the document. "I would not have thought you clever enough to think of this. Selfish enough, certainly, but not clever enough. Of course, now that your mind is no longer muzzy with drink, who knows what you are capable of?"

Lerryn's face burned and he clenched his fists. He forced himself to relax. He had been prepared for Larris's anger, but not to be accused of doing this for himself. Did Larris not see that this was best for the kingdom? Lerryn would never be fit to rule. He was fit only to kill and to die.

"This document binds me tighter than any chains ever could. I am now the sole heir. I could not risk my life if I wanted to. If I die, our house dies." Larris looked up at the sky, his lips compressed and his eyes searching. He took a long, deep breath and exhaled. Lerryn was painfully aware that every eye was on them, and everyone was straining to hear any part of what they were saying. Finally, Larris continued. "Very well. I can do nothing else. I appoint you," he spoke in a loud, clear voice, "to the rank of general, and order you to fulfill your King's command by leading the defense of our western border."

"I hear and understand, Highness." Lerryn thumped his fist to his chest three times, followed by a bow.

Larris did not return the bow. He returned, mounted up in silence, and rode away at a trot. Edrin and Hair followed behind him. Rinala handed the reins of her horse to Van Derin and stalked over to Lerryn.

"You are no a prince now, so I can speak to you as I like." Of course, a man's standing had never stopped the girl from speaking her mind before now. "You know he loves Shanis, and now he can no ever marry her. Either you did think of that, or you did no. In any case, he is right. You do be a selfish man." She turned on her heel and stalked back to her husband, who stood looking abashed. Neither of them looked at Lerryn as they mounted and rode to catch up with Larris.

Lerryn shook his head. She was correct. He had thought of Larris's feelings for Shanis Malan. That union could never have come to be, and the sooner Larris saw that, the better for the kingdom. He did not relish hurting his brother, but he had no doubt he had done the right thing. He had not, however, anticipated the sudden field commission Larris had given him. Another thing that did not matter. He would not be a general for long. He sighed and turned to address his men.

"I know that every man here will follow me into battle without question. I have witnessed your bravery many times before. The battle to which we now ride is, perhaps, the most hopeless we have ever faced. Our numbers are few, but our hearts are strong, and our cause is noble. I ask that you ride with me one last time. I ask this not as the man who was once your prince, or as your general, but as a brother in arms who will lay down his life for you, and for his king."

Khattre was the first to draw his sword and raise it in the air. In a heartbeat, forty-nine blades, including Lerryn's, glittered in the sun.

"White Fang!" Lerryn shouted. "We ride!"

CHAPTER 27

"The trail breaks up here." Heztus knelt and carefully inspected the ground. "It is as if the entire party scattered in different directions." He snapped his head up, his eyes scanning the surrounding forest.

"Ambush!" he shouted.

Shanis rolled out of the saddle as an arrow whistled through the air where she had sat only a moment before. Flat on the damp earth she looked around for her attackers. She saw flashes of color moving through the dense greenery. Their assailants were well-hidden.

A whisper of chill air passed over her, and suddenly the arrows were falling to the ground as if striking an invisible wall. Aspin raised his hand, and a flash of light burst forth. A surprised cry rang out, then fell silent as suddenly as it had arisen. Another flash, this time in a different direction, and another cry. Now the attackers were falling, the sounds of them crashing through the brush receding.

Shanis clambered to her feet and freed her bow from where it was tied to her horse's saddle. She strung it with practiced ease and sprang into the saddle. She urged her horse forward, determined to catch the attackers. Aspin was right behind her, while Oskar helped Heztus up onto his horse.

The going was slower than she would have liked. The ground grew soggier the farther they rode, and the undergrowth thicker. Soon they would have to dismount and lead their horses or risk a horse breaking its leg. Up ahead, angry shouts pierced the forest. They burst forth into a clearing and immediately reined in.

Dark clad men, some armed with spears, others with bows, ringed the clearing. The men they had been pursuing had dismounted and stood with their arms outstretched as they were relieved of their mounts and weapons. A rustle behind her caught her attention. She glanced back to see that they were now surrounded.

"We might as well join them," Aspin said, sliding out of his saddle. Taking care to make no sudden movement that could be interpreted as having ill intent, Shanis dismounted. Oskar jumped heavily to the ground. He offered a hand to Heztus, who ignored him and sprang down with ease.

Shanis took a long look at their captors. Though they were dressed alike, all in plain black clothing, they were clearly a mix of Monaghan and Malgog. Of course, Heztus was the only Malgog she had actually met, but these men fit the description: darker of hair and eye than their Monaghan cousins, their hair adorned with bones, claws, and teeth, but otherwise they were similar in build and facial features. Her eyes fell upon the biggest man in the group, and she had the sudden feeling that she had met him before. Then it struck her— give the man a bath, comb out his hair, and trim his beard, and he would look very much like... her father.

An angular fellow with a bushy beard and long hair stepped forward, interrupting her thoughts. He gripped his spear tightly, every vein on his lean forearms standing out in the mid-day sun that glistened on his sweaty skin.

"I am Ibram of the Gray Moss clan and an appointed guardian. Why are you breaking the peace?"

"They have stolen something that belongs to me." Her stare burned into the men who had ambushed them. She did not know their names, but she recognized them as some of the Monaghan who had broken away. "A sword."

"We no have any sword, save our own." One of the men whom they had been pursuing sneered as he spoke.

"It makes no nevermind to me," Ibram said. "You will not be breaking the peace of Calmut."

"Calmut!" Heztus muttered. "I've never approached it from the north before, so I had no idea. Stupid!"

"If you are coming in, you are almost out of time. The supposed bearer of the Serpent has not yet arrived. The elders are breaking the call on the morrow."

Shanis gasped. She was almost too late! And she still did not have the sword. She looked around at her companions. Oskar shook his head, but Aspin nodded.

"You must follow where your destiny leads and trust that all will be well." His voice was calm and reassuring.

Oskar swallowed hard and added, "It has all worked out so far. It will again. We should go in."

"All right." Shanis turned to Ibram. "We will enter."

"Ye will enter with no weapons," Ibram continued. "All of the Monaghan can enter." It took Shanis a moment to realize he was including her among that group. "And the dwarf as well. The seeker and this outlander must stay out."

Shanis felt the blood drain from her face. She had been nervous about going to Calmut and facing this Keeper of the Mists, whoever he was, but had not anticipated going alone. First she had lost Larris, Allyn, Khalyndryn, and Hierm, and now Oskar. She would be without any of their original group. Even Aspin's presence would have been some comfort. In fact, the seeker's wisdom and experience would have been much appreciated.

Heztus must have noticed the expression on her face. He stepped forward and offered his elbow as if he were escorting her into a ballroom. "My lady?"

The comical expression on his face broke the tension, and she laid her hand on his arm and followed the Monaghans, who were filing through an opening in the line of guards. She looked back at Oskar, who mouthed "Good luck," and at Aspin, who merely nodded, his face a mask of serenity. His steadiness gave her strength, and she turned to face what lay ahead.

The guards escorted them through a maze of crumbled stone buildings around and inside of which Monaghan and Malgog alike had set up camps. She could tell that this had once been a city of respectable size, though not as large as Karkwall, which was the only true city she had ever visited.

"So the entire nation is gathered here?" She wondered how an entire nation's worth of people could assemble in one city.

"No one in Karkwall considers her or himself part of a clan any longer, so they will stay put. Many from the eastern clans have aligned themselves with the imposter and will not be here. The Black Mangrove clan from the salt swamps keeps to itself. If they are represented at all, it will be a handful. I am told that the Mud Snakes have lost most of their number to the imposter. Many Malgog will stay put, because our settlements in the swamps are well-hidden and easily defensible. The Monaghan will be here in force, as they have no permanent homes any longer. The lands to the south and west, where the ground is more open and level than that through which we approached will be packed with people waiting to hear the news. There is clean water aplenty, but they cannot stay too long before food and sanitation become concerns. That is one of the reasons the elders will not wait much longer."

Shanis would never have even considered such details. She would have worried about conflicts breaking out, but had not thought about the mundane aspects of everyday life.

"That is a lot of people." She thought that she should have something more profound to say, and felt foolish.

"There are not that many of us, and not even as many as there were a few generations ago. There are twelve clans in all, none of great size. Swamps and hills do not provide the sort of arable land that allows a nation to thrive. Then, of course, there is the fact that we have been trying to kill one another for generations."

"I want to put a stop to that."

Heztus looked up at her, his expression now serious. "Forgive me… Actually, I never care if people forgive me or not for the things I say. Why does an outlander, one who has obviously spent a good part of her life learning how to kill people, care if we live or die?"

"Why do I care? Because I cannot bear the sight of children

suffering." She bit ber lip. "My mother died when I was a baby, and I was raised like a boy, and a spoiled one at that. I don't know why my father raised me as he did, though I am certain he had his reasons. Ever since I left home, it seems, no matter what I do, my destiny has taken control of my life. That bothered me at first. I was a selfish person who wanted what she wanted and, when it seemed like outside forces were controlling me, I felt enslaved.

"Now I realize that my destiny, or the prophecy, or whatever it was that was guiding my steps, was merely showing me a part of myself that I did not know existed." She looked down at Heztus, meeting his gaze. "This clan war is an abomination, and I am the person to end it. I will end it because I must, and because I want to."

"If words would be enough to bring us together again, I believe you would succeed. For what little it is worth, you have my support."

His words moved her. The whirlwind that had swept her life in this new and unexpected direction kept her mind overwhelmed with thoughts of what she must do. Often she felt less than human, like a piece in the gods' game. Heztus's simple declaration affirmed that what she hoped to do could make a very real difference in the lives of suffering people.

"Thank you."

"Shanis! It do be you!" Horgris drew annoyed glances as he pushed his way to her. "Do you have it?"

She shook her head.

"It no matter now. Time, it do be almost up. The clan leaders do be gathering in the circle as we speak. Follow me." He glanced down at Heztus. "You come, too. If the leaders do see that she is presented by Monaghan and Malgog, it will be well for her."

Heztus shrugged and followed behind them.

The circle was a ring of stones, each a span wide and the height of two men, with just enough space between each to allow someone to walk between them. The clan chiefs sat upon a circle of smaller stones around a pool of undulating liquid earth—quakewater, the Lothans called it. It was shady here, but the cool air seemed scarely to touch her. She felt hot and itchy all over and impatient for... whatever was about to happen.

She scanned the faces. Gerrilaw, the leader of the Three Oaks, met her eye and nodded. The other clan chiefs regarded her with varying degrees of suspicion in their eyes. One man stood out. His silver-sprinkled hair and leathery skin spoke of advancing age, but he exuded strength. His icy blue eyes shone with intensity, but his face gave little away, save a hint of cool disinterest.

"Krion, leader of the Black Mangrove clan," Heztus whispered. "He and his people rarely leave their clanhold. He will not be easy to sway, but if you can bring him over to your side, it will go far."

Silence fell upon the clearing in which the circle lay. Beyond the ring of stones, the Lothans were gathering. Malgog and Monahgan stood shoulder to shoulder, all feuds cast aside as they waited for... her.

Horgris broke the silence. "I, Horgris, chief of the Hawk Hill clan, do bring before you Shanis Malan, bearer of the Silver Serpent, she who be prophesied to unite the clans of Lothan."

He glanced at Heztus, who repeated the ritual words, naming himself son of the clan chief of the Red Water clan.

Horgris guided her into the circle of chieftains. A narrow footpath led to a small circle of solid ground in the middle of the quakewater. Refusing to let apprehension show on her face, Shanis strode across the footpath as Horgris took his seat among the chieftains. When she reached her destination, she was uncertain which direction she should face, so she settled on Krion. If he held as much sway as Heztus believed, she might as well start making an impression.

"By what right do you claim to be the bearer?" A Malgog chieftain asked in a level tone that suggested neither judgment nor suspicion.

"I recovered the Silver Serpent from its resting place in the mountains." She hoped her answer was proper. The only preparation she had been given during the trek to Calmut was to tell the truth. "I have used its power, and I bear its mark." She pulled down the neck of her loose-fitting tunic to display the silver mark on her breast. "I have witnessed the suffering this clan war has…"

She fell silent as Krion raised his hand. He nodded to Gerrilaw, who cleared his throat. "We did no ask your reasons for wanting to unite us. We ask only by what right you make your claim." The other chieftains nodded in agreement.

"Ye have the hair of a Monagahan," another Malgog chieftain spoke, "the eyes of a Malgog, and the tongue of and outlander. Who are you in truth?"

"I was raised in Galdora. My father is Colin Malan. He has never spoken to me of his home or family, but now that I have met the Malgog, I wonder if he might be of your blood. I never knew my mother, but I am told she looked much like me, except not so… large." Her height and strength had often been a source of embarrassment growing up, but the clan chieftains merely nodded.

"My son presented you," the chieftain continued. So this was Heztus's father, Jayan. Shanis could now see that he and Heztus had the same eyes, though this man was tall and muscular like most of the Malgog she had seen. She wondered how Jayan felt about his dwarf son. "So he believes in you, but I am not certain. A woman, and an outlander at that, the bearer of the serpent?" He shook his head.

"Man or woman, Lothan, or outlander. The prophecies no say anything about those things," Horgris protested. "Besides, the Keeper will choose her or no. She do have been spoken for and shown us her mark." Quiet muttering, both within the circle and without, rose up in response to his words.

"What of this other claimant?" Culmatan of the Blue Stag spoke up. "He has no come to make his claim."

"Yes he has." A new voice rang out. Shanis turned around to see Pedric Karst stride into circle.

CHAPTER 28

"They are coming in force!" Dannil's sweaty face was flushed from exertion. "Moving through the forest," he gasped, leaning against the table in the common room of the inn where Colin and Lord Hiram waited to receive reports and send instructions. "They are over near the Clehn farm."

"We will hold them, just as we have done every other time. That position is well-defended." In fact, Colin doubted they could continue to do so, but there was nothing to be gained by voicing that thought.

When attempts to parley with the invaders, or even communicate, with the enemy were rebuffed, the Galsburans had not wasted a moment. They sent messages to the king, prepared their defenses, and began harrying the oncoming army. The king had sent a single squad of foot soldiers. Their sergeant had not believed Colin's report of a large marauding force, and had set out with his small contingent of men to engage the enemy.

They had not returned.

For weeks now the Galsburans and the refugees from the frontier settlements had engaged in a campaign of delaying tactics against the force that moved inexorably toward Galsbur. They had taken the fight to their enemy, sending skilled woodsmen out to kill their scouts and conduct minor raids. Of course, such actions would have little impact on a force of any size, and the Galsburans had lost skilled woodsmen.

The enemy had now reached the banks of the Vulltu River at the westernmost edge of Galsburan farming land. Colin and his men had turned away several attempts to cross, but those had not been serious attempts. The enemy was probing their defenses. Soon, the real attempt would come, and Colin had no idea if they could turn back the tide.

"Colin!" Natin Marwel came dashing up. Having lost his hand the previous year, the young man was unable to fight, but he had a good mind, sharp eyes, and was a fast runner, so Colin had put him to work scouting and carrying messages. "They are crossing at the White Run!" A favorite fishing spot for catching silversides and redeyes, the White Run was a rocky stretch of water just north of Galsbur. The river widened at this stretch, and was thus shallower than the southern stretch, but was also perilous due to the fast-running whitewater that gave the spot its name.

"Tell me what you saw."

"There are about fifty of them fording the stream. They are raining down arrows on us from the opposite bank, trying to cover the crossing, but the range is too far."

"How many archers?"

"Ten or twelve, though they are putting enough arrows into the air for twice as many."

"It is a diversion," Colin said. "The true attack is the one by the Clehn farm."

"Are you certain?" Lord Hiram scowled. He had an annoying habit of questioning nearly everything Colin said, but to his credit, he seldom argued once Colin explained his thinking.

"I am. They are not sending enough men across at the White Run to make any difference even if they did make it to our side of the river. They hope to make us divide our forces so that their crossing at the Clehn farm is easier, that is all." He turned back to Natin. "Go back to the White Run. Stay out of range of their arrows. I shall need you to report back here if it looks like their crossing has even a chance of succeeding. Do you understand?"

"I do." Natin turned on his heel and dashed away.

"I am going to the Clehn farm." Colin told Hiram. "You have a dozen men at your disposal should you need to send them to White Run or anywhere else for that matter. Send a runner to me if you need more." Hiram nodded and Colin left the room.

A dark mass moved like an oncoming storm cloud through the forest on the other side of the river. The defenders of Galsbur waited behind the hastily constructed defenses of earth and sharpened stakes. A buzzing like angry hornets filled the air as a few nervous men loosed arrows at their enemy, their shots falling well short of their marks.

"Hold until I give the command!" Colin shouted down from his perch in the lower limb of a chanbor tree. They could not afford to expend arrows through futile volleys. Others down the line echoed his command, and soon an expectant silence fell over the defenders.

The shadow moved forward, and as it came into range, Colin saw that something was wrong. The line was too high, too uniform to be a mass of men.

"Hold!" he commanded. He needed to understand what he was seeing. And as they came into clear sight, his stomach fell.

"What is that?" someone muttered.

The defenders had constructed large wooden shields three yards high and two yards wide. It looked like a stockade wall was moving in their direction. Colin gritted his teeth. The enemy had to know that these oversized shields would do little good once the men were down in the river. What were they planning? The answer came as soon as the line of attackers reached the opposite riverbank.

The wall of shields stopped on the bank and came together into a solid wall. The soldiers on either end fell back, forming a box to protect their flanks. Unable to wait any longer, some of the Galsburans released their arrows, then others followed suit. The ragged wave whispered through the air with deadly intent, but most of the arrows bounced harmlessly off of the wooden wall, or off the upraised shields the soldiers farther back held above their heads for added protection. Scattered cries indicated that a precious few had found their marks.

"Hold until I give the command!" Colin shouted again. Lack of discipline was the bane of any militia, and this gathering of farmers could scarcely even be called that. He hoped they would stand their ground when they closed with the enemy. The attackers would have to ford the river, climb the bank, and break through their defenses. If the Galsburans held fast, they could break this attack.

A rhythmic beating sound arose from across the river, followed by another, and then another. Then the men were banging on their shields and crying out. The Galsburans did not answer the cry, but stood resolute.

From the back of its ranks, the enemy sent a volley of arrows at them. The defenders huddled down behind their defenses and weathered the assault. Colin did not know if anyone had been hit, so loud was the noise from across the river. The cacophony rose to a tumult, yet still the men did not charge down into the water and attempt a crossing. And then Colin realized the purpose of the noise. The first noise he had heard was the sound of axes biting into trees. He scanned the opposite bank, his heart pounding. And then he saw it.

A flash of movement. A glint of light on steel. A hollow thump. They were bringing down the trees! All along the opposite bank, boxed in by the protective wooden walls, groups of men were relentlessly hacking away at the tallest chanbor trees. If those fell…

He barked out a series of commands, indicated the locations, and young men with slings sent clay jugs filled with redroot sap hurtling across the river. Highly flammable, redroot sap was not as viscous as most resins. Most of the jugs fond their marks, shattering against the chanbor trees and spilling their contents onto the surprised men below. Fire arrows followed, and some found their marks, setting the resin aflame. Tongues of fire raced down the tree, igniting the men upon whom the liquid had fallen. They screamed and fell back, but were quickly replaced by fresh men, and the work began again in earnest.

Colin groaned. The sap was difficult to come by, and their supply was limited. They certainly did not have enough to burn every man who picked up an axe.

A cry went up as the first tree fell. Then another came down. In a matter of moments, four of the statuesque trees crashed onto their defensive positions. The huge trees, with no low-hanging limbs, were now bridges not only across the river, but over the Galsburans' defensive lines.

Quick as a flash, a furry gray form shot across the nearest bridge. An ice cat! Arrows sang through the air, but the creature was too fast. In an instant it was among the surprised defenders, biting and tearing at them. As Colin clambered down from his perch, he saw more ice cats dashing across the bridges. Warriors followed behind them, their faces painted blue and white, roaring out their battle cries. The defenders who were not occupied fighting the ice cats let loose a barrage of arrows and rocks, toppling the warriors in the front, but they kept coming across the tree bridges.

Colin reached the ground as the archers on the far side of the river sent a barrage of arrows into the defenders. Many found their targets. As the defenders fell wounded or took cover from the deadly rain, more warriors poured across the bridges.

And now the attackers were putting their wooden shield wall to a new use. Under the covering fire of their archers, the warriors dropped them into the river and began lashing them together, creating a floating bridge across the river. A handful of men fell to Galsburan arrows, but the invaders' numbers were too great.

"Retreat!" Colin shouted, brandishing his sword and sword breaker. "Back to the town!"

A warrior in blue face paint charged him, jagged teeth bared in a predatory grin. Colin turned the man's sword with ease and opened his throat with a tight slash. He kicked the dying man's body into the path of another charging warrior, who stumbled and fell. Colin ran him through, wrenched his sword from the body, and charged at the nearest cluster of enemies. *Strange how the old battle reflexes come back so quickly,* he mused.

All around him the Galsburans had taken up the call to retreat. To their credit, they fell back not in a panicked flight, but in the way they had been trained— weaving their way between the hidden pits and traps they had laid out well in advance, occasionally stopping to shoot down an attacker. Fortunately for them, the pursuit was minimal. The invaders were concentrating on clearing the defensive positions on the riverbank, and allowed the villagers to flee.

Colin fought his way clear and dashed after his comrades. The battle madness was upon him, and part of him wanted to stand and fight until they cut him down. The rational side of his mind reminded him that his leadership would be needed long after this first failed engagement.

A sound of unsurpassed wildness caused him to stumble, but he kept his footing and looked back over his shoulder to see an ice cat hurtling after him. The sweat that soaked his body seemed to freeze. He could never outrun the beast. It would catch up with him long before he reached the next line of defense.

Something whizzed past his head, hissing like an airborn serpent, and the ice cat snarled in pain and rage as an arrow blossomed above its left foreleg, but the wound served only to slow the creature, and not much at that. Another arrow missed its target, but a third caught it in its hindquarters.

Colin stole another glance behind him. It was still coming, and though its movement was obviously hindered, it was closing the distance fast. He scanned the ground in front of him. The defenses were a good four rods away—too far, but just ahead... He had to risk it. If it did not work, well, he was going to have to turn and fight in any case, so why not?

He sprinted four more steps, stumbled, and staggered to his left. He kept moving in that direction as he drew his sword and turned to face the creature's charge. Its eyes and teeth shone in the sun as it charged its prey.

And then the ground fell out from under it.

In a half a heartbeat, the roar of angry surprise turned to a feral cry of pain, and then fell silent. Colin did not spare a second glance at the creature that now lay impaled on the sharpened stakes, but hurried to safety before another monster from grandmothers' tales could chase him down.

Behind the safety of the wall they had constructed to protect the town, he sank to one knee and inspected his wounds. A few superficial cuts, nothing more. They could wait.

He rose to his feet and assessed their situation. Defenders, mostly young men with bows, lined the walls, ready for the next assault. A good twenty Galsburans were being treated for minor wounds. He hoped they had not lost too many men in the fight at the river, but he would not know until he took full stock of their defenses.

Suddenly feeling more tired than he could remember ever having felt before, he made his way back to the inn where Lord Hiram waited. The firstman fixed him with a grave look as he entered.

"Well?" He looked far older than his years. His face was taut, and his hands trembled.

Colin shook his head. "Too many of them. We bled them a little, but had no hope of holding them back."

"Do we have any idea of their numbers?" Hiram offered him a bottle of wine, from which Colin took a long drink before answering.

"Several hundred, I think." That was more than twice their number.

Hiram grunted and sat down heavily. He propped his elbows on the table and buried his face in his hands. "Who are they?" he asked, not for the first time. "What do they want here?"

"They are no nation of which I have any knowledge." He hesitated. "They have ice cats with them."

"What?" Hiram gaped at him. They had heard these rumors from the refugees from the frontier settlement that had been raided, but few of them had believed the tales. "But ice cats are just…"

"They are real. One almost killed me."

"The snows blind me! I just can't believe it. If they are real, what other tales might be true?" If Hiram's hands had trembled before, now they quaked. "Have I done the wrong thing? Should we all have fled to safety?"

"Everyone here chose to stay. They wanted to fight, in full knowledge that the worst might happen."

"What do we do, then?"

Colin moved to the window and stared out upon the town green where the wounded had been moved. All of the young women with children had fled to safety, at least he hoped they had made it to safety, but most of the women who were past childbearing years had remained behind. He watched as Marra Hendon bandaged Ham Lurel's wounded forearm. What was it about a home that made someone willing to die for it? There was dirt aplenty in Gameryah. They could plant their crops elsewhere. Why remain here, fighting a losing battle, all the while hoping for aid that might not come?

He almost laughed at his own cynicism. His wife had always chided him for his outlook on the world. He knew the answer to his question. In fact there were two. The practical answer was that the western frontier of Galdora was one of the rare places in which a man could be free from indenture. There was nowhere else these people could go where they would not live in near-slavery. The other answer, the true answer, his wife would have said, is that there was power in *home*. It was that same power that made him long, on occasion, for the black water and tangled swamps of his youth.

"We keep fighting," he finally said. "We hold them off as long as it takes for help to arrive. This is their home. They will do what it takes."

"It is your home too, Colin." Hiram's voice was surprisingly gentle. He rose from his chair and joined Colin at the window. "One day soon, our children will return to us. Let us make sure there is a home for them to return to."

CHAPTER 29

"I am the bearer of the Silver Serpent." Karst's voice was a viper's hiss. "I have come to be recognized as such and to claim my rightful place."

The clan chiefs exchanged dark glances.

"You no be presented?" Culmatan frowned. "This is no proper."

A young Malgog warrior stepped forward. "I, Padin of the Mud Snake clan, do bring before you Lord Pedric Karst, bearer of the Silver Serpent, he who is prophesied to unite the clans of Lothan." He grinned and stepped back behind Karst, who turned to glare at Shanis.

Her heart was in her throat. Karst was the imposter? How could he be? And then her eyes fell upon her sword. He wore it slung across his back, its hilt glittering in the sunlight. All thoughts of bringing peace to the Lothans vanished. Right now, the only thing she wanted was to snatch her sword away from Karst and run him through.

Someone coughed. She looked to see Horgris frowning at her. With a slight jerk of his head, he indicated that she should direct her attention to the chieftains, rather than to Karst.

The chieftains looked displeased. They all turned to stare at Krion, who in turn stared at Karst. Krion scratched his beard, cocked his head, and then gave a thoughtful nod. Apparently Karst's presentation was acceptable.

"By what right do you claim to be the bearer?" The same Malgog chieftain who had asked her the ritual question now posed it to Karst.

"I bear the Silver Serpent." He inclined his head toward the sword slung across his back. "I am the one." He held up his right arm, around which a serpentine band of silver coiled. "I already control most of western Lothan. Malgog and Monaghan recognize me as the true bearer, and flock to my banner."

Shanis was about to challenge him, but warning looks, this time from Horgris and Culmatan, froze the words before they passed her lips. It was plain to see that the chiefs were not pleased with Karst's words. Perhaps the wise course was to remain silent and let him continue giving offense.

Tell him to draw the sword, she thought. *Then you'll see.* Horgris knew! So did Culmatan and Gerrilaw! Why didn't they say anything?

"You be an outlander as well." The Monaghan chief who spoke was one whom she did not recognize.

Karst nodded, but did not elaborate. His usual sour frown was fully in place, and there was an air of impatience about him as he waited for the chieftains to deliberate.

"He could be of our blood from old." Padin, the young Mud Snake warrior, interjected. "He has the look about him."

"You are not to speak!" The eldest Malgog chieftain stood, shaking with rage. "Ye will not disgrace me like this."

"You are the disgrace, Father," Padin snapped. "Lord Karst makes us strong again, yet you abandon the clan."

"My clan abandoned me," the man rasped. "They have all forsaken their rightful leader."

"Peace, Labar," Horgris said. He signaled to someone outside the circle. Two warriors stepped forward and dragged Padin bodily from the circle. "We do have two outlanders. We can no exclude one but no the other."

What was Horgris doing? He knew Shanis was the true bearer, and he also knew Karst could not draw the Silver Serpent. Why did he not say so? She tried to catch his eye again, but he kept his gaze on Krion.

Finally, Jayan stood. An eager silence hung in the air as they waited for him to speak. "Both shall submit to the Keeper of the Mists."

One by one, each clan chief showed his agreement by standing, until only Krion remained. The chieftain of the Black Mangrove looked from Shanis to Karst and back to Shanis. Finally he nodded and stood.

Shanis felt as if she had been doused with cold water. So it was really going to happen. She was going to face the Keeper of the Mists, whatever it was. But Karst was going too! Again she wondered at the Monaghan chieftains' failure to disprove Karst's claim by simply challenging him to draw the sword.

The chieftains remained standing as Jayan approached Karst.

"You will remove the sword. It will be in the circle should you return."

If Karst was troubled by the suggestion that he might not return, he did not let it show. He unslung the sheath, careful to hold it only by the strap, and carried it to the center of the circle where Shanis stood. His eyes burned into hers with the same intensity as they had when the two of them had nearly come to blows over Natin's injury.

Shanis returned the glare double. Anger surged within her, and it felt like an old friend. How long had it been since she had let her temper run unchecked? She wanted to pummel Karst in front of all of these people. That would show them who was the imposter. She clenched her fists.

And then she remembered.

If an opponent can make you angry, he can kill you just as easily.

Master Yurg had understood her weakness better than anyone. If she gave in to her rage now, no telling what might happen. She had to remain calm. She forced herself to remain under control.

Karst saw the tension leaving her body and smirked. He took a step closer, doubtless thinking she was frightened, but Horgris stepped between them, turning her around and guiding her away.

"You do be chosen to submit to the Keeper of the Mists," he intoned. "Turn to the north." Shanis had no idea which way was north in this circle, but she quickly took note of the angle of the sun and turned around.

And the world went black.

She gasped. Someone had covered her head. Strong hands pressed her arms against her sides.

"It will be all right." Hogris's whisper was so quiet that no one could hear it but her. "Trust me."

He led her along a winding path. The air grew cooler and she no longer felt the sun on her arms. All was quiet, save the sound of muted footfalls on soft earth. They finally halted and Horgris uncovered her head.

She and Karst stood before an ancient tree. Knots in the shape of grotesque faces bulged from its twisted limbs. Two standing stones, like smaller versions of those that formed the circle, stood before the tree. Between them, the light danced on a curtain of mist. It undulated like a living curtain.

Krion moved to stand before them. "The way forward is there." His voice was deep and rich. "Ye will speak no words before you pass between the stones. The way back will show itself to you, if you are found worthy." He stepped back and motioned for them to continue.

It was too late to turn back now. Steady steps carried her to the standing stones, where the curtain of mist shimmered. It seemed so substantial that she wondered if she could truly pass through it. Only one way to find out.

She took a deep breath and stepped into the mist.

CHAPTER 30

"You inside! Open the gate! Open up in the name of the King!"

Confused faces peered cautiously over the makeshift stockade wall, speaking in low tones to one another. Lerryn caught the words "soldiers" and "help." One man finally mustered the courage to rise up and take a good look at the mounted force that waited outside.

"It can't be! Did the king send you?"

"Don't stand there gaping like a frost fool! It will soon be sunrise. Open the gate before I tear it down myself." Tabars had grown surlier each day as they taxed themselves and their horses to get to Galsbur before it was too late. Lerryn's abdication of his title had not set well with Tabars either, not that it made a difference. What was done was done.

The gate swung open and Lerryn led the way in. The faces that gazed at them in the waning moonlight showed both surprise and relief. Some grinned openly at the new arrivals. Clearly they had not been expecting relief of any kind.

"I would speak with the man who is in charge of your defenses. Take me there."

"Yes sir. This…" The speaker glanced up at Lerryn and was momentarily struck dumb. He regained his wits and dropped to a knee. "Your Highness! I remember your face from the tournament. Sorry we did not recognize you at first."

"We have no time for that. Show me the way."

"Yes, Highness. The inn. It is this way."

"I remember the way." Lerryn had stayed at the inn the previous year while holding his tournament in Galsbur. He winced at the memory. All that work for nothing. And yet another thing that no longer mattered.

Two men sat in the common room. He recognized Hiram Van Derin, who was the town's firstman and Hierm's father. The other, a physically imposing man with shaggy dark hair and beard, was unfamiliar to him. They both sprang to their feet as Lerryn stepped inside.

"Your Highness," Van Derin gasped. He bowed and then motioned for Lerryn to take a seat. "May I offer you a glass of wine?"

Lerryn's stomach wrenched at the very thought, and he gagged, though he thought he covered his reaction well. He was growing accustomed to these strong physical reactions to the sight, smell, or sometimes even suggestion of drink. How had that girl done this to him?

"Water or tea if you have it." Travel weary, he sank into the chair Hiram offered him. Hiram fetched him a cup of tea, and stood expectantly. Finally, Lerryn realized the men were waiting for his leave to sit. He motioned for them to join him at the table. Hiram introduced the other man as Colin.

"What can you tell me of the situation here?" Lerryn asked.

"It is grave, Highness. They outnumber us, and refuse to tell us who they are or what they want." Hiram glanced at the big man, who took up the explanation.

"We face what appears to be a marauding force of several hundred. They are well-armed, and fight reasonably well together, but lack the discipline of a proper army. No cavalry, no siege engines… not yet anyway."

Lerryn took a sip of the piping hot tea. It was dark and bitter, but it seemed to sharpen his thoughts at the first swallow. "From what I gather, you have been holding them off for some time."

"As soon as our attempts to parley failed, we began doing what we could to slow them down. Once they crossed the river, they have tried us each day. Yesterday, they almost breached our walls. We have bled them, but not enough. Every man we lose, however, deals us a great blow."

"What are our numbers?"

"Near two hundred healthy men and boys. Another thirty or so who are wounded, but can fight in a pinch. Fifty eight either dead or too hurt to fight."

"Add to that number forty-nine mounted fighting men— the best in Galdora. And subtract from theirs the three scouts we rode down on the way in."

The big man nodded grimly. He was clearly pondering the same question that troubled Lerryn. Would it be enough?

"His His Royal Majesty sent word to you? Orders? Promises of reinforcements?"

"He sent us one squad," Colin growled. "And the ice-encrusted sergeant was too great a fool to believe us when we said it was an army we faced, and not a band of highwaymen. He went off in search of them several days ago. We can only assume he failed."

Lerryn comtemplated this over another swallow of tea. The situation in the north must truly be dire if his father could send only a token force to aid these people. Then again, his own unit represented little more than a token response to so vast an enemy.

"Highness, if I may ask, why here?" Weariness dripped from Hiram's every word. "What does an enemy gain from attacking a farming town like ours?"

"I suppose they had to make their attack somewhere. Most likely this is a mercenary force hired by the Kyrinians in an effort to distract us from the war in the north." Seeing their confused looks, he explained the situation to them. They had neither heard about Kyrin's invasion, nor the rebellion in Kurnsbur.

"There is something I neglected to mention." Colin folded his hands and leaned closer to Lerryn. "There are ice cats with them."

Lerryn choked on his tea. He spat it back into the cup and glared at the man. "How many?" he rasped, coughing the liquid out of his windpipe.

"I personally saw eight of them on the day they crossed the river. We killed four. The others have not been seen again." He gazed up at the ceiling as if coming to a decision. "There are ref-

ugees from the mountain villages among us. When they first began arriving, a little girl told me a story that I dismissed at the
time, but upon seeing the ice cats, I am wondering if it is true."
He leveled his gaze at Lerryn. "I believe they have a shifter
among them as well."

Lerryn did not want to believe it, but if there truly were ice
cats in the invading force, it was not so far-fetched to believe
there would also be shifters.

"Find Captain Tabars," he said to Colin. "He will be waiting
outside. Take him and my squad leaders around your defensive
perimeter and let them assess the situation. Tell them everything
you have told me and answer any questions they might have.
They are good soldiers- the best, in fact."

The big man rose from his chair, gave a perfunctory bow, and
left the room.

"I should tell you," he said to Hiram, "that I have seen your
son, and he is well. He wanted to come here to join the in the
defense of your village, but I did not permit it. As we speak, he
rides with my brother to Archstone to enroll in the academy."

"That is welcome news, Highness. Thank you." Tears welled
in Hiram's eyes, but his countenance brightened, and he sat up
straighter. "His mother and brother have gone to Archstone.
Perhaps they shall find one another."

"When this is over, you can go there yourself and organize a
reunion." Lerryn doubted any of them would live that long, but
one could hope. "Oh, and congratulations are in order. You are
to be a grandfather." He resisted the urge to laugh at Hiram's
flummoxed expression. "He is married to a Lothan girl, a Monaghan to be exact, and she is with child." Hiram continued to
stare at him. "He married well, she is the daughter of a clan chief,
and I am told she can put an arrow through a deer's heart at forty
paces, and skin it as well as any hunter."

Stunned silence filled the room as Hiram gaped at Lerryn.
Then he burst into a fit of laughter. He slumped back in his chair,
the tears now trailing down his cheeks. When he recovered himself, he sat up and wiped his face.

"Forgive me, my Lord, but I wish I could be there when my
wife meets her new daughter."

Lerryn had to laugh as well. He remembered Faun Van Derin well and could imagine how she would receive Rinala. Now that he thought about it, it seemed that everyone who knew Mistress Van Derin had made a similar comment. "You are not the first person to make that observation."

"Have you news of Colin's daughter, Shanis, and the others who left our village?"

"That is Shanis Malan's father?" Lerryn wondered how much to tell either of the men about what the girl was doing in Lothan, and how she came to be there, but that decision could wait until after the battle. "She is well. Last I saw her, she was in Lothan with the other young man from your village. I believe his name is Oskar."

Hiram nodded. "And what of Khalyndryn Serrill. A pretty blond girl."

"The news is not good." Lerryn saw no need in softening the blow. This was not the girl's father. "She was killed. An accident," he added. He saw no harm in the small lie.

"A shame. Her family also fled, so there is no one to whom we need to break the news just yet. Colin will want to know of his daughter, as will Oskar's father. I shall let them know."

Lerryn glanced out the window. The first brush of dawn was painted low upon the horizon, a dusty orange trimming the horizon.

A shout arose outside, followed by other cries of warning. *Attack! Attack!*

Lerryn sprang to his feet, his fingers searching out the comfort of his sword hilt. Not sparing a glance at Hiram, he dashed out the door.

CHAPTER 31

Shanis expected the sheet of mist to be damp and chilly, but instead it felt like a warm bath. It wrapped her up and drew her in with unseen hands. She seemed to drift forward, enveloped in an ever-darkening cloud.

As gray surrendered to black, she once again felt the earth beneath her feet. The sensation of drifting dissolved, and she took a tentative step forward. The spongy ground gave a little as she put her weight down, but it held her. She took another tentative step, wondering where she was and what might be hiding in the blackness.

Moving one cautious step at a time, she discerned a faint glow up ahead. She could now see that she was inside an earthen tunnel. Thick, gnarled roots, worn smooth with age, formed the walls and ceilings, and held the black earth at bay. At least she hoped they were holding it back.

A crystalline sphere filled with a glowing yellow substance sat atop a cracked stone pedestal. Approaching it with caution, she peered down into the sphere, where the shining substance whirled about inside the container. It put her to mind of thousands of fireflies dancing within the sphere. The thought warmed her heart and gave her comfort.

Behind the pedestal, the tunnel branched off in three different directions: one leading upward, one going straight ahead, and one descending. She took a long look at each one in turn. There was nothing to indicate which was the proper path. Next she examined the pedestal itself, but found nothing on the aging stone cylinder to give her guidance. She examined the walls, ceiling, and even the floor of the tunnel, but found nothing but unrelenting earth and roots. No symbols, no writing, not even a footprint in the soft earth.

She looked around again, suddenly remembering that Karst should be here too, but she did not see him. Beyond the circle of golden light, there was nothing but unrelenting darkness and silence. Why wasn't he right behind her?

"So," she said aloud, unable to abide the silence any longer. "I suppose it is up to me." Her words were braver than she felt, and they rang out in the stillness. She looked again at the tunnels. They appeared to be identical, save the direction in which each led. The tunnel on the left sloped upward, while the one in the center ran on a level with the passage in which she now stood, and the one on the right disappeared down into the darkness.

"Which one? Which one?" Her whisper sounded like shouts. She narrowed her eyes and thought of what each direction might symbolize. She dismissed the upward-leading tunnel as the way of a coward who sought only to escape from destiny. But what of the other two? The tunnel in the center might symbolize staying the course, or it could represent someone who was unwilling to change.

She reflected on her life since leaving home. Nothing had remained the same. Every time she came close to something she desired, it was snatched away. She still resented it, but she now accepted that her destiny was not her own. And she held in her heart the hope that someday things would be as they should. Perhaps the time would come that the gods, or whoever was pulling at the strings of her destiny, would release her, and let her live her life. But for now, change was her reality. Her life must change. The Monaghan and Malgog must change. The world must change.

It was possible that the tunnel on the right, the one leading down into the darkness, symbolized someone who would sink to any depths to get what they wanted, but she did not think so. To her, it was the only courageous choice—the only choice for one who was willing to embrace any path upon which the gods placed her. And had she not already experienced the depths of pain and despair in this quest? Losing Khalyndryn, almost losing Allyn, witnessing the tragic lives of the Lothans... She supposed being brought low was sometimes a part of following one's destiny.

Her decision made, she entered the tunnel on the right and began her descent into darkness.

Pedric Karst wanted out of this place. Each step was a labor as he tugged his boots from the muck that was the floor. Cold, slimy water dripped down from the ceiling. He raised the hood of his cloak, but it was a poor barrier against the persistent dampness. All about him was filth. Serpentine roots coiled up the tunnel walls, glistening in the pulsing red light that oozed forth from the crystal vase that sat on the stone pedestal.

He had no idea how long he had been standing here, staring at the three tunnels, trying to choose his path. His search had provided no clues as to the proper choice. Obviously, each tunnel held symbolic meaning, thus the three directions. He gazed at each in turn, imagining himself passing through each.

And suddenly he understood.

The way down was a way of subservience, the path of the lowly. The way ahead was the path of one who was content with his station, and sought to climb no higher. He was neither of those things. He would rise high. A warm sense of self-assuredness now flowing through his bones, he chose the tunnel on the left, and began his ascent.

The passage spiraled down into the blackness, but the air remained warm and dry as Shanis descended, feeling as if some invisible force was drawing her ever forward. After what seemed an eternity, she emerged in a gloomy chamber that somehow was familiar. The floor was smooth stone, as if hewn by a master craftsman, and the walls arched up in uniform perfection. An ancient woman, her face lined and cracked, sat behind a small fire. Shanis knew her at once. This was the old woman whom she had encountered in a mountain cave during the search for the Silver Serpent.

"Hyda?" she gasped.

"I do be the Keeper of the Mists." Her voice creaked like a rusty hinge. "That do be the only name by which you shall call me."

Shanis noted that the woman did not explicitly deny the name by which Shanis had called her.

As she drew closer, she noticed subtle differences in the woman from her memory and the one who now sat before her. The lined face and silver hair were the same, but where Hyda's eyes had been yellow, her hair unkempt, and her clothing ragged, the Keeper's eyes sparkled like precious gems, her hair was a silken cascade, and her robes a snowy white. Still, it was the same woman.

The old woman set a stone bowl filled with water into the midst of the flames. Shanis sat down and reached up to pluck a hair from her head, just as the old woman had asked her to do at their previous encounter.

"No!" The woman seized her hand and pulled it toward her, stretching Shanis's arm over the bowl. She pushed back the sleeve of Shanis's tunic, baring her fair skin. "Blood," she whispered. The Keeper drew a small knife from inside the sleeve of her robe and pricked Shanis's wrist. The blood glistened like the ruby eyes of the Silver Serpent. Shanis watched impassively as it trailed down her wrist and dripped into the bowl.

Steam billowed up, angry orange like sunset after a storm. The Keeper released her hand.

"Now, you shall submit to the mists." She placed a gentle hand on the back of Shanis's head and drew her face down toward the bowl of water. The steam wrapped around her, and she was falling... falling... falling...

CHAPTER 32

"Their main force is in sight, Highness." Colin grimaced, his fingers working as if seeking someone to throttle. "We shan't hold them long. Our supply of arrows is almost exhausted. All we have left are shafts sharpened and scorched at the tips." He bit his lip, putting Lerryn in mind of Colin's daughter Shanis. It was the first time he had noticed a resemblance between the two of them. "They must know we are on our last legs."

Lerryn was careful not to allow concern to show on his face or in his voice. "I do not think they know about my men, however. Surprise is in our favor. Perhaps we can hold them long enough for you and your men to flee into the forest."

"We will stand and fight, and perhaps die, but we will not flee." Determination glowed in Colin's dark eyes, and he threw Lerryn a challenging look, as if daring him to order the men to make their escape.

"Very well." He had suspected that would be the answer, and he admired the townspeople for their resolve. "See to it that your men hold their fire when we charge. We do not need to be struck by our own arrows." Colin's impatient nod was little more than a jerk of his head. "Another thing, Colin. There is too much to tell at the moment, but I want you to know that your daughter is well."

Colin gaped, stupefied by the words. He recovered from the surprise and bowed. "Thank you, Highness." The display of respect did not suit the man at all, which made Lerryn appreciate it all the more. "Forgive me, but, is she in Lothan?"

Lerryn nodded, wondering how Colin had known this. Having no time to spare for such puzzles, he turned and barked a series of clipped orders to his men. One of the soldiers brought Kreege to him, and he mounted up. His men formed up behind the makeshift gate.

For a moment, Lerryn considered making a final speech by which he could be remembered, should anyone survive to tell of this battle, but he discarded the thought as quickly as it had come. He was here to fight and die. Words would only delay that purpose, and the longer they waited, the greater the likelihood the enemy would spot them, and they would lose the element of surprise.

He signaled to Colin, who instructed his men to loose one volley on his command, and then hold. The order came, arrows sang through the morning sky, the gate was flung open, and the White Fang rode forth for the last time.

Up ahead, the enemy soldiers ducked beneath upraised shields, or just ducked, as arrows rained down. Lerryn and his men were almost upon the enemy before someone raised a warning cry.

There were defensive measures infantry could take against mounted men, but the marauding army had taken none of them. The head of the White Fang charge ran down the first men who tried to stand before them. Riders on either side broke off from the formation, sweeping around the flanks, looking for targets for their short bows. Lerryn and those supporting him went after anyone who looked like he was giving orders. Lerryn opened the throat of a man who was trying to regroup his confused troops. Tabars split another man's skull just as the fellow called for his men to rally.

All around him, warriors began a clumsy retreat. Lerryn did not waste his effort on those who were fleeing, unless they ran in front of Kreege, in which case they found themselves trampled beneath the warhorse's hooves. Instead, he concentrated on disposing of those who offered the most resistance, reasoning that breaking their will first, or simply breaking them, might cause even more men to flee.

A burly man with one eye thrust a spear at Lerryn's head. He batted the spear aside, slashed the man across his good eye, and wheeled around, looking for his next victim.

His battle senses had never been so clear. He supposed he had the Malan girl to thank for that. A shame this would be the last time he would get to use them. He spotted a cluster of men trying to drag Khattre from his saddle. The squad leader fought with sword and dagger to good effect, but there were too many of them for one man to hold off for long. Lerryn charged them, running down two and killing a third with a deft stroke of his sword. Khattre used the distraction to dispatch another attacker, and the two of them broke free.

Lerryn scanned the battlefield. His men were doing their job well. Only two of the White Fang lay among the dead that littered the open ground. All about him, his men were hacking or shooting down the enemy with reckless abandon.

But there were too many.

Despite their efforts, the marauders were regrouping, and finally using their numbers to their advantage. They attacked the riders in groups, seeking to encircle them and drag them from their mounts. At Lerryn's command, Khattre blew the rally order on his warhorn, and the riders began to fight their way free from the throng. Some had charged too deep into the ranks and were pulled down before they could break loose.

Another horn sounded in the distance, so shrill that it pained the ears. Lerryn saw the fleeing invaders slow, and then, one-by-one, turn and reluctantly head back toward the fray.

A tall warrior clad all in gray strode behind them. Flanked on either side by three ice cats, he held a sword in his right hand, and a crescent-shaped moon knife in his left. His form seemed to ripple as approached.

A shifter!

"You and Tabars take the lead!" Lerryn shouted to Khattre. He put heels to Kreege and charged.

The shifter saw Lerryn coming and ran to meet him. Meanwhile, the ice cats broke away from their master, charging into battle.

As the intervening space narrowed, Lerryn took in every detail of the creature: the catlike eyes, its predatory face that shifted back and forth from flesh to fur, the bared fangs.

And then he was on it.

The shifter sprang aside, deftly avoiding Kreege's charge. Its sword whispered in a deadly arc, and Lerryn deflected it with a desperate parry. As he wheeled Kreege for another charge, the shifter sprang forward. The thing could leap like a mountain lion, and it cleared Kreege's hind quarters in one bound, slashing at Lerryn with its moon knife.

Lerryn twisted away from the strike and felt the blade skitter across his chain mail. Alarmed by the creature's attack, Kreege kicked out and struck the shifter a solid blow to the chest. The shifter cried out in a feral shriek of rage as it leapt back and crouched to spring again.

Knowing the beast was too quick for him to fight from the saddle, Lerryn leapt down, ducking behind Kreege as the shifter hurtled through the air where Lerryn had sat astride his mount an instant before. Sword in one hand, dagger in the other, he turned to face the creature.

The shifter sprang forward and thrust its sword at Lerryn's chest. He had known the thing was quick, yet had underestimated just *how* quick it was. He used his dagger to turn his opponent's thrust, pivoted out of the way, and struck back, but the shifter danced out of reach, its fangs bared in mocking laughter.

It went on that way for what felt like an eternity: thrust, slash, dance away. Lerryn had taken several superficial wounds and had inflicted none on the beast. He was breathing from his mouth, but the shifter seemed fresh. Lerryn would not last much longer.

The shifter attacked again, slashing at Lerryn's thigh. This time he did not try to parry the blow, but charged in at the moment the shifter committed to the attack. He felt the blade slice into his leg, but his timing was perfect. He caught the shifter off-balance. It raised its moon knife an instant too late—deflecting Lerryn's strike instead of blocking it, and the stroke that was intended for the shifter's neck banged off the creature's temple, denting its helm and sending it reeling back.

Abandoning his weapons, Lerryn dove onto the beast and bore it to the ground. Shifters were lightning-fast, but not as strong as a man, and this one was stunned from the blow to the head. He pushed the creature's arms apart as they fell. When they hit the ground, he shifted forward, pinning its arms. It thrashed and snarled, but could not break free. Mustering his remaining strength, he struck the shifter on the jaw. Its eyes clouded, and its form began to waver. He struck it again and felt the fight go out of the beast.

The battle fury full upon him and rage coursing through his veins, he wrapped his hands around the shifter's throat. He felt the flesh change to fur and the chest cavity narrow as it reverted to its true form. It struggled weakly for a moment, and then the life left its eyes.

Lerryn staggered to his feet and looked around, too weary to care if he was in danger. The attackers had rallied, and the battle had shifted to the walls. The bodies littering the field testified that his men had done their job well, but what remained of his force was now pressed back against the wall, fighting for their lives against the teeming mass of humanity that surged forward. Desperate townspeople manned the walls, struggling to keep the attackers at bay. They had to realize that hope was rapidly fading, yet they fought on. Where there was breath, a little hope remained.

He retrieved his sword, but forsook his dagger in favor of the shifter's moon knife. In a different time and place he would have admired the craftsmanship of this rare treasure from beyond the Claws, but there was no time. He was only one wounded man, but he would fight until the end. His eyes fell on two ice cats savaging a fallen soldier. Fury renewed his strength, and he charged.

If it is my day to die, I shall make it a day to remember.

The walls were holding. Colin was surprised they had held out for this long, but the attackers' lack of discipline, plus the heavy bite the White Fang had taken out of the enemy, was working to the Galsburans' advantage. Furthermore, the determination that came with fighting for home and family, and the reality that they all would surely die should they not emerge victorious, had strengthened their resolve. He now dared to hope that a few of them might survive this day.

He had only just permitted himself to entertain this thought when a cry of alarm arose from the eastern side of the town—the side opposite the mountains and farthest from the attack. A modest contingent of guards was keeping watch on that side.

He dashed toward the sound and caught sight of an ice cat as it pounced onto one of the few defenders who had maintained his post. The man's surprised shout was cut off in a strangled cry of pain as the cat ripped his throat open. As the remaining guards closed with the cat, another of the creatures clambered across the wall, sprang to the ground, and dashed away toward the town's center.

Colin had feared that a detachment of the enemy might try to circle away from the main attack and slip over the wall at a more vulnerable spot, but he had counted on the guards spotting the attack and sounding the warning in time for him to send support troops. These ice cats could move like the wind and melt into shadows when it suited them.

"Reserves to the east wall!" Hiram had been holding a few youths in reserve. They would make little difference if a larger force crossed the wall, but against two ice cats they could be of help, provided they kept their nerve.

Hiram came dashing out of the inn, his sword at the ready. He immediately spotted the ice cat, which had veered toward the very center of the green, putting the surprised firstman right in its path.

So fast was its attack that Hiram had time only to brace himself before the cat was upon him. Hiram went down in a blur of gray, his sword falling uselessly to the ground. The cat opened his throat with a single swipe and continued on its way.

Colin had never heard of an ice cat fighting with such precision. His question was immediately answered when the beast stopped just short of the sacred oak. Its form blurred, and suddenly a man stood in its place. The shifter raised its hand and fire burst forth, engulfing the sacred oak around which the town green was centered.

The shock caused Colin to stumble as he ran. A mage shifter? Here? Any remaining doubt he had that this was more than a marauding army was now gone.

The oak showed no damage from the burst of fire, but the ancient symbols carved into its trunk now glowed like iron in a forge. The mage shifter sent another burst at the tree, with no more discernible effect than the first blast.

And then Colin was on him.

The creature moved in a blur, dancing aside as Colin's sword sliced through empty air. He kicked out, and his foot met bone. The mage snarled as its leg went out from under it and it fell heavily to the ground. Colin stabbed at it, but it scrambled out of the way again. Colin pressed the attack, knowing he had no chance if the mage could gather its power.

The mage slipped a long knife from its belt, but Colin's ferocious stroke battered it from the creature's grip. His back stroke bit into the mage's chest, but not deep enough. The creature was wearing some sort of mail beneath his robes. It wasn't enough to completely stop his sword, but it prevented the stroke from being a killing blow. Colin yanked his blade free, but now the mage was on him, its fingers clutching at his throat. Colin lifted the mage bodily and slammed it to the ground, but it held on, pulling him down on top of it.

The hands gripping his throat suddenly felt like ice. It was gathering its power. Colin battered the creature's hands away and raised his fist to pound it into unconsciousness.

And he froze.

The shifter had him by the wrist, and the feeling was like an icy mountain river in the dead of winter pouring through his body. He could not resist. Somewhere nearby, he was aware of people running toward him, but he could not call out, could not turn to see who was coming to his aid. He could do nothing but stare into its eyes.

"Where is the girl?" The mage's voice was a primordial growl. "We can no longer see her. Our eyes grow cloudy and our senses dull. Where is she?"

Colin did not know the girl of whom it spoke, but his lips could not form the words. He tried to answer, but only a low groan rose from his throat.

The creature placed his other hand on Colin's temple. Colin's memories seemed to fly backward in a blur too fast to follow. Shanis swam to the surface, and the visions slowed. He relived their last argument in agonizing slowness, wishing he had taken her in his arms and held her close. And then the visions blurred again, this time moving forward, stopping at the moment just prior to the battle, when Lerryn had told him that Shanis was in Lothan.

The mage shifter snarled and pushed Colin off of him. The icy feeling that had engulfed him immediately melted, and Colin drew his knife, but the creature was now running away, this time toward the front gate. He scarcely had the energy to pursue it, but he forced his legs to move.

Up ahead, the mage shifted back into the form of an ice cat and dashed toward the gate. It was going to take the men at the gate from behind and let the attackers in. Colin shouted a warning, but the defenders could not hear him over the tumult of battle.

But the cat did not attack. It took the gate in one leap, bounding over the sharpened stakes and disappearing from sight. Its cry rang out above the din, startling the defenders who had not noticed it. Even the attackers trying to cross the wall seemed to freeze for a moment at the sound. Colin kept running, the creature's cries growing ever more strident, but receding fast. It seemed to be running away.

He reached the wall, sagged against it, and slid slowly to the ground. He had no strength left to fight. The mage power had drained him. His vision clouded, and sounds faded. He sucked in ragged breaths, filling his lungs with sweet air, and waited to fade into unconsciousness.

But he did not.

Gradually, his strength returned, and he was finally able to regain his feet. His head felt like it would split in two, but he otherwise felt strong and well. He scanned the walls and was surprised to see puzzled-looking defenders standing all along the line, weapons hanging loosely at their sides. Natin Marwell stood on a mound of earth a few paces away, staring out across the wall. Despite having only one hand, he had joined the defense of the town when it looked like the walls would be breached. His face was battered and filthy, and blood stained his long knife. He caught sight of Colin and shook his head.

"They left. That... thing jumped over the gate and started roaring at them. Some of them seemed to understand, and they started calling for a retreat. Next thing I knew, they were all disappearing into the forest." He brushed a sleeve across his face, smearing the dirt and sweat. "A few of them made it across, and we killed them. But then there was the fire on the green, and I suppose we were distracted, because more of them came across. And then they were gone. Why did they leave?"

"I don't know for certain, but I suspect our defenses finally proved to be too much for them." Colin suspected he did, in fact, know why the enemy had called off the attack, but he saw no reason to tell the townsfolk. They had fought bravely. Let them feel they had won the victory. "But I don't think they will be back."

CHAPTER 33

Shanis drifted in clouds of gray vapor. She felt as if she was without substance, a mere consciousness within the shifting mists. Shadows drifted toward her, little more than dark outlines within the endless grayness.

The mists swirled and then opened to reveal a forest. She floated among the tree limbs. Looking down, she saw a young man and young woman clutched in a tight embrace. Her heart lurched. It was her and Larris on their last night together. She watched as Larris wiped the tears from her cheeks. She tried to turn away, to flee from the agonizing scene, but the mists held her fast, forcing her to live that painful night again. When it was over, and the two of them had gone their separate ways, the mists spun again.

As if an invisible hand was drawing back a curtain, the mists parted again to reveal a new scene. She held Khalyndryn in her lap as the girl gasped for breath, an arrow lodged firmly in her chest. Blood oozed from the side of her mouth. She looked up at Shanis with fading eyes and whispered, "I finally found my purpose."

She cried out in anger and pain as the mist engulfed her. Wrapped in their cocoon, she was powerless to escape as it carried her deeper into the past.

Now she saw her father kneeling at the bedside of a beautiful auburn-haired woman. Mistress Anna stood at the foot of the bed, holding a baby wrapped in swaddling. Colin's eyes glistened with unshed tears as the woman stroked his cheek.

"Now, do no be like that." The woman's voice was weak. We do have us a beautiful little girl. You must take good care of her and teach her right. She will be someone very special some day."

"You are someone special." Colin could scarcely speak, so choked with emotion was his voice. "I don't want to lose you. You are my treasure."

"Now," the woman whispered, "you do be sweet to say so." Shanis cried insubstantial tears as her mother closed her eyes and passed away.

What was this cruelty? Why was she being forced to witness these excruciating scenes? Was it a test of her ability to endure pain? If so, she would not relent. She was made of stronger stuff than that.

The visions continued.

She watched Aspin draw a metal band from his wrist and hurl it to the ground. A dark-skinned soldier scowled and fingered a fox medallion underneath his cloak as he watched an aging priest place a crown on a young man's head. An old Malgog dashed into a burning hut and staggered out moments later carrying a squalling baby.

And then the mist spiraled like a whirlpool, sucking her down into the midst of a high mountain range. Their snow capped peaks seemed to reach up toward her like icy claws, threatening to snatch her, but she plummeted down through them and into the very rock of which they were formed.

Now she drifted in pulsating ripples of blue light. In fact, she *was* the light, ebbing and flowing in the darkness, filling every space with her power.

Five men and one woman stood in a semi-circle, all bathed in blue light. Behind each stood a priest chanting words Shanis could not quite discern. The woman, a tall, blonde wearing a golden tiara stepped forward to face a young man who could only be her son. He wept openly, but his mother laid a hand on his shoulder and spoke to him in reassuring tones. The young man nodded and raised... a *stone sword*? He placed the tip against her heart, his hands shaking so that he could scarcely hold it in place. He hesitated, but she nodded and spoke to him again. He bit his lip, took a deep breath, and thrust. Her expression barely changed as the sword pierced her heart. As she crumpled to the floor, her son dropped to his knees, letting the stone sword, which now glimmered as if dusted with stars, fall from a limp hand.

Next, a lean man wearing a golden circlet with a raven set in its center stepped forward. A weeping girl picked up the stone sword and placed it against his chest, but froze. He whispered words of comfort to her. Then, placing one hand over hers, and gripping the cross-guard with the other, he forced the sword into his own heart.

She watched as the ritual was repeated four more times. Each person stepped forward to be killed by a reluctant young person who appeared to be her or his son or daughter. Each time, the stone sword shone brighter.

When the last person had fallen, the priests stepped forward, each continuing his chant. As one, they took hold of the sword and raised it into the air. Six tiny sparks of light whirled in the air above the sword, growing brighter as they circled one another. The light grew to the intensity of a tiny sun until, with a flash, it shot down into the sword, which burned brightly for a moment, then fell to the ground amidst the ashes of what, moments before, had been six priests, where it glistened in the blue light. The serpents on its blade looked alive, and the ruby eyes on the stylized hilt flashed dark red.

Shanis gasped as she realized she had just witnessed the creation of the Silver Serpent.

Before she could wonder at what she had just seen, the mist carried her up into the sky. Far below, she and Pedric Karst faced one another, each backed by an army of Lothans, but behind Karst's army loomed a dark specter, its sinister form growing ever larger as it rose above the horizon. As it grew, it formed into a vaguely human shape that towered over the army. Power emanated from it in dark waves, and wherever it stepped, the land was made barren. She turned to see a figure standing above the mountains behind her own army. Snow and ice raged within it, and whatever it touched froze and shattered.

She saw herself raise a sword and cleave the land between her and Karst. Where she smote the ground, a river grew between them, pushing the armies apart. She broke the sword over her knee, tossed it into the river, and turned to face the thing in the mountains.

It looked down upon her with eyes of ice, reached out a hand, and all was black.

CHAPTER 34

"Have you any food, my lords?" The dirty-faced woman grasped at Larris's leg as he rode by. "We are starving." Others took up the cry, and the crowd began to press in on the riders. Allyn rapped the woman across the knuckles with the flat of his sword, and she sprang back with a cry of pain, sticking her fingers in her mouth. She fixed them with a reproachful stare, and others muttered their disapproval, but they now gave way as Allyn rode to the front of the group and led them down the road to the gates of Archstone.

"Swords out," Larris instructed, keeping his voice low, "but do not use them. We only want the people to leave us alone until we reach the city."

"Forgive me, Highness, but could we not give them what food we have? Surely we will not need these meager rations when we are inside the city." Hair frowned down at two skinny children sitting in the dirt staring up at them, too weary to even play. His shoulders sagged as he looked into their hopeless faces, and he thought he understood a little better why Shanis had made the choice to remain in Lothan.

"We no have enough food to feed all of the people. Look at all of them." Rinala made a sweeping gesture that took in the veritable city of humanity that had sprung up outside Archstone in the form of tents, lean-tos, and shacks as refugees had poured into the capital from the north and the west. "At the first sign of food, they will tear each other apart to get it, and maybe do tear us apart, too. And even if they did no do that, how would we choose who do get fed and who continues to starve?"

Larris continued to be impressed by Hierm's wife. She was perceptive, and had a greater breadth of knowledge about the world than he had expected from a Monaghan tribeswoman, whom he had always imagined to be fairly primitive.

"Your wife is a wise woman, Van Derin, even if she does interrupt on occasion." After parting ways with Lerryn, he had explained to the others the need for him to adopt a more formal way of interacting with them. Once inside Archstone, it would not do for the first prince to interact with commoners as if they were his equals. Everyone had understood and all, save Rinala, had complied.

He did not truly mind. The closer they drew to the capital, the heavier the duties of his new rank seemed to weigh upon him. He was going to miss the easy interaction and camaraderie of the trail. That was far from the only thing he would miss, but he shoved those feelings as far from his conscious mind as he could. Freeze Lerryn for doing this to him!

"I am no wise." Rinala shook her head. "I have known too many hungry people, that do be all." The melancholy in her voice was matched by her downcast expression.

The sun shone brightly on the city walls, atop which bright banners snapped smartly in the crisp breeze against a clear blue sky. He wondered how such a beauty could hang above a scene of such sadness, as if the gods were taunting the wretched and downtrodden.

The city gate, colossal double doors of iron-bound wood, loomed before them. Sentries manned the gate towers on either side, their bearing alert and suspicious. Larris felt their gaze upon him, and was painfully aware that one false move, or an impulsive decision by an archer on the gates, could spell doom for him or one or more of his party.

A contingent of guards stood sentry outside the gates. They waited until Larris and the others had reined in before one guard approached them.

"Name yourself and your business." His bored expression indicated that he did not particularly care who they were or what their business was; he would hear what they had to say, and then turn them away.

Larris drew from within his cloak the document naming him First Prince of the Sword. He unrolled it far enough to reveal Lerryn's seal and signature, and held it up for all the guards to see.

"We are on the prince's business. We will require an escort to the palace."

The guard frowned. "Does that document state that all of you must go to the palace? If you are merely delivering a message, there is no need for all of you to enter the city."

"Can you even read?" Allyn interrupted, his voice dripping with scorn.

The guard's face reddened, and he took a step toward Allyn, his hand on the pommel of his sword. "You can watch your tongue or you will enter the city in chains. These gates are closed by order of the king himself, and none may enter, save they have a very good reason."

A second guard joined them, holding out his hand to Larris. "I have my letters, M'lord. Let me see that paper."

This would not do at all. Larris had hoped the seal would be enough to gain him entry to the city without questions being asked or his identity being revealed. That was no longer a possibility, but he positively could not have news of Lerryn's abdication whispered about the city before he could deliver the news to his father.

"Enough of this!" He threw back the hood of his cloak, and then stripped the glove from his left hand. He held up his hand, displaying his signet ring that was the sign of his office. "I am Prince Larris Van Altman. You will escort us to the palace immediately, and you will speak of this to no one." He knew the latter command was futile- soldiers gossiped as much as any chamber maid.

That did it. The guards babbled apologies and explanations as they scrambled to open the gates.

"I thank you for your assistance." Now that these men were compliant, there was no need to browbeat them. You never knew when the loyalty of even the most ordinary man might prove to be useful. "I shall commend you to my father for the seriousness with which you have taken the responsibility of guarding these gates." The relief in their faces was almost comical.

They passed through the main gate and into the barbican. An aging man, uniformed, but armed with a quill, recorded their names in a ledger. He frowned at the name Van Derin and turned back several pages in his records with trembling, liver-spotted hands.

"Are you any relation to a Mistress Faun Van Derin and Laman Van Derin?"

"They are my mother and brother. Why do you ask?" Hierm squeezed Rinala's hand.

"They took up residence in the city prior to the King's closing of the gates. I remember your mother asking to be notified if word came of her other son. I assume she meant you."

"And what of my father, Hiram Van Derin?"

The guard took a second look at his book. "I fear I have no record of anyone by that name entering the city, at least not in recent weeks." His mouth crinkled in a poor attempt at a sympathetic frown. "I can have one of my men escort you to your mother if you like."

"That is a fine idea." Larris turned to Hierm. "You should see your mother and let her meet your wife. I shall send for you soon."

Rinala and Hierm bade them goodbye. Next, Larris had Edrin and Hair, or Mattyas, as the young man would be called upon entering the academy, taken to the nearby barracks to be fed and outfitted for service. Finally, he took a deep breath and looked at Allyn.

"I suppose it is time, Your Royal Highness." Allyn made a mocking bow.

"That it is." Larris signaled for the guards to lead the way, and they trotted out into the city. In the distance, the spires of the royal palace were just visible. He frowned. He remembered all the times he had rued his position as second prince, wishing he could one day be king. And now he was first prince, and it was the last thing he wanted.

"Are you unwell? You look as if you have eaten a dozen green apples." Allyn's sardonic grin was back—a sure sign he was recovering.

"I am all right." It was a lie, but what did it matter? Right now, he could see no way to redirect the course of his life. The path the gods had laid out before him was not of his choosing, but he must follow it, at least for now. "I was just thinking that nothing is ever going to be the same again."

Chapter 35

"Oskar, you are not concentrating! You have parried that stroke hundreds of times before." The anger fled Aspin's face as quickly as it had come. His expression softened, and he laced his fingers over the end of his staff and leaned on it, staring through the trees in the direction of Calmut.

"It has been three days and still nothing." Oskar spun his staff as he, too, gazed into the distance. He had almost forgotten what the sun looked like, so cloudy had it been since the day Shanis entered Calmut. Dense clouds blanketed the sky above them, hanging precariously low like a hammer about to fall.

He was not sure what he hoped to see as he stared toward the ruined city. Shanis emerging from the forest with an army of Lothans at her heels? Shanis walking along, having failed in her quest, but ready to return to their old life, to be his friend again? He dismissed that thought. There was no returning home for him, whatever path Shanis took. Though he felt a touch of home-sickness, village life had never been for him. He had gotten his first taste of the larger world, and though it had sometimes been bitter, it had whetted his appetite. He wanted more.

"Regardless," Aspin reproved, "you must always concentrate on the task at hand. Push your worries to the back of your mind and focus your thoughts on the task at hand."

"What if I can't do that?"

"Then one day someone will kill you." Aspin's voice was conversational, but his face mirrored the gravity of his words. "Your heart is your strength, but if you cannot master it, it will be your undoing."

"You sound like Master Yurg," Oskar grinned at the memory of the old swordmaster chastising Shanis and Hierm, but his heart fell. He still could not believe the man was gone. Shanis and Hierm had been closer to Yurg, and thus had taken the news much harder than he, but Oskar had admired the man, and keenly felt his absence at moments such as this.

"Yurg was a good man. One of the finest you or I will ever meet. And he would not want you to let Shanis distract you from what you must do."

Aspin had never explained exactly how he had known Yurg, but this was not the time to ask. Besides, he doubted Aspin would answer him.

"I want to help her." Oskar's throat tightened as he spoke. "I could not help Allyn. He asked me to help him, but I thought what happened to us in the mountains had addled his mind, so I did nothing. I slept through the raid when Shanis's sword was stolen. My home is being attacked and I sit here playing with sticks, pretending I shall be a sai-kur some day."

Aspin's eyes, so like a bird of prey, bore into Oskar, and he smiled.

"Your story is not yet written. You are strong of mind, body, and heart, and I have no doubt you will be a sai-kur one day, provided you can learn to believe in yourself as others believe in you."

"No one believes in me." Oskar kicked at a pebble. He was being childish, but just now it felt good to indulge his emotions a little bit. "I was always the odd one: in my family, in town, among my friends…"

A cry rang out, followed by what sounded like a multitude of voices calling out as one. A column of silver-gray mist shot up toward the sky from the direction of Calmut. Straight up it climbed, spinning like a maelstrom, until it met the low-hanging clouds. Flecks of silver spread across the cloud cover, setting the blanket of gray to sparkling. All around them, guards dropped their weapons and dashed toward the column to see what was the cause.

Oskar hesitated only a moment. "The winter take me if I am

going to stand here a moment longer!" Clutching his staff, he dashed off behind the guards. He did not know what he would find when he got there, but no longer would he sit passively by and wait. If Shanis should have need of him, he was going to be there for her.

The chamber was empty. The fire was reduced to cold ash, and the bowl was dry. All about her was black, save the faint light of the passage in front of her.

The way out.

She tried to stand and found herself weak as a newborn babe. She took several deep breaths and gathered herself for the effort. She forced herself to her feet, head spinning, and staggered on unsure legs to the arched tunnel that she somehow knew would take her back to Calmut.

Warm, fresh air with the scent of rain and earth clinging to it welcomed her as she stepped out of the chamber and into the tunnel. It seemed to renew her strength and steady her steps as she began her ascent.

She had taken only a few steps when someone called out. She froze. The sound came again, a cry of pure despair that pierced her soul. And it was coming from behind her. She turned back to the chamber from which she had just come, and stopped short.

The cavern floor was now a morass of black mud and filthy water. Water dripped from the walls, and moss dangled from the ceiling. The fire was burning again, a sick, smoky green, and in its glow Pedric Karst writhed, his face twisted in agony. Though she detested the young man, she could not leave him writing in the filth.

Returning to the cavern, she slogged through the thick mud and grabbed Karst by the wrist.

"Get up Karst! It is time to go. Come with me. I'll help you up and we'll get out of here." She would rather have asked Mistress Faun for dancing lessons than speak to Karst in such a friendly, encouraging manner, but she knew she was doing the right thing. He was her enemy. She could leave him here to die, but there would be no honor in it. Master Yurg would never have approved.

Karst looked up at her with blank eyes. Blood oozed from deep scratches where he had clawed at his own face. He gaped at her, slack-jawed and bewildered. For a moment she wondered if he had lost his mind, but finally he spoke.

"Not you." His voice was a groan of abiding agony. "Anyone but you."

"There is no one else but me. Come with me or die here. Your choice."

Where her kindness had met with rejection, her blatant disregard for his well being prodded him to action. He permitted her to help him to his feet, but refused further assistance until he stumbled and fell flat on his face in the mud. Grimacing, she grabbed him by the belt and collar, hauled him up to all fours, and half-led, half-dragged him through the mud and up the tunnel. The way grew steeper, and Karst could bear little of his own weight.

As their climb grew more difficult, he grew more and more surly, muttering deprecations under his breath in a hollow voice. By the time her eyes fell upon the dancing silver mist curtain that she hoped marked the way out, she was ruing her decision to help him at all. She released her grip on Karst and he dropped to the ground like a sack of grain.

"The way out is there," she said. "Stand up and walk out on your own like a man."

"What does a girl know of being a man?" A drop of his characteristic venom returned to his speech.

"More than you do. If it were not for me, you would still be down there wallowing in the mud, and crying like a newborn. Now stand up!"

Karst raised his hand as if to shield himself from her words. He gaped at her for a moment, and then life slowly returned to his eyes. His flinty stare was soon back. He took a deep breath, shuddering as he let it out, and then rose on unsteady legs. He braced himself against the wall and closed his eyes. He was a muddy, bloody mess.

"Why do you care what happens to me?" She could not tell

if it was suspicion or hatred that marred his face—probably a healthy dose of each.

Shanis did not have to mull the question over. There was only one honest answer.

"I don't." She turned her back on him and passed through the mist.

CHAPTER 36

A clamor arose from the throng pressing toward the center of Calmut. Oskar whispered one of the few spells he had mastered, and a sliver of air snaked through the mass of bodies. Another word and it pushed apart, shoving people to one side or the other and opening a path through a wall of startled onlookers. He was too focused on his destination to be amused at the confused and even angry expressions that turned his way as he lumbered by.

"Very good!" Aspin shouted from behind him. "Not as discreet as one might like, but nicely done."

He stopped at the edge of a stone circle that seemed to mark a line that the clanspeople dared not cross. Inside, the chieftains sat around a pool of quakewater from which the silver mist poured on its way to the sky.

The mist dissipated, and a figure gradually appeared. No. *Two figures came forth!* Shanis and Karst both stood before the chieftains, but the two could not look more different. Shanis stood confidently, a hint of her old temper flaring in her eyes. Karst was caked in mud, and his face was cut, but his glare was as defiant as ever.

A hush fell over those assembled, broken only by confused whispers. Perhaps they had expected only one of the two to return. The chieftains exchanged long looks, but no one seemed willing to be the first to speak.

Oskar wanted to ask them what they were waiting for, but knew it would be foolish to say anything just now. He was not even supposed to be here.

After what seemed an eternity, a Malgog chief addressed Shanis and Karst. "You have submitted to the Keeper of the Mists, and you both have returned. What words have you for us?"

"I am the one." Karst stepped forward. Despite his present state, he held his chin high. "A walk through the mud in the darkness did nothing to change that. I am the same man I was when I entered."

Several of the chieftains exchanged whispers behind their hands, disapproval clearly evident in their eyes. This was obviously not the reply they had been expecting. Horgris rocked back and forth, tapping his toe and chewing his lip. He appeared torn between the desire to speak and the need to give no hint of partiality.

Culmatan finally broke the silence. "We do be asking what did the Keeper show you?"

Karst flinched at the question, and his complexion grew even paler, but he did not waver. "She showed me that, without me, you will surely die." He let that sink in, looking around at each leader in turn, and then extending his gaze to the masses that pressed in close to hear his words. "All of you. I am your only hope."

His words had no visible affect on the chieftains, but a ripple of whispers flowed through the throng of Lothans who watched the proceedings. Oskar ignored them. He was waiting for Shanis to speak. In fact, he was surprised she had held her tongue for this long.

Culmatan turned to Shanis. "And tell us what the Keeper did show *you*."

Keep your temper, Shanis. Just hold on to your temper. Don't do anything to give offense. Oskar tried to send his thoughts across the intervening space, though he knew it to be foolish. Karst had not made a good showing so far, and Oskar sensed that Shanis could persuade the Lothans to accept her if she could just present herself as a calm, confident leader.

Shanis's expression was unreadable. She took her time in answering Culmatan's question. "She showed me things about my past that are not for you to know."

Oskar grimaced, wondering how best to get himself and Shanis out of here alive should she let loose with one of her tirades in the midst of all of these people. He saw no way out through this mass of humanity. He supposed he would have to use the air spell again.

"A few of the things she showed me I do not yet fully understand. But I can tell you this much with certainty." Shanis took a step forward, ignoring Karst's offended stare. "Your greatest threat is no longer your neighboring clan. I have seen the shadow of a grave danger rising in the east, and the frost is marching in the west. Clan war ends today, whether you wish it or not. Unite now, or Lothan shall be crushed between the hammer and the anvil."

These words should have offended at least some of the Lothans, Oskar was sure, but to a man, Shanis's words had silenced them.

"Many here have seen me heal your injured. The power of the Silver Serpent can work through me to mend the direst of wounds, but it is foolishness to heal one person at a time, only to watch you cut them down again. No one has been spared in your foolish wars. Women, children, your elders... all of them suffer and die along with your young men. I have seen your suffering. I have seen the remnants of once proud cities now fallen to ruin." She paused again, letting the words sink in. No one was paying any attention to Karst now.

"I did not come to Calmut to convince anyone that I am the rightful bearer of the Silver Serpent. I did not come here to claim the right to lead you in battle." She let the words hang in the ringing silence. "I came to Calmut to heal a nation."

Oskar's blood sang, and he found himself drawn in by her words as much as everyone around him. He had never heard Shanis talk this way. Where had it come from? Then he remembered all the evenings she and Larris spent alone, deep in quiet conversation. Perhaps the young prince had given her lessons in how to inspire one's followers. Whatever he had done, it had wrought an amazing change in Shanis.

"But I swear this to you—if I must, I will take up the Silver Serpent and bend each of you to my will if that is what it takes to make you stop killing your children and scourging your land. Lo-than will once again be one nation, and will stand as one to weather the storms to come."

Oskar bit his lip. So much for the diplomatic, inspirational Shanis. Leave it to her to issue a challenge to several thousand people at once. He glanced at Aspin, whose blank stare revealed nothing. Fortunately, they did not seem angered by her words—only thoughtful.

"I am the one!" Karst shouted into the silence. "I bore the Silver Serpent to Calmut. I have already united the east, and I come with an army at my back. What does she come with? Nothing!"

"Then take up the sword." Shanis's voice was a calm counterpoint to Karst's rage. "Draw the Silver Serpent from its sheath, raise it up for all to see, and call upon its power. I will not try to stop you. Show us you are the one."

Karst was dumbstruck. His lips moved, but he spoke not a word. His knuckles shone white and his clenched fists trembled. His eyes flitted to and fro like the mouse cornered by the snake.

"Endgame," Aspin whispered in a voice almost too low to be heard. He smiled and nudged Oskar. "Look! Krion is holding the sword."

A Malgog clan chief stood, holding the Silver Serpent by its sheath. "Come, Pedric Karst. You claim to be the bearer. Take up your sword."

The young man had no choice. Making his way across a footpath that spanned the quakewater, he stood almost nose-to-nose with Krion. He turned to cast a defiant glance at Shanis before grasping the hilt of sword.

The effect was instantaneous.

Karst gasped and tremors racked his body, but he did not release his grip on the sword. With spasmodic jerks, he inched the gleaming sword from the scabbard. Sweat poured in rivulets down through the dried dirt and blood on his face. Using his left hand to steady his right arm, he lifted the sword above his head.

And then he screamed.

The sword clattered to the ground, and Karst fell next to it, clutching his right hand against his body and convulsing. When the spasms abated, he rolled over onto his side and vomited into the quakewater. Afterward, he did not try to rise, but lay trembling in the dirt.

Krion ignored the young man, but instead looked expectantly at Shanis, who took her time crossing the quakewater to stand before the chief.

At this moment she was every bit the girl Oskar had grown up with, her face shining with a self-confidence bordering on fearlessness, and her eyes issuing a challenge to all who met her stare. Keeping her eyes on Krion, she knelt down, took the sword in her hand, and stood. She now turned about, looking each clan chief in the eye, as if daring any of them to speak.

She thrust the Silver Serpent into the air. Sparks danced around the blade for an instant, and then a bolt of pure white light erupted forth from the tip. It shot skyward, piercing the gray clouds, which rolled back like ripples on a pond, letting blue sky shine through.

The silence broke all at once as every man and woman cried out as one. All around him, people jumped up and down, raised their hands in the air, and cried out in triumph. This outpouring of sheer joy was so unlike anything he had previously experienced with these people, who had always seemed so morose and downtrodden.

When the tumult died down, the clan chiefs rose. Krion spoke first. "Shanis Malan is the true bearer of the Silver Serpent."

Every clan chief repeated the affirmation, until only Horgris remained. The big Monaghan did not merely speak the words, but raised his fists and shouted for all to hear.

"Shanis Malan do be the bearer of the Silver Serpent!" As the crowd roared again, he dropped to one knee and bowed his head. Soon, others followed suit, until Oskar and Aspin were among the few who remained standing.

Some of the Lothans, however, apparently had no intention of kneeling to Shanis. The young men who had arrived with Karst remained standing, as did a few others scattered throughout the crowd. None of them looked directly at her, but stole glances out of the corners of their eyes and whispered amongst themselves.

Shanis did not notice. The Lothans were showing no signs of rising, and the silence now bordered on interminable. She looked at Oskar, frowned, and mouthed, "What should I do?"

Oskar could not help but grin. He shrugged and looked to Aspin, who motioned that the Lothans should stand.

"Y-you may rise!" Though her voice was uncertain, she had once again drawn the mask of supreme confidence over her visage.

A roar went up again as the Lothans stood as one.

"What do we do with this one?" Culmatan had to shout to be heard above the din, and his voice carried to where Oskar stood. He indicated Karst, who was now sitting up, still clutching his hand against his chest.

Shanis scowled at Karst. "See if someone can treat his hand; then let him go."

"I need no help!" Karst clambered to his feet, his face beet red. "I am leaving here for now, but mark my words. I shall be back to take my revenge." He tried to stagger away, but Horgris grabbed him by the collar and held him fast.

"Kill him!" One of the nearby Lothans bellowed. Others quickly took up the cry.

Shanis held up her hand to stymie the shouts. She stepped directly in front of Karst, so they were almost nose-to-nose. It seemed to Oskar that the space between them might erupt in flames, so intense were their stares.

"You may go and none shall harm you." The crowd fell silent at her words. "But if you or yours should dare take up arms against any Lothans, I promise you shall die by my hand." She continued to stare unblinking at Karst, whose jaw worked, but he made no sound.

For a moment, Oskar feared Karst would try to attack Shanis. He took a step toward her, and immediately felt Aspin's hand on his shoulder, pulling him back.

"She is doing fine. Do not interfere."

Of course there was no need for Oskar to try and help. Horgris still held Karst by the collar, and he and the other chiefs could intervene should they deem it necessary. Oskar released the breath he was unaware he had been holding.

Karst stared for a moment longer before muttering a curse, turning, and trying to pull away from Horgris, who maintained his grip for a moment, then let go, causing the young man to fall face-first to the ground. A few jeers and guffaws rang out, but most continued to watch in silence. He wasted no time regaining his feet and stalking away. Some in the crowd moved aside to let him pass, but others took obvious pleasure in making him worm his way through.

Oskar noticed that those who had not knelt to Shanis were also leaving. "How can they follow him?" he muttered. "He has made a fool of himself."

"Some people will only believe that which they want to believe." Aspin kept his voice low as he spoke. "Some will not accept a woman as a leader."

"But they revere Badla—almost worship her. She is the reason they have been at war all these years." He still could not believe that the dispute over whether to commit the great warrior queen's remains to water or earth had led to so much death and devastation.

"For some, she is merely their excuse to go to war. There is a difference. Many will follow Karst because conflict is all they know and all they care about. I fear we have not heard the last of him or them."

Somewhere in the distance, a cry arose, followed by a chorus of shouts, some gleeful, others indignant. The sound drew closer, and Oskar could make out chants of "Badla! Badla!" amidst the cacophony. A dark shape wended its way through the throng, coming ever closer to the circle where Shanis waited with the clan chiefs.

A dozen Monaghan men were carrying what looked to Oskar to be an ornately carved tree trunk, worn smooth by weather and age. And then he remembered— the Lothans used tree trunks as coffins. They were bringing forth the mortal remains of Badla, the celebrated warrior queen. He remembered that, after her death, while the Lothans argued over where her mortal remains should be interred, sorcerers had magically preserved her body. Oskar shuddered at the thought that she lay inside that hollowed-out tree looking exactly as she had on the day of her death. There was something unnatural and almost sinister about the thought.

As they entered the circle of stones, the warrior in the lead called out for all to hear. "The warriors of the Green Mountain Clan do bring Badla to Calmut! All honor be to the Green Mountain!" The few shouts of approval from the other members of the clan were drowned out by derisive cries from the rest of the Lothans.

"The Green Mountain did steal Badla from the Mud Snakes!" one Malgog shouted. "They did take her while under the peace of Calmut!"

"Badla was no inside Calmut." The Green Mountain spokesman shook his fist at the accuser. "You did encamp far from the city!"

Suddenly, it seemed everyone was shouting. Oskar could not make out a single word in the din. Even the chieftains were arguing. He could read Shanis's lips as she shouted for everyone to stop, but no one heard her. Her face was beet red, and Oskar could tell that she was moments from doing some damage with that sword of hers, but he could think of nothing he could do to help.

A group of Mud Snakes charged the Green Mountain men who held Badla high overhead. Above the throng, Oskar watched the casket move to and fro with the ebb and flow of the crowd. It wobbled, teetered…

…and crashed to the ground.

Those who saw what had happened uttered a collective gasp and stood in mute surprise. Those who could not see continued their arguing, but word quickly passed through the crowd, and peace reigned again.

The craftsmanship of the log casket was such that it had looked to Oskar to be one single piece, but as it struck the ground, a previously indiscernible lid came free and the body inside tumbled to the ground.

Oskar gaped at the remains of the warrior queen. She lay contorted like a grotesque marionette, gazing up at the sky through sightless eyes. He could not stop himself. He approached the body, drawn forward as if pulled by an unseen force, his gaze never leaving the face that was so like....

Shanis pushed her way through the crowd, but stopped short when she saw Badla. "What madness is this?" Her voice quavered and the blood drained from her face as she stared transfixed at the body that lay before her.

"Shanis," Oskar whispered, looking first at Shanis, then down at the body, and then back up at Shanis. "She's... you!"

CHAPTER 37

The soft knock startled Jowan from his quiet reflection. It was well known that no one was to interrupt him during this time, save for matters of only the greatest importance. His heart pounding and his neck prickly hot from annoyance, he took a moment to gather himself before responding. As High Priest, he went to great pains to always apper to be in complete control, regardless of how he truly felt.

"You may enter."

Gemel entered, looking abashed. He dropped to one knee and lowered his head.

"You may rise. Now, what is it, Gemel?"

"Holiness, there is word of the prince." Gemel's words came out in a rush. "He entered the city a short while ago and is being escorted to the palace as we speak."

"And which prince would this be?"

Gemel's face reddened. "It is Prince Larris, Holiness. The second prince."

Jowan suppressed a smile. If only Gemel knew the truth. It was too bad Larris was not attempting to slip through the city on his own, which would be very much in character for the impulsive young prince. Were that the case, Jowan could simply send out the temple guard to bring Larris to him. With the prince guarded, however, that was not an option. Too many potential witnesses. If he could not take Larris, he would have to settle for the document.

"Word must be sent to those inside the palace. The prince is in possession of a certain document that I must have before it reaches the king."

Gemel screwed up his face as he always did when he was trying to decide how to phrase an objection in a way that would not offend Jowan.

"The prince will doubtless need to bathe and make himself presentable before being received by the king," Jowan continued before Gemel could interrupt. "Considering the unique position of one of our agents inside the palace, it should be a simple matter to take the document then, should it not?"

Gemel smiled. "That it will, Holiness. I shall send word immediately." He paused. "May I ask why this document is of such great importance?"

Now Jowan did smile. He folded his hands, leaned toward Gemel in conspiratorial fashion, and lowered his voice to a whisper. "The prince has been corrupted by the wildlings of Lothan. He has abandoned the Seven, and now he seeks to spread his heresy to Galdora. If I could stop him from reaching the palace, I would, but I cannot do so without rousing the king's ire. It is essential that we have that document before great damage is done. Can I rely on you?"

"Absolutely, Holiness." Gemel's eyes gleamed. "I promise; it shall be done."

"Highness, you are dirtier than I have ever seen you." Melina scrubbed Larris's back with a coarse wool cloth. The trail dirt came away in broad streaks, revealing swathes of skin turned pink from the scrubbing. "And I have seen you quite filthy in your lifetime." She poured warm, scented water over his back, sluicing away the grime.

"You don't have to remind me." Larris grinned up at her. Melina had tended both princes from birth, and they treated her, if not like a mother, then like a member of the family.

Orphaned as a young child, she had been taken in by the Temple of the Seven and raised there, first helping with the cleaning, and later the cooking. She had been spared the life of a ritual prostitute, the fate of most of the desperate young women who found their way into the temple, when Timmon, a kindly old priest who worked as a healer, had taken a liking to her. Contrary to the rumors whispered around the temple, there was nothing unsavory about their relationship. Amused by her sharp tongue and strong will, Timmon had taken her under his wing, and taught her to read, write, and do sums. Eventually, he permitted her to assist him with his daily work.

When Melina was fifteen, Timmon was called to the palace to attend to baby Lerryn. The child had a high fever which no one had been able to bring down. While Timmon puzzled over the illness, Melina held and comforted the baby. She had leaned down to nuzzle his head when she spotted something everyone else had missed—two tiny red dots behind his ear. The child had been bitten by a rare spider, and Melina's discovery saved his life. The king and queen had been so impressed by Melina they had made her Lerryn's nurse that very night. She had not wanted to take the position, but Timmon had insisted. It was not long before she learned why.

"I do think I am perhaps too old for you to still be giving me my bath." Larris's voice brought her thoughts back to the present.

"Royals do not bathe themselves, Highness. I am, however, satisfied that no sores or injuries requiring my attention lurk beneath this layer of dirt." She glanced at the serving girl who had just entered carrying a fresh set of clothes for the prince. "Sarill, will you finish for me?"

Sarill took the cloth from Melina and began scrubbing. The weary prince sighed and let his chin fall to his chest, and his eyes close. Melina scooped up his soiled clothing and his leather bag and made to leave.

"You may leave my bag here," Larris called. Apparently his eyes were not completely shut.

"I can leave it in your chamber for you, if you like." Melina tried to keep her tone nonchalant. Obviously, the document was in this bag.

"There is no need."

Melina laid the bag down, her mind working at a rapid clip. She moved back to Larris's side, her eyes narrowed and her mouth twisted into a grimace, as if she had spotted something distasteful. He looked up at her and arched an eyebrow. She pretended to give his hair a close inspection. After a minute's probing, she sighed.

"Vermin," she muttered. "Have you perhaps been sleeping in barns?"

"Since leaving home, I have slept in every sort of place you can imagine." He shook his head, a look of resignation on his face. "Let me guess. Lye soap?"

"Precisely." Melina looked at Sarill and adopted a commanding tone. "Two washings should do it. Use a towel to keep the lye out of his eyes, nose, and ears."

Sarill winced as she handed Larris a towel and took up the bar of the strong lye soap they kept on hand to kill lice, mites, and skin pests. Larris covered his face and ears with the towel, and Sarill began to scrub.

"It stings!" Larris grumbled. "Isn't there anything else that can do the job without burning my skin off?"

"Why do you think it works so well, Highness?" Melina smirked. The soap would do him no harm, though his skin would be red and tender for a day. Making certain Sarill was concentrating on her task, she opened Larris's bag and quickly found what she was looking for. She slid the rolled parchment into her baggy sleeve, retrieved the bundle of dirty clothes, and left the bath chamber.

She left the soiled clothing with the laundress and went directly to her suite of rooms, all the while expecting Larris to come chasing after her, demanding to know what had become of his stolen paper. When she reached her quarters, she locked the door behind her and sat on her bed, catching her breath and listening for approaching footfalls.

The temple had frequently asked her for information, and she had always been happy to provide it. Her devotion to Timmon, and gratitude to the temple for saving her from the streets, had made it easy for her to comply. But they had never asked her to take anything. What was so important that they would instruct her to steal from the prince?

She took the document out and held it in her lap, staring at it. *I should return it to Larris's bag and tell the temple there was no document.* She immediately dismissed that thought. She doubted she could come up with another ruse that would distract both Larris and Sarill long enough for her to return it.

The document was not sealed. She unrolled it with care and read it hastily, her eyes constantly flitting to the door. She gasped as the meaning of the words sank in. Lerryn had abdicated? It could not be!

Before she could contemplate the weight of that news, she heard approaching footsteps in the corridor. Whispering a curse, she hurried to the window. The mortar around one of the stones below the sill no longer clung to the stone, though it still fitted perfectly in place. She removed the stone, and slipped the rolled parchment into a hollow space behind it. Replacing the stone with care, she waited, her pulse pounding in her ears as she listened. The footsteps passed her door and kept going, and she allowed herself to breathe again.

What was she going to do? What would Larris do when he found the document was gone? How had the temple known, and why did Jowan want it so badly?

She sagged onto her bed and propped her head in her hands. She needed to think.

CHAPTER 38

Shanis looked down in numb disbelief at the face of Badla, the famed warrior queen of Lothan. She did look like Shanis, but it was like looking at her reflection in a rippling pond- it was an imperfect image of her. The differences were subtle, but they were there. Aside from being older than Shanis when she died, Badla was leaner, her shoulders not quite so broad, and her hair a lighter shade of red. Overall, Shanis thought Badla looked just a shade more feminine than her. Otherwise, however, the resemblance was frightening.

The clan chiefs stood transfixed as Shanis knelt beside Badla. Culmatan leaned over to Horgris. "Could Badla have been her vardoger?"

"Nah. A vardoger do be a ghostly thing—a premonition come to life, and no very long before the person it do represent. Badla did live." His voice was filled with wonder. "It can mean only one thing."

Before he could elaborate, Aspin strode into the circle. "Badla is your great-grandmother, Shanis."

Shanis gasped and sprang to her feet. How could it be true? Her father would have told her. It was impossible.

"Badla did have no children!" Culmatan's voice lacked certainty even as he disputed Aspin's words. "She did no marry, and she did die childless."

"I am afraid you are wrong on both counts." Silence reigned as everyone strained to hear Aspin's words. The sai-kur raised his voice. Shanis could tell by the tingle that washed over her that he was magically enhancing his words so all could hear. "As you know, Badla was the daughter of a Malgog clan chieftain and the daughter of a Monaghan chieftain. She was the last ruler to be recognized by both peoples of Lothan." Aspin was a masterful speaker, and he paused just long enough to whet the appetites of those listening.

"Badla foresaw the conflict which has plagued your nation. She knew that neither the Malgog nor the Monaghan would accept any man as king save one of their own. It seemed to her that she was destined to die alone. Her fate would permit her no other choice."

Shanis felt a lump in her throat. It seemed she had more in common with this woman than physical appearance.

"But fate had other plans for her. She fell in love with a young man, whom she married in secret. Her enemies learned of her new husband, and murdered him, but not before the two of them conceived a child."

Shanis found herself just as engrossed by this tale as everyone else. She held her breath, waiting for him to go on. The faint tittering of a threshel was the only sound she could hear.

"Badla hid her pregnancy, and after her daughter was born, she placed the child in the care of a select few—a Lothan secret society. She gained her revenge on those who had slain her husband, but at great cost. She was killed in the fighting that ensued, and the kingdom was torn asunder by her death.

"Badla's descendants were kept safe. Her daughter, Bennell, married a Malgog, and they bore a son, Addan. Addan married a Malgog woman, and they had two children: a son who died young, and a daughter, Janel, who married Colin, a Malgog of the Black Mangrove clan." Voices from out in the crowd expressed surprise at this news. Apparently there were those here who know, or knew of, her father. "They had one child." Aspin turned to face Shanis. "Shanis Malan, the Bearer of the Silver Serpent, and Badla's true heir!"

In the space between heartbeats, Shanis contemplated Aspin's words. It was not possible. Then again, how many times had she thought that very same thing since leaving home? Already she had come to accept her role as Bearer, and as leader of Lothan, and she had suspected for a while now that Colin was of Malgog descent. Really, was being Badla's descendant truly that far-fetched in light of all the things that had happened?

Culmatan was the first to find his voice. "Begging your pardon, Seeker, but how can we accept this? It do seem like a Seeker's trick, meaning no offense, of course." Muttered whispers floated through the air, but no one else spoke up.

Aspin did not react to the words, but stared at Culmatan until the man lowered his gaze. "I do not lie. And there is at least one other here who can attest to the truth of my words."

An expectant hush settled on those assembled, until, finally, Krion stood. The clan chief of the Black Mangrove slowly turned, as if he could look every Lothan in the eye. The suspense stretched like a bow ready to loose.

"The sai-kur Aspin speaks the truth." The sudden flurry of surprised conversation cut off the moment he raised his hands. "Long has the Black Mangrove Clan protected the secret of Badla's line. We protected this secret even from our own. Colin's name was not always Colin Malan. He is my son."

Shanis felt her knees sag, and she only just caught herself before she crumpled to the ground. Her father was the son of the Black Mangrove chieftain? That meant that Krion was...

"I am Shanis Malan's grandfather. And I am proud to stand before you and declare that she is not only the Bearer of the Silver Serpent, the one prophesied to unite the clans, but she is also Badla's true heir."

His words hung in silence. It seemed that everyone was as surprised as she. Finally, Horgris raised his fist and cheered. Soon, everyone joined in.

"Let them hear us in Karkwall!" Horgris cried. "Let Orbrad know that Lothan do have a true queen!"

As the triumphant cheers cascaded over her, Shanis took a tentative step toward Krion. His steely eyes softened, and he dropped to his knees and bowed to her.

"No, Grandfather," she whispered, taking him by the hand. It felt more than a bit odd to name him such. "Please stand."

He rose, and looked into her eyes with an expression that seemed to take in her entire being. "You are a fine woman," he whispered. "I am humbled to know that I had some small part in bringing you into this world."

There was so much she wanted to say, so many questions she wanted to ask him, but the words would not come. She squeezed his hand and felt him return the gesture, his callused palms rough on her skin.

"You must do something about Badla." His lips barely moved, and his voice was low enough that only she could hear. "You are the only one who can."

She looked down at Badla's body, and the memories flooded her mind: children dead, cities destroyed, all over where a body should be put to rest. Earth or water? Was it truly so important that it was worth ripping apart a nation? Anger coursed in her veins, warming her body that had been numbed by shock at Aspin's and Krion's revelations.

Earth or water?

Her first instinct was to draw the Silver Serpent and burn the body right there. She had never used the sword to create fire, but she somehow knew she could do it. It was as if the sword was whispering to her, eager to share its knowledge. That would not do, though. Fire was of Arscla.

Earth or water?

And then her eyes fell on the quakewater. Yes!

She knelt and gathered Badla into her arms as gently as if she were picking up a newborn. She carried her great-grandmother to the edge of the pool of quakewater, the liquid earth at the center of the ring of stones. As gently as she had picked Badla up, she laid her in the water, and silently watched as she slowly... slowly... sank beneath the surface.

As if a spell had been broken, angry shouts arose and men pressed in on all sides. She sprang to her feet, drew the Serpent, and swept it in an arc. All around her, men fell back as if struck by an invisible blow. How had she done *that*?

"Enough!" Her voice boomed like thunder. She supposed Aspin was aiding her. "Badla's body has been returned to the earth and the water, that Dagdar and Boana might be pleased." She knew little of the god and goddess, but it felt right to invoke their names. "The clan war is ended. No more are we divided as

Malgog and Monaghan. Lothan is a single, united land! We are one people!"

"All praise the wisdom of Shanis Malan, Bearer of the Silver Serpent and Badla's true heir!" The cry arose from somewhere in the crowd. Shanis realized immediately that it was Oskar who had called out, but the fact that it was not a fellow Lothan seemed to be lost on the crowd, who gradually began to chant Shanis's name.

"Shanis! Shanis!"

The chanting subsided as the clan chiefs circled her, and all dropped to their knees. She was thankful it was at an end, for she had felt more than a bit foolish standing there, receiving the kind of praise reserved for royalty. She needed to say something, but what? Larris had filled her head with advice, but nothing about how to tell a cheering throng to go away and leave her alone without offending them.

"You honor me." That was weak. "A great task stands before us, and I must consult with the clan chiefs." That was a little better, though not much. How to disperse them? "I ask that you return to your camps and pray that Dagdar and Boana will grant us wisdom." That was the best she had to offer, and thankfully, it appeared to be working. Some continued to cheer, but gradually, the crowd broke apart as the onlookers drifted away. Doubtless, there would be more merrymaking than praying, but it made no difference to her, as long as they were not killing one another.

She felt a firm hand on her shoulder, and she turned to see Krion smiling at her. "You did well."

"Thank you, Grandfather." The name still felt strange on her lips, but she supposed she would grow accustomed to it.

"There is a place nearby where we can meet."

Shanis signaled for Aspin and Oskar to join them. The remnants of the crowd gave way as the chieftains made their way to a stone roundhouse with a south-facing door and narrow, vertical slits set all around. The conical roof was made of poles, mud, and leafy branches, and appeared to be brand-new.

Horgris noticed her staring at it. "We did hope we would have reason to use this meeting house again. I do be glad we were right."

As the last person entered, guardians of Calmut took up positions outside, assuring they would remain undisturbed. When all had settled around a rough-hewn wooden table, another obviously recent addition, Culmatan cleared his throat.

"I can no believe you did do that to Badla." He paused. "I do think it was wise. Shocking, impulsive, but wise."

"Shanis is nothing, if not impulsive." Oskar's face reddened, perhaps feeling he was the last person who had a right to speak in this group. The chieftains seemed to feel the same way. Some frowned at him, while the rest ignored him entirely.

"Oskar is here because he is a trusted friend and I value his opinions," Shanis said. "He is also well-read, and he knows me better than the rest of you put together. For those reasons, he has leave to speak his mind whenever he sees fit." That had been one of Larris's suggestions; have someone close to you whom you could trust to always tell the truth, even if the truth hurt. "And he is right about me. If I know something is the right thing to do, I am not one to dawdle." A few of the men chuckled uneasy, forced laughs.

"I would like to know what you plan to do about Karst." Labar scowled, clearly bitter over the defection of most of his Mud Snake clan.

"Nothing right now." She knew this would be unpopular, so she hurried on. "Our first order of business is to rebuild our kingdom. Generations have been decimated by these wars. For Lothan to be a powerful nation again, it must be allowed to grow, and its people to regain their former strength."

"But how can we regain that strength with Orbrad sitting in Karkwall and Karst sitting in the east? We must not be weak in the face of our enemies." Jayan argued.

Shanis gritted her teeth. How could these people continue to look for reasons to fight? Had they not had enough yet? "I have made it clear that I will heal this land. The clan wars are over." She also suspected, based on what the Keeper of the Mists had shown her, that Pedric Karst was not their greatest threat, but she did not feel that this was the proper time to discuss it. The vision had been too nebulous. She needed to understand the vision for herself before she could persuade anyone else. "If Pedric Karst makes war against us, or so much as crosses the Igiranin, we shall fight him. Otherwise, we will deal with him in due time. Right now, our goals are to reunite and rebuild."

"If I may be heard?" Aspin's voice was serene, but it carried a tone of insistence. Shanis nodded to him.

"The situation in Gameryah has become precarious. Kyrin and Galdora are at war, and there is concern that a new frost-march is at hand."

The men let this news sink in. Horgris and Culmatan, having traveled with Aspin, were already aware of the happenings outside of Lothan.

"And what of these threats?" Jayan asked.

"There is much I do not understand," Shanis admitted. "But these threats are further evidence that we must no longer fight amongst ourselves. We must be strong for what is to come. In the meantime, I need to learn more about our people, the history of this sword… about everything, really."

"Karkwall." Horgris folded his arms and looked around at the other chiefs. "That do be where we must go."

The fool man! After what Shanis had just said, he still wanted to go after Orbrad. She was about to upbraid him, but Aspin cut across her.

"Why do you say that, Horgris?"

"Two reasons. First," he held up a thick finger, "we can no be truly united without a properly crowned queen. We do accept you," he nodded to Shanis, "but many of the people will no accept you until you do be properly crowned, and rule from the throne." Shanis was ready to tell him just how foolish those people were, but she could see in his eyes that he already knew what she was going to say. "Second, Karkwall do have an extensive library. There be no better place to begin if you do want to learn about our people and… other things." His eyes flitted to the Silver Serpent and then back to her.

The other clan chiefs nodded in agreement. Of course, they probably saw this as nothing more than an excuse to make war on Orbrad.

"But Larris and Oskar searched that library thoroughly." She turned to Oskar. "You said there was virtually nothing there about the Serpent."

"That is true. Larris was surprised and disappointed at what we found. He felt the library did not live up to its reputation. Sorry," he hastily added. "I intended no offense."

"None was taken." Krion made a placating gesture. "Orbrad would not have permitted you to see anything of true worth. The location of the real library is a closely guarded secret. If you want to learn about the Silver Serpent, that is where you must begin your search."

"You want to lay siege to Karkwall? I've been there and seen its fortifications. That city could hold out for an eternity. Besides, I don't want the citizens to suffer. They are Lothans as much as any Malgog or Monaghan." The darkened faces around the table indicated that the others did not necessarily hold to this opinion.

"We might no have to do much fighting at all," Horgris said.

"What do you mean?" Shanis's blood raced. Though she fully intended to make peace her priority, she knew that, at some point in the future, she would have to deal with Orbrad, and probably Karst. Was it possible to remove Orbrad without a protracted siege, and more of the suffering she'd witnessed.

"Certain plans have been in place for quite some time." Krion exchanged glances with Horgris. "We have already sent the necessary messages. If you will accept our counsel, it would be wise to take a strong fighting force and move in that direction with all due haste. It will make you appear decisive, and put you in a position to take advantage of the situation, should our plan prove fruitful."

Shanis met each man's eyes in turn. Was this merely a ruse by which they hoped to continue fighting? She didn't think so. Though a few of the chieftains appeared surprised at Krion's words, most of them looked at her with expressions that were both grave and earnest. She recalled another bit of Larris's advice: *You have to trust someone. Choose your advisers wisely and listen to them.* She believed she could trust Horgris. He had given her no reason to doubt him. And somehow, she knew she could trust Krion.

"Very well. You may tell me about these plans, and then I have some plans of my own that we shall put into place as soon as this council has concluded."

The sun had hidden its face by the time the meeting ended, a ruddy smear across the horizon the only evidence of its passing. Shanis lounged by her campfire, thankful for Oskar's presence. Her friend lay stretched out on a bedroll, tossing crumpled leaves into the fire. Her campsite was now ringed by guards—something to which she would have to grow accustomed now that she was to be queen.

"I have to confess, I loved the looks on their faces when you told them that each clan would have to provide a young man and young woman from among their clan's leading families to be married to members of opposite tribes. Even Horgris looked like he was going to choke."

"It was Larris's idea. Not only will it form ties, tenuous though they might be, it produces healthier children to marry outside of your own circle. I intend this to be the first of many such marriages."

"They liked your rebuilding plan a little bit better, but not much." Each clan had been assigned the task of rebuilding a city or town within their own lands. Shanis's added wrinkle was to pair each Monaghan clan with a Malgod clan, and those clans would be responsible for rebuilding both towns. It was a small thing, but her father had taught her that working alongside a man was the best way to get to know him. Any inroads she could make in turning two tribes into one nation would be progress.

"It occurs to me," Oskar hesitated, his eyes still on the campfire, "that you will soon be a noblewoman, royalty even."

"That occurred to you only now? We've been talking about it all afternoon."

"No. It just occurred to me that you and Larris could wed if you wanted to."

It was as if an icy hand had squeezed the breath out of her. She couldn't marry Larris! It was impossible. "I don't think so." Her voice was scarcely a groan.

"Think about it. He's not going to be king. Lerryn is first prince. Consequently, Larris will simply need to find a suitable match. And what better way to solidify relations with Lothan than to marry the queen?"

"But…" She cleared her throat. "How would they feel about

me marrying an outlander? They bowed to me today, but many of them have to be suspicious of me because of my upbringing. Marrying Larris might seem to them proof that I want to bring Lothan under Galdora's influence."

"Possibly." Oskar rolled over onto his back and stared up at the sky, tapping his chin as he thought over the problem. "But if you marry a Lothan, you will have to choose either a Malgog or a Monaghan. Either way you're going to offend half of your populace."

Shanis let her chin fall to her chest. The full impact of the day's events seemed to finally sink into her very being. She heaved a sigh that bore every ounce of weariness and hopelessness she had ever felt.

"Why did this happen?"

"What do you mean?" Oskar continued to stare at the sky. Despite his words, she suspected he knew exactly what he meant. She got up, walked over to where Oskar lay, and nudged him with her toe.

"Move over."

Surprise filled Oskar's eyes, but then a smile split his face, and he scooted aside to make room on the blanket.

Shanis stretched out next to him, and together they lay gazing up at the heavens.

"Do you remember when we used to look up at the stars and you would tell me the stories of the pictures we saw there?" She could almost believe they were ten summers old, lying in a field in Galsbur with Hierm on her other side, all of them hoping their parents would not realize they had slipped out during the night.

"I remember."

"Promise me," she swallowed a lump in her throat. "Promise me that, no matter what else changes, our friendship will be like the pictures in the sky. I need one thing in life that I know will always remain the same."

She felt Oskar take her hand in his and give it a firm, reassuring squeeze. No words were necessary.

CHAPTER 39

"Ambassador Amil to see you, Highness." Bertram bowed to Orbrad, King of Lothan, who acknowledged him with a frown and an almost indiscernible wave, indicating that the ambassador should enter.

Amil did not wait for Bertram to usher him inside. He swept through the door and into Orbrad's private study. Bertam closed the door behind him. He seemed to be the only person the king trusted anymore.

"Your Highness, I appreciate your seeing me on short notice." There was no trace of irony in his words, and his bow was respectful, but the three of them knew Orbrad had no choice but to receive dignitaries from the surrounding kingdoms. Their acknowledgment of his kingship was as tenuous as his hold on the capital city and the surrounding land. He had never been a true king.

"I have come to inform you that Diyonus can no longer stand by as an army masses on its western border."

"Army?" Orbrad gripped the arms of his wooden chair and leaned toward Amil. "There is no army. It is the same rabble it has always been. Malgogs stirring up trouble."

"I beg to differ, Highness. The fighting among clans that you have been unable to quell has ended." Orbrad shifted in his seat but did not contradict him. "An organized force of Malgog, Monaghan, and even a few Galdorans has taken control of the lands surrounding the Igiranin River from the Galdoran border to the salt swamps near the coast. They are rebuilding the cities that were abandoned during the clan wars. This is permanent."

He paused to let his words sink in. Bertram already knew all of this and more. He had let Orbrad in on as much as Amil seemed to know. Doubtless, the ambassador was holding back information as well. Amil drew a rolled sheet of parchment from his cloak.

"In the interest of its own security, Diyonus shall take control of the Harriland before this new army does so. This document cedes that land to Diyonus. We shall, of course, pay you." He reached into his cloak again and withdrew a small leather pouch. "Your signature is required to make this… official."

Orbrad, red in the face, reached out his trembling hand to take it, but Amil drew it back.

"I respectfully suggest that His Royal Highness should think long and hard before refusing to sign this document, much less tearing it to bits or tossing it into the fire.

Orbrad froze. Amil had obviously read his mind. He took two deep breaths and sat up straight. He was barely maintaining his composure.

"That is my land." His voice shook with rage. "Mine!"

"I tire of this." Amil turned to Bertram. "Leave us."

"You will not give orders in my chamber!" Orbrad looked as if he would explode from rage.

"By your leave, Highness." Bertram made a quick bow and slipped from the room, thus creating at least the minutest illusion that it was Orbrad who had dismissed him. Turning the corner, he slipped into an alcove behind a faded tapestry. He pressed his ear to a small hole in the wall.

"…both know that you have no kingdom. At best, you are the equivalent of an earl, maintaining control of nothing more than the lands within a day's ride of your castle. The Diyonan council has been exceedingly patient, waiting to see if you would give them any reason whatsoever to believe you could one day take control of your kingdom. You have not."

Bertram winced. Those who dealt with Orbrad on a regular basis went out of their way to maintain the fiction that he ruled Lothan in more than name. This would be painful for him to hear, and the ambassador's words had rendered him silent.

"You have two choices in this matter. You may cede the Harriland to us, in which case we will continue to recognize your kingship, and maintain diplomatic relations with your court. Your other option is, of course, to refuse to sign this document, in which case we shall make it our official position that you are a failure and a pretender to the throne, and we will make our peace with whomever emerges as clan leader from the gathering at Calmut."

"How do you know about that?"

"Never you mind how I know. I must have your answer. I suggest you choose the former."

"I will have to think about it." Bertram had never heard Orbrad sound more defeated than he did right now.

"Very well. I shall give you until you get up out of your chair to make your decision."

A ringing silence filled the air, as Amil's words sank in.

"Very well. I'll sign your freezing document, and to the snows with you and your council."

"I am pleased that we have been able to reach an agreement. I have two more copies here, if you will sign them as well. You may keep one for yourself, of course."

Bertram could no longer bear to listen. Orbrad was a fool, and was getting what he deserved, but he took no joy in listening to the man being humiliated. Amil was taking much too much pleasure in his work today.

He slipped out from his hiding place to find a young man in livery waiting for him. The boy looked embarrassed and would not meet Bertram's eye.

"What is it?"

"Master Carl sent me. He said if you were not with the king, I should wait by this tapestry. I was not meaning to spy."

"It is of no matter." Carl was an ostler, but he also kept Bertram's pigeons- those that carried messages outside the normal channels of communication in and out of the castle. Perhaps more important, Carl was a member of the Order of the Fox, a group dedicated to the reunification of Lothan. "I assume you have something for me?"

The lad bent down and drew a tiny roll of parchment from

inside his boot, and handed it to Bertram.

"Give Carl my thanks. And you are not to speak of this to anyone."

The young man frowned. "The pigeons or the tapestry?"

"Both. And if you do not hold your tongue, I shall hear of it. Am I understood?"

"Yes." The young man bobbed his head. He took a hasty look up and down the corridor before pulling down the neck of his tunic, revealing a fox medallion on a leather cord.

Bertram smiled. This one could be trusted.

When the young man had gone, he unrolled the slip of paper, knowing he could easily hide it should anyone approach. The message was not surprising, but still his heart pounded as he read it.

The fox bites its tail.

Glossary of Characters

Allyn- Friend and traveling companion of Larris Van Altman. A member of the original group of six.

Arlus- A Monaghan warrior who refuses to accept Shanis as the bearer of the Silver Serpent. He now leads a reble group known as "clanless."

Aspin- A sai-kur, or "seeker" as some people refer to those of his order.

Bertram- Steward to King Orbrad of Lothan.

Bull- A member of Lerryn's group of six. Is called 'Bull' due to his size and strength.

Colin Malan- Father of Shanis Malan.

Culmatan- Chief of the Blue Stag clan of the Monaghan.

Denrill- Prelate of the Order of Sai-Kurs.

Edrin- A member of Lerryn's group of six.

Faun Van Derin- Wife of Hiram Van Derin. Mother of Laman and Hierm.

Gerrilaw- Leader of the Three Oaks clan of the Monaghan. Father of Gendram.

Granlor- A young man of the Hawk Hill clan of the Monaghan.

Hair- A member of Lerryn's group of six. Is called 'Hair' because of his long hair, of which he takes great care.

Heztus- A dwarf of the Red Water clan of the Malgog. Son of Jayan.

Hierm Van Derin- Friend of Shanis Malan. A member of the original group of six. Son of Hiram and Faun Van Derin. Brother of Laman.

Horgris- Chief of the Hawk Hill clan of the Monaghan, and a member of the Order of the Fox. Father of Rinala. Husband of Miliana.

Hyda- A witch woman whom Shanis met during the search for the Silver Serpent.

Jayan- Chief of the Red Water clan of the Malgog.

Jayla- A refugee from a Galdoran frontier village.

Jowan- High Priest of the Temple of the Seven in Archstone.

Khalyndryn Serrill- Friend of Shanis Malan, though the two have been at odds for most of their lives. A member of the original group of six.

Krion- Leader of the Black Mangrove clan of the Malgog.

Labar- Chief of the Mud Snake clan of the Malgog. Father of Padin.

Larris Van Altman- Second prince of Galdora. Brother of Lerryn. A member of the original group of six.

Lerryn Van Altman- First prince of Galdora. Leader of the White Fang. Brother of Larris. Led his own group of six in search of the Silver Serpent.

Malaithus- A sorcerer and an adviser to Pedric Karst.

Oskar Clehn- Friend of Shanis Malan. A member of the original group of six.

Orbrad- King of Lothan. He rules in name only, and controls only the land in the immediate vicinity of Karkwall, the capital city.

Padin- A Malgog warrior, formerly of the Mud Snake clan, and the son of Labar. He is now a devoted follower of Pedric Karst.

Pedric Karst- Son of Duke Rimmic of Kurnsbur. A member of Lerryn's group of six, and a rival to Shanis Malan.
Rinala- Daughter of Horgris and Miliana of the Hawk Hill clan.

Rimmic Karst- Duke of Kurnsbur. Father of Pedric.

Shanis Malan- Daughter of Colin Malan. Raised in the village of Galsbur in Galdora. Bearer of the Silver Serpent.

Tabars- Captain of the White Fang.

Xaver- A sorcerer from the Isle of the Sky. Vizier to Prince Lerryn.

About the Author

David Debord began writing at age twelve after reading *The Hobbit*. He made it two pages intothe story before giving up in frustration for nearly twenty years. His love of the fantasy genre was renewed years later when he discovered the works of Robert Jordan, David Eddings, Raymond Feist and George R.R. Martin. The world of Gameryah and the *Absent Gods* series is a byproduct of his love of epic fantasy inspired by these literary giants.

A proud wearer of "Fat Elvis" ties, David lives in metropolitan Atlanta, Georgia with his wife and two daughters. When not writing, he attempts to teach Language Arts to teenagers. He also coaches youth sports and is a fan of minor league hockey. Writing under his "real" name, David Wood, he is the author of the Dane Maddock thrillers and the co-host of the ThrillerCast podcast.

Visit David on the web at www.daviddebord.com

16337367R00156

Made in the USA
Lexington, KY
17 July 2012